Everybody Takes The Money

DIANE PATTERSON

To Rob, who said he was buying dinner for four at Manresa if I
ever finished this.

Pay up, dude.

EVERYBODY TAKES THE MONEY

CHAPTER ONE

"THE THINGS I DO FOR money," Anne da Silva said as we drove into the parking lot of Mason's Motel. Mason's was a cheap but clean-looking two-story motel on 6th Street near Los Angeles's Koreatown district. Mid-century, featureless architecture, with a sea of asphalt outside the downstairs doors. The exterior was painted this weird mix of beige and orange. There was no glass in the parking lot, all of the cars there were in fine condition, and the exterior of the motel was well maintained. It might have been low budget, but it was well taken care of.

She parked by a small row of bushes and then looked at me. "What's the worst thing you've ever done for money?"

I shrugged. "I know I wouldn't kill anyone," I said.

She blinked at me through her blue cat's-eye glasses. "Drusilla? Seriously? That's the first thing that comes to mind?"

Mentally I slapped myself. Anne's only exposure to murder

had been the death that had introduced us to one another, when my husband Colin was murdered two months ago. In the course of figuring out who killed him, I'd met his girlfriend, Anne.

They were a much better couple together than he and I ever had been. I was truly sorry for her loss.

Anne's response reminded me that, to many people, murder is a simple conversational gambit. I have a much greater familiarity with homicide than she does. Than most people do, to be honest, and that fact can freak them out if I'm not careful. One more thing to hide.

"What's the worst thing *you've* ever done for money?" I asked.

"I asked you first." She wiped her glasses on her blouse. "C'mon. Tell me the worst thing."

The motel's exterior had looked deserted when we arrived, but it turned out there was a guy loitering in the shadows, standing between the Coke machine and a bush. He seemed kind of gangly and highly strung, shifting his balance back and forth as he looked at us. First he stared at us, then he watched cars going by, and then he checked us out again. His attention skipped here and there. He wore one of those unkempt beards that young men who don't have office jobs seem to like. If he'd been wearing a wool cap I wouldn't have been at all surprised.

"Take a gander at that bloke," I said.

Anne leaned forward and studied him. "That's who we're here to meet."

"Are you joking?"

"You didn't bring any shuriken or anything with you, did you?"

"Forgot to pack them before I left the house this morning. Are you certain you want to continue? This fellow seems rather sketchy."

"He's waiting for us."

I stared at her. "Again I ask: are you joking?"

She shook her head. "Are you okay with doing this?"

This? This was much easier than our adventures in Baldwin Park had been. Still, wouldn't do to seem too eager. "Are you still paying me?"

Anne was shorter, rounder, and less athletic than I was. I was taller and more physical, without appearing especially aggressive. I made a good companion on these sorts of trips. She knew my talents at self-defense and liked having me around when she was going to do anything remotely scary. Which made sense for the trips we'd taken for her articles over the past two weeks: a religious commune in Ojai led by a charismatic and definitely creepy punk who liked to quote Buddhist philosophy and use the women as his harem, a hellish brothel in Baldwin Park staffed by unwilling, undocumented Cambodian immigrants, and a meth bust in a small nothing town north of San Diego. The drive there and back had been pleasant, at least.

This day's assignment had disappointed her: back on the fake, fluffy entertainment beat. She had told me this assignment was a minor affair involving a reality show starlet I'd never heard of. She wondered if she'd done something to disappoint her editors; I wondered if an assignment involving a celebrity meant there would be cocktails at the W or something. Instead we were here at this motel in Koreatown. Made sense why she'd need me along with her to feel secure.

These days I had so few reasons of my own to meet sketchy men in motels. I always looked forward to Anne's phone calls.

She nodded. "Yes, of course I'm paying you."

"Good. Here are the rules. It's a short list, one rule. If I say we leave, we leave. Do you need to write any part of that down to remember it?"

She nodded as she slung her camera over her shoulder. "Understood."

The fellow's name was Roger Sabo and he was Anne's contact for her story. She wanted to do a "Where are they now?" article on some of the figures from reality shows that had been popular for fifteen seconds and then disappeared, taking all of their newly minted "celebrities" with them. There wasn't much of a market for the actual celebrities themselves, mind you, but stories about whatever had happened to them after their fame had flitted by were wildly popular.

Anne, a celebrity journalist, liked working on popular stories, as getting published kept her employed.

Roger had been a producer or production assistant or something on *Girls Becoming Stars*, a reality program about young women who moved to L.A. to become (what else) celebrities. Not my sort of thing, but Anne told me the show had been a train-wreck success, a guilty pleasure watched and torn apart by millions every Tuesday night on Twitter. Clothes, morals, and friendships had been cast off easily and frequently. The girls had competed with one another, on camera and off, to get the most attention from anyone calling himself a producer.

In Los Angeles, everyone's a producer. Everyone has business cards and their CV at the ready. The print shop is everyone's first stop after crossing the county line.

I shook my head. "You said we were here to talk to that girl."

"Yeah. Courtney. Roger is Courtney's boyfriend and she wants him here."

"And Courtney is...?"

"She was one of the stars of *Girls Becoming Stars*. The cute Oklahoma girl with a down-home drawl and Daisy Duke shorts."

"Wait. Let me guess. Turned out that, in fact, she couldn't act worth a damn."

Anne made a clicking noise with her tongue. "A common and usually fatal ailment among wannabe movie stars."

"But now she's back."

"They're doing a reunion show. You know. For the nostalgia."

"A reunion show? How long was this show on the air?"

"Four seasons. But reality show seasons are different. They did two seasons per year, so really it only lasted about two years."

"How long has it been off the air?"

She glanced at her notes. "Two years."

Los Angeles and the entertainment industry gave me a headache twenty-four-seven. "Mother of Apollo. This show that was on the air for two years—"

Anne smiled. "—on a cable network you've never heard of—"

"—gets a reunion show and this is what passes for *nostalgia*?"

She nodded.

My family owns a lot of media and entertainment companies. I wouldn't have been at all surprised to find out that someone in my immediate family tree owned *Girls Becoming Stars*. Early on, my family taught me the joy and beauty of taking money from people who keep waving it at you.

I gave the nervous Nellie in the shadows a once-over. "Everyone in this town has a posse."

She nodded. "And you're mine, cutie. We want to talk to Courtney, we go through Roger."

"There were other girls on the show, right? Ones who don't

hang out in motels with sketchy blokes?"

"I drew the Courtney straw. As soon as I heard where we were meeting, I called you." She poked me in the shoulder.

We got out of the car and Roger scowled at us until he recognized Anne. At least, he switched to a less flagrant method of doing it. "Hey. She's waiting."

As we walked toward him, something bothered me enough to make me put my hand on Anne's arm to stop her. While at times in my life I have accepted money for psychic readings, I have never actually been psychic, so when my internal alarms go off I immediately figure out what's set them off.

It had to be our anxious, twitchy little friend, stuck between the Coke machine and a bush.

His right hand kept scratching at his nose—a bad habit at the best of times, but the recurrent way he kept doing it said "drugs" or "nerves" or maybe both. His left hand was jammed in his coat pocket, not moving. He also kept licking his lower lip, right before he chewed on it a little. Overall he had a weird and unsettling combination of nervous motion and stillness going on.

Drugs. Fabulous.

"Roger, I need to ask you to take your hand out of your pocket."

He squinted at me. "Who the hell are you?"

"My name's Drusilla Thorne. Did you hear what I said, Roger?" Always keep repeating their name. It gives the person something to focus on.

His right hand, still scratching the side of his nose, stopped moving, and as he pulled it away he stared at it.

"The *other* hand, Roger."

"Oh." He pulled his left hand out of his pocket. He wasn't

holding anything. He must have jammed the hand in there and then left it as though it were stuck. "Court's really looking forward to this." He rapped on the door to Room 11 with his knuckles. When the door remained stubbornly closed, he slammed his open hand on the door a few times. "Open up," he yelled.

The curtains on the room's window, which had been pulled all the way across, twitched at a corner. Then the door opened.

Roger pushed the door all the way open, revealing a standard motel room with all of its lights on. "Jesus, takes you long enough."

The young woman who answered the door was definitely one of the L.A. species known as "a bobble-head doll." She was pretty, with symmetrical features and big eyes, and she had bright blonde hair that fell in giant, soft waves around her face. Her head appeared even bigger than it normally would have, though, because her body was so thin her head ended up too large for her frame. She had awesome cheekbones, most likely due to her low body fat. But she still had huge breasts, which stretched against the fabric of her tight pink V-neck t-shirt. Her face was lovely, but for someone so young—early twenties?—she was wearing way too much makeup.

I glanced at Anne. She nodded. This was Courtney from the show, all right.

Roger pushed his way into the motel room, right past Courtney, and then he turned to wave us in. "Come on, come on," he said, like we were backing up a truck full of vegetables onto his loading dock.

"Courtney Cleary?" I said.

"Yeah, hey there. It's so great to finally meet you." She pulled open the door to make space for us.

As we had discussed, Anne waited for me to go first.

Before entering the room, I scanned the place: there was one of those standard-issue motel-room coffee pots, a couple of pens on the desk, a pair of white headphones on the floor. A suitcase with most of its contents dumped out took up most of the queen-sized bed. Roger sat on the free space next to the clothes. By the window were two plastic chairs and a small table. I didn't know what sort of things they might have in the bathroom, but I could make do with most of what was at hand here, if things went bad.

"You're the writer?" Courtney asked me.

Anne stuck her hand out. "Hi, I'm Anne da Silva, I'm the journalist."

Courtney shook her hand out of obligation. Her fingernails were ragged. "Who are you?" she asked me.

I didn't offer my hand. "Drusilla."

When I didn't offer any more than that, Courtney nodded. "We're going to take pictures first, right?" The way she said *right* took five syllables.

"Where do you come from?" I asked.

The blonde woman's smile was immediate and infectious. I could see her being a cheerleader. "Broken Arrow, Oklahoma. You ever been there?"

I shook my head.

"It's outside Tulsa."

Every time she spoke, I memorized how she slurred her vowels in case I ever needed to pretend to be from Broken Arrow, Oklahoma, outside Tulsa. The vowels are the key to accents. After I'm confident of those, I practice the diphthongs.

"Oh, no," Anne said. "Let's talk a little bit here and then go outside. That okay?"

Anne and Courtney sat in the chairs by the window. Courtney

pressed the sides of her cutoffs into her legs as she sat down, which seemed slightly bizarre. She also hunched herself forward. It might have looked like she was pushing her breasts up and out, but to me it looked as though she were trying to protect herself.

I leaned against a corner of the desk, forming a triangle between the women on the chairs by the window and Roger on the bed. He kept watching me, his eyes narrow.

"And you're Roger, right?" I asked.

He flapped his hand at the desk I was leaning against. "Hey, move away from the desk."

Telling a complete stranger what to do and not even saying, "Please." Alarm signal number one.

"Move?" I asked.

"Just...there. Move. Over there." He waved in the general vicinity of Anne and Courtney.

I had no intention of crowding us all into one area. "I'm comfortable here, thanks." I pulled out the desk chair and sat down, the chair's back to the desk. The coffee pot was within reach, albeit I'd have to bend backward slightly to get to it.

"Where are you from?"

"London," I lied. At the moment, in this life, I was using a British accent. My normal speaking voice is probably standard American, but I haven't used it in so long I'm not even certain anymore. In real life, I hail from New York. Manhattan. Upper East Side of Manhattan, to be exact. Also, my birth name isn't Drusilla Thorne. Anne was the closest thing I had to a friend in Los Angeles, and she didn't know any of that about me. Most of the people I've known in my life haven't heard my real voice or my real name and I was perfectly content to let the situation remain that way. "Have you been?"

He wasn't paying attention to me. He was bouncing in place on the bed, watching Courtney and Anne. "Want to party while they talk?" he asked.

Everything is about the drugs for drug users. They're so boring. The users, that is. Sometimes the drugs are, too, depending on what they are. Even when the drugs are exciting, however, they usually come with users attached, most of them hoping for a free ride, and every single one of them is beyond boring.

"No, thank you, not interested," I said.

"Man, you make a simple 'no' sound snotty."

I shrugged. "It's eleven in the morning."

"Time for a pick-me-up." His grin most decidedly didn't make me feel warm.

Courtney and Anne were still talking. Courtney's mouth was downturned and her blue eyes were wide and wet, like she was about to start crying. Whatever was under discussion was making Courtney upset.

Dammit. Anne did not need to go in-depth here. How long did it take to get a silly interview?

"C'mon, let's party," Roger said.

"You go ahead."

"You want to get something to take with?"

A good salesman wants to get the customer to stop saying "No" and start saying "Yes." A great one knows when to back off. "No, thank you," I said.

Roger kept glancing over at them, paying attention to whatever Courtney was saying. She was talking about how she and Roger were going to use the money from the reunion special to move and start a family.

"Courtney! Shut up about that!" he yelled.

The girl flinched. Anne looked up in alarm.

I wondered what she'd said. But I didn't care that much. What I cared about was that he'd just given alarm signal number two: yelling at someone who wasn't already yelling at him. I tapped my fingers in a V across my mouth. Anne looked at me and nodded. She'd picked up that things were not good. If I got to three—and that seemed likely, given how hard Roger seemed to be pushing the drugs on me—we were gone. We hadn't had this much trouble in Baldwin Park.

"What do you do now?" I asked Roger, as though he hadn't screamed at Courtney three seconds before.

He was still eyeing her. "I'm on a show." The vaguest of all possible job descriptions in a town where everyone I ran into was peripherally involved with the movie/TV business. Of course, I lived with a famous actor, and it was amazing how fast people became peripheral around a star. "What about you?"

"Not much yet. I only moved here a few months ago." My lack of steady employment was as much by design as it was anything else.

"Oh? Where from?"

"Las Vegas."

"Yeah? Cocktail waitress?" He grinned. His teeth seemed stained. Perhaps he was a cigarette smoker. The discoloration seemed darker than the usual yellowish smoking tint. Probably used products more serious than tobacco. Meth was a possibility.

"Psychic advisor."

His foot dropped to the ground by the bed. "No shit?"

"No shit."

"Yeah? You really psychic? You got the second sight?"

Courtney swiveled around in her chair, whatever she was

saying to Anne completely forgotten. "You're a psychic? Really?"

That accent. I could see why she'd have trouble getting work in Hollywood, because the words were nearly impenetrable. But it remained unadulterated by the American Standard accent everyone was rushing to adopt. I rolled her vowels around in my head.

Her teeth didn't look so great, either. Not a great look for someone who wanted to be known for being beautiful.

"Can you read me?" she asked.

Roger jumped off the bed and yelled "No!" at Courtney.

There's two kinds of people who don't want to talk to psychics: those who think psychics are frauds, and those who are worried the psychics know something. People who think psychics are frauds are, for the most part, annoyed by them, not deeply angry toward them.

Roger's immediate anger—signaling the accompanying fear that I was going to learn something—worried me. Alarm signal number three, everybody scramble into the lifeboats. Now.

"Anne." I stood up.

She reached for her bag. "It's okay, we're done."

Roger pointed at me, his arm extended and held rigid. "Hold on a minute."

I held up both hands, palms out. "We're going now. You two have fun."

"Roger, calm yourself down," Courtney told him.

Her placid voice seemed to enrage him further. "Shut up, Court." He stalked toward me, crowding me up against the desk. "Why are you here?"

"Get away from me," I told him.

He stood right in front of me. "Shut the fuck up, bitch." Spittle flew out of his mouth and landed on my face.

He wasn't someone on my list to French kiss anytime soon. He didn't rate having his saliva anywhere on my face.

I held his gaze and didn't blink. "My friend and I are leaving. Back away."

"You looking for something here?" he yelled. He reached for the desk drawer.

Which was right behind me. So he had to press up against me to get to it. And he put his hand on my stomach to pin me in place.

Yeah. That wasn't happening.

I raised my leg and stomped down on his foot as hard as I could, and when he startled I elbowed him in the stomach sharply. Then I did it again. He staggered back against the bed with the clothes on it.

"Roger!" Courtney screamed.

"Jesus Christ," Anne added.

I looked at Anne. "The car!"

She opened the room's door. "Come on!" she yelled at Courtney, which surprised me. Not only was she trying to get Courtney out of there, but she'd clearly decided I could handle myself.

"Roger, stop," Courtney said.

And Roger reached out and shoved her, this wispy girl who probably didn't weigh over one hundred pounds. She flew backward and her head cracked against the edge of the table she'd been sitting at with Anne. Her head made a dull *thwopp* when it hit, like a fat softball at a slow speed.

I kicked Roger in the crotch, hard. I'd worn boots for a reason. If I'm going to fight, I plan on inflicting permanent physical injury. When it's down to me or the other guy, I plan on being the one to walk away.

Roger folded into a tight ball and vomited on the carpet. Great. I could ignore him for a bit, then.

Anne ran over to where Courtney lay, moaning. That she was making any noise was a good sign. If someone doesn't make any noise or move within a very short time after getting hit in the head, they might have a serious brain injury or cranial bleeding.

"Get in the bloody car!" I yelled.

Turned out Roger wasn't quite as incapacitated as I'd thought he was. He reached out and grabbed my ankle, which pulled me backward to the ground. I landed on my back and my head hit the floor. He launched himself with a surprising burst of energy on top of me, landing a weak but stinging punch to the side of my ribcage, followed by a hit to the side of my face. That one hurt much more than the ribcage one did.

"Bitch!" he yelled.

Bitch: the modern version of the *kiai* from martial arts. Tiresome.

Instead of taking advantage of his superior position and really hammering me into the thin carpet, he reached up, toward that desk drawer he seemed so damned fixated on.

His agitation about that desk warned me I'd better keep Roger from getting into that drawer if any of us were going to get out of here alive.

"Call 911!" I added.

Behind me I heard Anne finally jump up and run out of the room. The sounds of traffic on West 3rd Street nearby were loud and the warm outdoor breeze wafted over me, so the door was open, thank God. Perhaps someone passing by could create enough of a distraction that I could really lay the hurt on Roger.

I reached up and jabbed my fingers into the underside of his throat. He twisted away from the drawer and toward me, which gave me enough time to push him backward into the desk chair. Which took him off me and allowed me to scramble to my feet and take stock of the situation.

Anne: outside. Good.

Courtney was pushing herself into a sitting position, holding the side of her head and squinting in pain. Tears leaked out of her eyes without any sobbing motion on her part. And she was looking at Roger. Instead of, you know, getting the hell out of there.

I wasn't going to waste time saving her if she wasn't invested in saving herself.

I dashed out of the room and into the parking lot, where Anne's car idled, waiting for me, pointed toward the exit. I yanked open the door, jumped in, and said, "Drive!"

She drove. I didn't have my seatbelt on before she took the first right and I damn near flew into the driver's seat. Hermes Trismegistus, my entire left side hurt. He must have gotten a good punch in.

"Are you okay?" Her voice was wavering, like she was about to lose her entire mind.

"I'm okay. Drive somewhere public. And fast."

"He had a gun," she said. She pressed her hand over her mouth and started hyperventilating. "I think he had a gun!"

So I was right about the drawer. I was willing to bet he had a few other things in there, but I didn't care. We were out.

Now that the adrenaline rush was over, I realized my back hurt from where I had hit the floor. The back of my head hurt, too. And my jaw was beginning to throb with pain from where he'd punched me. My left side hurt from where I'd bashed into Anne. Today was not my day.

Anne kept turning her head to look at me, which terrified me given how erratic her driving was right now. Up ahead was the familiar large red oval marking a Ralph's supermarket. I jabbed my finger at the parking lot. "Drive! There! What are you looking at? Is he behind us?"

She shook her head, vibrating back and forth. "Oh God oh God oh God."

"Park, would you?" My stomach felt like crap.

The car thumped over the uneven curb cut into the Ralph's parking lot. The jostling made me feel like I was going to vomit all over myself. "Park, and stop moving this car."

She parked the car. I don't think she lined it up between the lines very well. L.A. drivers tend to be cavalier about following parking space recommendations.

"Did you call the police?" I asked. My side was really starting to hurt.

"I have to call an ambulance!" she yelled. Anne was really sliding into hysteria now, with tears washing all over her face and her eyes scrunched up.

"An ambulance can wait. Call the—"

"You're *bleeding*!"

As soon as she said it, I tasted copper in my mouth. My fingers touched the corner of my lips and came away red. Dammit, I was bleeding. My teeth felt secure, though—it was probably a cut on the inside of my mouth. I wouldn't be able to drink my coffee hot for a few days.

Then I felt the trickle on my forehead and reached up to feel wetness. My fingertips were covered in a decent amount of blood.

"Don't worry," I said. My words began to slur and I had to concentrate to keep using the right accent. Now would be a very bad time to start sounding like someone from Broken Arrow, Oklahoma. "Head wounds always bleed the worst."

"Not *that*," she screamed, and then she pointed to my ribs. "*There.*"

A large red spot had bloomed on the gray fabric of my sweater.

I licked my lips. "Stevie's going to murder me if I ruin my clothes."

Then I stopped talking.

Chapter Two

EVENTUALLY THE PARAMEDICS CUT THE sweater off, so I no longer worried about whether Stevie would complain about the stains. When they lifted me out of Anne's car, the passenger seat was painted with blood. I had enough awareness of what was going on to feel guilty about that.

One of the paramedics was white and the other one was black and I still lost track of who was doing what. One of them gave me a few stitches in the side before the ambulance took me to a hospital. I told them I'd rather be treated in the Ralph's parking lot, because frankly I'd had worse injuries that I'd left untreated and I'd rather not deal with hospitals. But no, they wanted to get x-rays of my side, because something, maybe a rough blade I hadn't even seen in Roger's hands, had given me a serious slice over my left ribs.

Anne had become hysterical at the sight of blood. Not being able to do anything while the paramedics worked on me made her incoherent. When she wasn't allowed to come with me in the ambulance, she was crying so much I had to touch her hand to get her attention. I told her I'd text her to tell her what hospital I was at, and did she have anyone who could come get her to drive her home? For some reason, saying that made her completely lose it, so today's lesson was that Anne could not deal with blood and violence. As my stretcher went into the ambulance, a police officer introduced himself and asked for a statement. My final words to Anne were, "Call your lawyer before saying anything, you idiot," but she didn't seem to hear me. Or perhaps I wasn't saying them very well.

I took my own advice to heart and called my lawyer from the ambulance. He said he'd come find me. Which meant, he was coming to take care of me.

I love my lawyer. Not in a sexual way. That would just mess up what was a stunningly useful relationship for me.

Obviously, I didn't call Stevie. If I thought Anne was on the verge of madness about the fight and my injuries, my sister Stevie would have immediately entered a comatose state, reversible only by divine intervention. She had never dealt with my more serious altercations well, and there have been a fair number that have driven her into hysterics over the years. The moment she heard my mission to help Anne with a story had ended in a fight that landed me in the hospital, she would demand my promise to stay home with her forever and ever, only the two of us, where it was safe.

Or some definition of safe, at any rate. After all, not too long ago someone had tried to kill me at the fabulous Pacific Palisades estate where we lived. I've inspired that sort of reaction a few times too many in my life.

At the hospital, the residents cleaned me up, x-rayed me, and did a CAT scan to see if any of the blows to my head had had any serious effect. The whole time, a uniformed cop kept telling them loudly, within my earshot, that he needed to take my statement on this matter right now.

I wondered why my little squabble with Roger Sabo might be so important he needed to talk to me right now, before I finished receiving a medical examination.

My lawyer, Nathaniel Ross, finally showed up and told the cop to leave me the hell alone until such time as I was ready to talk. Which on Nathaniel's calendar would be penciled in under "never." That made the police officer mad. I didn't care. The Vicodin was starting to kick in and my mood began to show significant improvement. The wonders of narcotics.

Nathaniel closed the curtains around my bed for a modicum of privacy as we spoke. We both knew the officer was standing right outside—the side of his black shoe was clearly visible. He rolled his eyes, as if to say, *Can you believe this guy?*

I hadn't felt much like smiling since I'd arrived at the hospital, but my lawyer's arrival cheered me up immensely.

Nathaniel didn't have the drop-dead good looks so many people in Los Angeles do—he was in his late thirties, and his blond hair was thinning on top, and his face wasn't completely symmetrical. If we met at a party I'd have passed him over and moved on to see who else was there. But he was comfortable staring me directly in the eyes, without flirtation or menace or lust or any of the usual emotions I've gotten from men over the years, and his directness was both reassuring and attractive.

Nathaniel Ross was incredibly secure in how good a job he was doing being the one and only Nathaniel Ross.

My flirtations with him were merely perfunctory. Our

relationship was fine as it was, and he never flirted back, which was for the best. And it was comforting having someone take care of me for once, even if it was only because at the moment I couldn't take care of myself.

He leaned close to me so he could whisper. "What the fuck happened this time, Drusilla?"

"You should see the other guy," I whispered back.

"If you want to press charges, we need to do it as soon as possible. However, circumstances being what they are...."

I knew what he meant.

On the one hand, Roger Sabo was an abusive fuck who deserved absolutely everything I could hit him with, physically and legally. He had assaulted me. He'd thrown Courtney across the room like a rag doll. He was so comfortable doing it, he'd clearly done it before. On top of all that, he was a terrible conversationalist.

There was nothing about Roger Sabo I didn't hate.

On the other hand, filing charges could mean publicity, and publicity meant exposure. I was quite possibly the only person in Los Angeles who didn't want her face on the evening news. While trapped in the City of Angels, I had exactly one job to do: avoid attention.

"I'm high right now. I'll make a bad decision, no matter what I do."

He nodded. He was well aware of the sort of restrictions I chafed under. As long as I lived here under the name of Drusilla Thorne, Nathaniel Ross was my prison warden.

At least I wasn't the one paying his hourly rate.

I motioned him closer. "Will you call Stevie for me?"

"And tell her what?"

Good question. I smiled. "Tell her I met a man in a motel this afternoon and we got busy."

Nathaniel snorted under his breath as he shook his head. "Okay. I'll think of something. Something better than that."

"Thank you." I patted his hand. "You take such good care of me. I should marry someone like you. My stepfather would be thrilled."

Nathaniel dragged his hand away from mine.

Since I wasn't up to much physical movement, I had to settle for mentally slapping myself for saying something so stupid.

No, not the marriage proposal. That didn't even rate on the idiocy scale compared to the other thing.

Did I say *stepfather* out loud? Nathaniel was a smart guy. He had to have figured out the relationship between Roberto Montesinos and me, but no one was supposed to acknowledge it. Especially as Roberto Montesinos's stepdaughter was alive and well and probably partying in South Beach this weekend.

"What I mean is—"

Nathaniel stood up. "The dope's kicking in. Don't say another word. To anyone. At all. I mean it."

The curtain was pulled to the side and one of the residents walked in. "How are we doing?" she asked.

Had I seen her before during my visit? I had no idea. The drugs the hospital had put me on were magnificent.

Now, if Roger had offered me some of these without the accompanying beating, I might have been interested.

"Your tests are clear. No internal bleeding. No concussion."

Nathaniel folded his arms. "Do you need to keep her here?"

The resident shook her head. "We can keep her here overnight, but—"

"What do I need to do to check her out?" Nathaniel said.

The resident handed him a couple of forms. "Here's her prescriptions."

A diminutive brown woman in a form-fitting blue skirt suit and holding a thin plastic shopping bag walked up to my bed. Her kitten heels clicked against the white vinyl floors with a dancer's rhythm. Carmela Tanner, Nathaniel's scarily effective assistant.

"Hello, Ms. Thorne," she said. She put the bag on a chair near Nathaniel and pulled a camera out of it. Still in the bag was a set of clothes. "How are you feeling?"

"I've been worse," I slurred.

Nathaniel said, "We need to document what happened if we're going to file."

Carmela took a set of photos of the worst of it—the cut on my side, the bruise on my stomach, the side of my face. She checked them on the screen and then nodded.

Nathaniel took a powder blue, oversized t-shirt and matching sweatpants out of the bag and tore the tags off. He tossed the clothes to the foot of the bed. "I'll get your pills from the pharmacy."

He disappeared into the hospital while two nurses prepared me to go home. They checked all my bandages and helped me dress. The clothes were soft and loose and still irritated my skin next to the dressings.

"You ready to go?" one nurse asked me.

I nodded.

An orderly wheeled me into the elevator and took me downstairs to the loading area, where Nathaniel and his Mercedes sedan were waiting for me.

He helped me put the seatbelt on.

"He's going to hear about this, isn't he?" I whispered.

No need to explain who I meant.

Nathaniel put on his turn signal. "He pays my invoices. Remember that."

⁂

Stevie freaked out when she saw me. It's not that hard to predict my sister's reactions in certain circumstances, and my ending up in the hospital was one.

By the time Nathaniel got me home, it was seven o'clock. We drove through the electric gates installed only two months before. Gary had had the gates installed after someone tried to kill me— actually, more than one person had made the attempt, because I'm quite the overachiever. Nathaniel swung his car around the fountain in the center of the cobblestoned courtyard in front of the Tuscan-style mansion and parked next to Anne's car.

The doors to the garage building were closed, which meant Gary was here, too. Unless he'd taken the car service to the movie set that morning, in which case he wasn't back yet and maybe hadn't heard what had happened to me. Zeus almighty, I was so disoriented I couldn't even remember where Gary was supposed to be that day. One of the reasons Stevie and I had this cushy little setup living at Gary's house was that one of my jobs was to take care of him and know where he was at all times. If I messed that up, my life would be more difficult than it already was. Dammit.

My lawyer helped me out of the car as the front door opened and Stevie came running out of it, still wearing her favorite pink-and-purple floral apron. While waiting for me to come home, my sister had channeled her energies into whipping up one of her seven-course meals. "Dru!" she yelled.

Anne appeared behind her. She did not come running across the courtyard.

When my sister got close I held up one hand. "Don't hug me," I told her. She had a nasty tendency to hang on to me like a cobra when she needed reassurance.

She flopped her arms out a few times. I gave her a quick, loose hug, careful to keep her to my right side, which hurt a hell of a lot less than my left. It wasn't easy: my sister is twenty centimeters shorter than I am. We make an odd pair for hugging.

When she pulled away, she was saying, "Are you okay?" over and over again. It sounded like an incantation.

I nodded. "I'm fine. They wouldn't have let me out of hospital if I weren't."

"Anne told me...." Her voice cracked. "She told me what happened."

I made a mental note to make Anne understand she should not tell Stevie things. Ever. I put my hands on Stevie's shoulders and stared at her. "Ask Nathaniel. He was there when they let me go. He knows precisely what they said."

We turned to look at him.

He gave me an absolutely flat look before nodding. "Clean bill of health. Just...you know. Take it easy." He held out my bag of prescription medications. "I'll give you a call and check in."

Stevie took the drugs from him. Because she knew me all too well. "Please join us for dinner. There's plenty."

"My sister likes to prepare for any uninvited guests who might join us," I said. "For instance, the Russian Army."

Nathaniel's quick smile did not show his teeth. "I have heard about your cooking. But I can't."

"Sweetie, he's been sitting at the hospital all afternoon with me. And the man doesn't get paid ten thousand dollars an hour to sit in hospitals."

Stevie's head cocked to one side. "Twenty million a year, that's —"

"That'd be a good year," Nathaniel said.

"You didn't calculate overtime," I said. "You only figured for an eight-hour day."

He laid his fingers on my arm lightly. "I'll call you tomorrow —"

"Wait!" Anne's voice bounced off the facade of Gary's manse, echoing around the courtyard. She was waving her phone in her hand as she came running down the wide front steps and over the brick inlay of the courtyard. "Don't go! Don't go yet! Did you hear about this already?"

"What the hell," Nathaniel said.

When Anne joined us, all of her attention was on him. Her eyes were as open as they could get and she was breathing heavily. "Did you know about this?"

"Know about what, Anne?" I asked.

She sucked in huge quantities of breath, trying to catch up. "Roger Sabo's charging us with assault."

"Us?" I said.

"And there are restraining orders. And did I mention assault?"

"What?" I said. Too loudly: I strained my stomach muscles.

Nathaniel shook his head. "Did you get a case number?"

She nodded rapidly and handed him a piece of paper.

"Okay. I will look into it. In the meantime, don't—"

"—talk to anyone," the four of us said in unison.

"Yes. I understand." I looked over at Anne. "Remind me never ever to help you out with a story."

"Are you kidding?" she said. "I'm never leaving my house again."

CHAPTER THREE

IN THE MORNING THE PAIN in my head was throbbing unmercifully, and that was only the hangover pain from the Vicodin. My side hurt. My jaw hurt. And I was being charged with assault by a lowlife who liked to beat up women.

If I wasn't careful, I might overreact to recent circumstances and lash out in a reckless and ill-advised manner. And now I had some prescription and completely legal drugs in my possession. Well, they weren't as yet physically in my possession. Stevie had them, which meant I would need to moan enough for her to retrieve one or two from their hiding spot before doling them out to me. I would pay careful attention to where she went, at which point maybe I could figure out where they were.

However, she'd be expecting that and might have already stashed them in various locations around the house.

It's a toss-up as to who's sneakier, me or my sister. I get points for quantity; she gets points for no one believing she's capable of it.

My best course of action was to hunker down at the estate for the day, watch *telenovelas*, moan from time to time, and have painkillers handed to me.

My ribcage hurt when I took a shallow breath, so I forced myself to take deeper ones. Every step out of bed and into the bathroom shook my body and I tensed up, waiting for the pain. A shower was probably more trouble than it was worth. The mirror showed the injuries: the bandage on my left side, the fist-sized purple bruise on my right. That was already turning green, so that was good news. The cut at my hairline had steristrips layered over the stitches. Lifting my arms was unpleasant, but I arranged my hair to hide the bandage.

I dressed—carefully—in floppy, comfortable clothes and headed downstairs—slowly.

Anne was on the oversized sofa chaise, arms and legs stretched out like a giant pink beached sea star. The bright pink flannel pajamas were Stevie's. They had ruffles on the cuffs. She was out like a light.

After we enjoyed Stevie's dinner feast, Anne drank herself silly and I made a mental note of how many cocktails I had to forfeit because of these circumstances. Anne became more and more morose as the evening went on, upset about how crazy the whole day had been and how she was sorry for everything and how scared she'd been and how she didn't know what she was going to do now that Roger Sabo was filing a lawsuit against her.

If I were to begin a life of crime, I would not invite Anne to be my sidekick. She would confess quickly, to everyone, adding as many details as she could.

Stevie was unlikely to confess at any time, so I had chosen

well. Also, she can cook, which is always a valuable skill in a partner.

From the living room, my nose followed the delicious siren song of smells. Coffee, plus something yeasty, along with the distinctive smells of rum and pineapple. In the kitchen, Stevie was perched on a stool at the counter, staring at her laptop screen, the tip of her glossy black braid in her mouth. When she looked up at me, she immediately pointed at the coffee machine.

My sister knows me very well.

I sat on the stool next to hers with my large cup of black coffee and discovered the source of the smell: Stevie had made a giant Caribbean Bundt cake, which sat on a rack on the counter. "Where are the plates?" I asked.

"It's cooling."

"Your so-called rules fill me with hilarity. I'll only get the one plate then, for me."

"Dru. Have some toast. Better for your digestion anyhow."

I rolled my eyes. "What are you investigating with such single-minded determination?"

"This person who's suing you for assault."

"Don't bother, Stevie. Nathaniel has people on it." I looked through the counter window into the living room. Anne hadn't budged. Even so, I lowered my voice. "And even if he doesn't, certain other people in New York will see this goes away."

It's fun to act confident of events you have zero actual trust in.

Mentioning New York made Stevie inhale sharply, because she knew as well as I did what that meant. New York would take care of me. It did not take care of her.

There was a series of short raps on the front door of the house.

"What time is it?" I asked.

"Eight."

"Early for Gary."

"Maybe he has to be on the set early today," Stevie said.

"Or maybe he didn't sleep." Those days are always the most fun for us. He's either a little manic or on the edge of a precipice, and one of us has to sit with him all the time. Since I don't like leaving Stevie alone with anyone, let alone a male, that's usually me.

My sister retrieved the giant pill box filled with pharmaceutical goodies from its usual storage place on the shelf above the tea cups. It was a wooden box with twenty-one separate containers in it, each with its own little wooden lid and tiny hinge. It was probably originally a jewelry box, but Stevie had repurposed it to sort Gary's daily medicine intake. The three rows represented the time of day, the seven columns the day of the week. Gary had picked it up from a vendor in Old Town Warsaw while filming a fantasy movie there and then added it to the pile of *tchotchkes* he never looked at again. Stevie, an inveterate tidier, had pulled it out and made use of it. She popped open the box for Monday AM and tilted the drug cocktail into her hand.

"You haven't been over there today?" I asked.

Stevie pointed to the clock. "It's not time yet."

Usually when Gary came to visit us, he let himself in, but perhaps after hearing my story last night of an interview gone very, very wrong, he'd decided to be a bit more cautious and respectful. Or perhaps Gary was having a down cycle in his moods and was afraid we didn't like him anymore. Sir Gareth Macfadyen was a riddle, wrapped in a mystery, trapped inside the body of a crazy man. However, he let us live on his estate rent free, so he was one of my most favorite people in the entire universe.

And if he was in a good mood, he'd enjoy a nice cup of tea

with us. Plus, I was certain Stevie would let *him* slice up the Bundt cake if he asked nicely enough.

I opened the door, prepared to ask how he'd slept after last night's dinner. I should have paid more attention to the fact that the shadow behind the door curtain was taller than I was, not shorter.

"Hi," said Detective Samuel Gruen, still as tall and gorgeous as ever, wearing his usual sports coat, shirt, and tie. Work day, then. And he had to be looking good to pull off a plaid coat—muted and tan, but still plaid. His gaze checked me out quickly and clinically, starting at the cut at my hairline and going all the way down.

I was still in that powder blue set of sweatpants and a large t-shirt. At least I'd kept my dignity and wasn't wearing the fuzzy slippers Stevie had left out for me.

My immediate response to seeing him was surprise. Delighted surprise, not the wary or guilty kinds. After all, I hadn't seen him for two months. And a frisson of anticipation twitched in my stomach at seeing him after such a long time. We'd had a somewhat tumultuous start to our relationship: the detective had suspected I might have murdered my husband. I'd helpfully closed the case by being the killer's next target. I'd had high hopes we'd work out our differences in the time-honored fashion of getting drinks and then perhaps doing a few other things together. He never did follow through, though.

Come to think of it, neither had I.

I leaned across the doorway, which had the double benefit of showing that I still had a figure under the loose-fitting clothes and denying him entrance. "Detective, to what do I owe the pleasure of this social call?"

In the kitchen, Stevie's laptop clicked shut.

He put his foot in the doorway, as if I'd invited him in. "I heard what happened. You have a minute?"

"Ah. Well, as you can see over my shoulder, someone is sleeping on my sofa, and she may not appreciate the intrusion."

He glanced past me and saw Anne, still spread-eagled and out like a light. His lips quirked but he avoided an outright smile. He brought a finger up to his lips. "I'll be quiet."

"Let's go out here." I used my fingertips on his upper arm to push him back onto the guest house's front porch. The man had a body made out of solid muscle. If he'd chosen this moment to declare his overwhelming passion for me, he had terrible timing: I was in too much pain to reciprocate. At least, not to the degree I wanted to. I could be creative, but my mobility was limited for the time being.

I looked back at Stevie, who nodded. "This way."

One edge of Gary's property had a view of the Pacific Ocean, with a number of chaises and chairs set up for late evening viewing of yet another gorgeous California sunset. This spot on the property was undoubtedly what had sold him on the place. They aren't making more scenery like this.

Gruen sat on the low stone wall. I took one of the padded chairs, facing the ocean and him. This early in the morning, the Pacific was still at low tide. I knew how many runners would be down there. There was no running for me for a couple of days, but soon enough I'd be back on the sands.

"Are you okay?" he asked me.

I shrugged. Telling him "I've been in worse fights" might not help the conversation any. Feeling warm and fuzzy and maybe a little sticky that he'd shown up out of nowhere to find out how I was doing wouldn't help me, either. "It shook me up. No serious injuries, though."

He raised an eyebrow.

"Honestly." I raised three fingers in the Girl Scout salute. I'd actually been a Girl Scout when I was in the fifth grade. For one meeting. Then they asked me to sell cookies.

"Tell me what happened," Gruen said.

I tapped him on the knee in mock censure. "Detective. You know my lawyer's name. You need to call him first."

"Maybe you noticed I didn't even call you before coming over."

If I didn't receive a phone call on any lines that could be traced back to Detective Gruen, no one could prove we'd talked. "Is this what an off-duty police officer looks like?"

"What can I say. The badge says Detective. I'm a nosy guy."

I put my feet up on the stone wall next to him. "What's in it for me?"

He leaned forward. I honestly thought he might kiss me, which while unexpected would not be unwelcome. The first time I'd ever seen him, he was getting out of a car to come interview me about my husband's murder, and my very first thought about him was how good-looking he was. The second was that he didn't wear a wedding ring. The third was that the wife was the most likely suspect in homicides, and in the case of my husband's murder, I was the wife, and Detective Gruen was the one looking for suspects. Our relationship started off on the wrong foot, but how else would we have ever met?

After Colin's murderer was found, I should have done the polite thing and called Gruen for drinks. It had been two months. Anyone would consider me single at this point.

He didn't kiss me. Instead, he said, "You owe me one."

Well.

Already calling in his favor. Interesting.

I did, in fact, owe a very large debt to him. In the middle of trying to find Colin's killer, I had run into a problem mostly unrelated to my husband's death. A problem involving some other people who were looking for me, possibly in a homicidal sort of way. The detective obscured my trail. I had been hoping I could pay off my debt using inappropriate and intimate methods. And frankly, he turned me on so much that spotting him an extra favor was no hardship.

I adjusted my legs and pulled up the edge of the sweatpants. I have nice ankles. "How did you hear about yesterday's frivolities?"

"John saw your name on the report, handed it to me. He thought it was interesting that it involved you and Anne."

John Vilar was Gruen's partner. "Does Robbery-Homicide usually have a lot of interest in assault cases?"

"We agreed it's strange you and Anne are still buddies. You got to admit, it's kind of weird." He jutted his chin toward the guest house. "But it's true. You two still spend a lot of time together."

Nice deflection. Whatever reason he was here visiting me, it wasn't official and he wasn't going to tell me what it was.

"Anne self-medicated last night. She's sleeping it off."

"Did she get hurt?"

I shook my head.

"I'd like to talk to her after she wakes up. What about you?"

"I don't have a hangover. Well, Vicodin gives me a minor headache, but if I keep taking it the headache goes away, plus my mood improves."

"Drusilla. Tell me what happened yesterday."

"And then we're even?"

He nodded.

"If anyone ever asks, you and I never spoke. Particularly if the person asking is my lawyer, all right? If anyone asks why you were here at eight a.m., it wasn't about work."

He smiled. "I can do that."

I bet he could.

I gave him the background of going to the interview with Anne. Gruen hadn't heard of *Girls Becoming Stars* either. Honestly, was he trying to be my Mr. Perfect?

"Why did she ask you to go with her?"

"The bloke she'd been dealing with setting up the interview made her nervous. For good reason, it turned out. She thought if things went badly, I could help."

He nodded. He had seen some of my handiwork with aggressive types. He'd stopped me from killing someone with my bare hands. It would have been self-defense that time, too, I might add. I try to avoid conflicts, but I can hold my own. "How did the fight start?" he asked.

"While Anne talked to Courtney, I chatted with Sabo. He offered me drugs, I said no."

"You sure about that?"

"That he offered me drugs or that I said no? I'm quite certain of both. He didn't make a great salesperson for his own product."

"You thought he was high?"

"I had no doubts about him being high. He was twitchy and abusive and I told Anne we needed to leave. Roger pushed up against me, I pushed back, we started fighting, Courtney tried to get in the middle of it, and he tossed her across the room like a used tissue. Then he and I fought some more."

"I saw the pictures. You're good."

I wasn't going to deny it. I am good. "Anne said she saw he had a gun. However, I didn't see it. So that I can't confirm or deny or tell you what kind it was."

Gruen rubbed his forehead for a moment. "Did you see the drugs?"

I shook my head. "But he was high. Tough to fake that level of twitch."

He tapped his fingers on the table in a regular rhythm. Made me wonder if he'd been a drummer.

Gruen wasn't interested in the assault or what I'd done. His curiosity was about Sabo. To find out what he was up to. Why would he be so interested in a lowlife like Sabo? Obviously Sabo had been around the criminal block once or twice, but Gruen didn't work Narcotics. And it would be comforting to think that if Sabo were doing bad things all the time, he would have been arrested. That he hadn't been told me two things: he was either an exceptionally talented criminal, or he was valuable to the police. A confidential informant, perhaps?

Whatever he was, it was important enough to get Gruen to knock on my front door.

"Did you know Sabo's filing assault charges against Anne and me?"

Gruen swore. He hadn't been expecting that. Sabo was definitely important to the PD somehow.

"Which is further evidence he was high, because it wasn't my fault. I was fine with leaving." I lifted the edge of the t-shirt I was wearing to show him the bandage over the knife wound. "Roger Sabo had other ideas."

His gaze flicked down to my stomach. He reached out and then drew his hand back before making contact.

The anticipation of feeling his skin against mine completely upset my thought processes. Zeus in a sidecar, I needed to find someone to date, and soon. Perhaps later, when my skin wasn't purple and green and covered in bandages.

"Why is this important to you?" I asked.

He shifted backward on the stone wall, moving away from me. Moving away from temptation, perhaps. "Something about the police report read wrong to me," he said.

His voice cracked on the word "report."

Liar, liar, pants on fire, I thought, and then I took a moment to enjoy the mental image of Detective Gruen removing burnt trousers.

"Is this about the drugs?" I asked. "I don't know what kind he had."

"I don't work Narcotics."

I nodded. "Is Sabo a CI?"

Gruen's gaze flicked up to me damn quick. I was on to something there. "Why do you say that?"

I leaned toward him. "'Cause there's a lot of things I would have done for that favor and you called it in on something stupid like this."

We didn't say anything for a few moments. The morning light made Gruen's tan skin glow and I focused on my enjoyment of observing him, rather than think about why he'd actually come here.

"You think Anne's going to wake up anytime soon?" he asked.

"Let me give her a shake and stick some coffee in her. What time do you have to be at the office?"

"I'm flexible."

Did Gruen have any idea what kind of images that sentence

evoked? Now he was just being mean, making my imagination work overtime. "I'll go see about that coffee."

Anne woke up slowly and stupidly and with much blinking. She went upstairs to shower and dress. When she returned I stuck two cups of coffee in her hand and sent her out to chat with Gruen for a while. She returned really quickly, the detective right behind her.

"Have everything you need?" I took his cup from him. "Lovely to see you again, Detective. Don't let so much time go by before our next meeting."

"Stop getting into trouble."

"Seems to be the only way I can get your attention."

"You have my attention."

I leaned forward and whispered, "I was hoping to get a different sort."

When the door closed, Anne rounded toward me. "Well, that was interesting. He mostly asked me about you. You two are going to make great-looking babies."

"I have to get him horizontal first. Or vertical. Whichever. I'm not picky, but apparently he is. Tell me what you talked about."

Anne giggled. "He wanted to know who started the fight. Why you were there. What you said afterward. I'm almost totally sure our stories match up."

"Given that I didn't lie and you're terrible at it, they were the same story."

She glanced at her phone. "Oh my God. Guess who called me." She held up her phone in my face.

If I were made Queen of the Universe, my first decree would be to outlaw the practice of shoving a cell phone in someone else's face, as though what it's showing you is important. Or at the right focal length for your vision. Or something you can read. I used my usual trick of moving the phone back and forth, as if trying to find the proper distance, while hiding the text under my thumb and then revealing it letter by letter. *C - O - U - R* "Courtney called you?"

Anne nodded. "Yes, she did." She tapped a few buttons and the voicemail message started playing on the phone's speaker.

"Hi. This is Courtney. I...I really need to talk to your friend Priscilla."

"She probably means Drusilla," Anne said.

My gaze met Stevie's and we both struggled to avoid smiling. I actually had been a Priscilla once. Priscilla, Drusilla. Whatever. "What a remarkable guess. Shhh."

Anne batted me on the shoulder. It actually hurt, which was unexpected.

"I'd like to talk to her about...you know, what happened. This is all crazy." Courtney rattled off her phone number and hung up.

"What do you think she wants?" Anne asked. "Maybe she's had time to consider that Roger is a bad guy?"

I shook my head. "She's delusional. Like I would spend any time talking to her."

My cell phone rang in the kitchen. Anne and I looked at one another.

"Perhaps she's also very determined," I said.

Stevie came running out with the phone. "Mr. Ross," she whispered.

I took it back into the kitchen, out of earshot of Anne and Stevie.

"How are you feeling today?" Nathaniel said.

"I'm still alive."

"Great. We're still on for one o'clock today. Actually, make it a quarter to."

Goodness, was it Monday morning already? Time for my regularly scheduled transcontinental phone call.

When I returned to the living room, Anne asked, "Everything okay?"

"Forms and paperwork. I have to go to Century City at one."

"I have to go get the money I said I'd pay you...." Anne's voice trailed off, like maybe I was going to contradict her and say it was okay, she didn't need to pay me.

To hell with that. I needed it even more now.

"Let's get together and talk later today," I said.

The door to the guest house opened and Gary, our esteemed landlord, walked in. He looked like a middle-aged man wandering around in search of a golf course, with a slightly puzzled but still happy aura. He'd gotten into the habit of walking into the guest house at all hours of the day, probably because Stevie and I enjoyed the run of his house and he felt entitled to return the favor. He was dressed casually and seemed fairly aware of his surroundings, so today might be a good day.

He was better known to the public at large as Sir Gareth Macfadyen, star of stage and screen, as royalty-crazed Americans and entertainment shows liked to refer to him. He hated the name Gareth, hated anyone using it, definitely hated using the title he'd been granted by the Queen. But depending on the day, his mood, or the alignment of the stars, he might also hate owning furniture, being famous for doing something as silly as acting, or most varieties of cheese. He had two Oscars for Best Actor and was so convinced no one liked him he'd developed a bad habit of taking inappropriate women home with him, mostly in the hopes that they'd do something terrible to him.

Which was where I had entered his life. I decided I was going to be the last one of those inappropriate women. As things worked out, we didn't hook up and become lovers; we worked out a much better interdependent state. I stood between him and the trouble he could get himself into, and he let me live rent -free at his house and monitor his moods and keep him out of trouble. He got to tell people—women, mainly—that he had a live-in girlfriend, which stopped them from getting too clingy, and his pretend girlfriend was perfectly happy for him to date other women in the meantime.

The arrangement worked out swimmingly for both of us.

"Gary, how fabulous, you're awake, come join us," I said.

"Hm?" His eyebrows knit together, as though he were startled to find himself in our house at all. Which he very well might.

"Stevie made a Bundt cake."

"Oh, that's terrible news," he said. "Is there any left?"

Stevie popped her head out of the kitchen. "I'll make you a cup of tea to go with it," she said. She also had his medications ready to go, which was probably half the reason he was at our house anyhow. My sister and I managed a number of tasks for the famous actor, some minor and some more important.

For one thing, since Stevie and I had taken over his care and feeding, he'd had an uninterrupted string of days on his meds. Which was probably worth more than any rent we might pay him.

He humphed and headed toward the kitchen but stopped when he was about to walk past me. He stared at my face, his famous green eyes focusing on the cut at my hairline. "This is why the police detective was here this morning, wasn't it? You certainly do like to live on the edge."

"No worse than a rollerblading accident on the boardwalk."

Perhaps if boardwalks fought back, with knives.

"The police were here. I want to hear the full story. Particularly before your dead body washes up somewhere."

"After you have some tea, Sir Gary."

He nodded and headed off to the kitchen.

Anne leaned in. "It's so cool you live with him."

"Technically, we live adjacent to him."

She poked at my shoulder and I turned away to avoid contact, in case it hurt. Anne had lived her whole life in and around the movie industry, and if there's one thing Angelenos are jaded by, it's famous people. That Anne still thought our proximity to Gary was marvelous was a testament to the aura around the man.

"Let's go have cake," I said.

CHAPTER FOUR

STEVIE AND I ARRIVED AT Nathaniel's office ten minutes before one. This was not because of my usual passive-aggressive behavior, but because I once again underestimated Los Angeles traffic. Eventually I was going to remember to add forty-five minutes to my expected drive time instead of a simple half an hour.

Carmela came out to the reception area with a tray holding a small pot of English breakfast tea and a small bear claw. Stevie nestled into her favorite spot by the window, ready to read a five-hundred-page Portuguese epic about a fisherman. Then Carmela led me into the law offices, stopping at the door of Nathaniel's office. He sat facing a mountain of paperwork. Sometimes Nathaniel worked for other people as well, but I did my best at keeping him completely busy on my behalf. He waved me over to one of his ludicrously comfortable overstuffed armchairs while he finished up whatever he was doing. I did my usual casual survey of his office, to see if there was anything that would tell me something about Nathaniel's personal life, other than his college degrees on the wall (one was from Harvard and one was from Yale, and I could never keep straight which was the JD). No shellacked newspaper articles about him and famous clients. No pictures of a wife or girlfriend or kids or anything. The only thing I was sure about Nathaniel was that he wasn't gay. At least, he liked women enough to check me out when he thought I wasn't looking, at least on days when I could wear something shorter and tighter than these horrible, formless sweats.

Nathaniel dropped his pen onto his yellow legal pad. "Here's the good news. Sabo has a history of involvement with disputes and physical altercations."

"Somehow your phrasing doesn't inspire relief. What's the bad news?"

"Usually he doesn't even get charged. When he has been charged, it's always been dropped."

That seemed to line up with Gruen's visit to me that morning: Roger Sabo had to be some kind of confidential informant. "He has friends in the police department or the DA's or maybe both."

Nathaniel nodded.

I did not mention Gruen's visit to my house. When I don't know if sharing a piece of information will make my life better, I tend to shut up. Telling the lawyer about the detective could wait. "What about the restraining orders?"

"Do you have any plans to go near him?"

Good point. I shook my head.

"My advice about filing charges is not to do it. We want it to go away, not escalate. Which might be hard." He picked up a piece of paper on his desk. "Courtney is planning on filing an affidavit supporting Sabo's version of events."

"She what?" The sight of Sabo throwing Courtney against the table flashed through my mind. "He beats her up and she supports him?"

"Not your problem, Drusilla. Your problem is Roger Sabo. Whatever this chick's mental state is...stay the hell away."

Roger Sabo and Courtney Cleary against Anne and me. He had some kind of magic touch with the cops, and she was looking for publicity. I didn't want any publicity whatsoever. That put me on the defensive.

"Dammit. What did He-Who-Must-Be-Obeyed say about...this?"

"As of this morning, Sabo hasn't officially filed any paperwork. Right now he's making threats and that's it. And speaking of threats...."

The lawyer was referring obliquely to the reason I came to his office every Monday morning: my stepfather, Roberto Montesinos, insisted I check in with him weekly. I ran away from home when I was sixteen and managed to stay hidden until just a few months prior—when I also got to meet Nathaniel Ross. Now that I had been found, it was like I was still sixteen and under house arrest. All the time. "You haven't told him what happened."

Nathaniel reached up and turned the giant screen of his computer toward me. The screen was blank except for one black window. "He knows you were in the hospital."

"Does he know why?"

He said nothing as he stood up and buttoned his jacket.

"My version needs to match up with yours. Or we're both in deep, Nathaniel."

My lawyer cracked a smile. "I said you were in an accident."

"What kind of accident?" When he didn't say anything, panic set in. "What kind of accident did I have, Nathaniel?"

He picked up one of his perfect bound notebooks that had the numbers stamped on the corners of the pages, and opened it to the page where the green silk bookmark was nestled. He wanted to remember his story exactly. "You told me you wrecked a Vespa. I expressed doubts about whether that was true."

Doubts I could deal with. I smiled at him. "Now we're engaged in a conspiracy. That's devious and underhanded. And so incredibly hot. I am immensely turned on right now. Do you want to do it here on your desk? You have a really sexy desk."

He ignored me and settled on the corner of his desk (which was sleek and very attractive, much like the personality, if not the person, of its owner). "The second this Sabo guy files suit against you, I'm going to be shocked, *shocked* to find out you lied to me."

I nodded. "Fair enough."

The clock ticked over to one o'clock, and the computer rang. More of a buzz, perhaps. Nathaniel typed a few things on the keyboard. Then he said, as he did every week or two during these meetings, "This is Nathaniel Ross. I have someone here to talk to you." Then he walked out of his own office and shut the door behind him.

"He's gone," I said.

The black window in the center of the computer screen turned into an image of a middle-aged man with dark olive skin and salt-and-pepper eyebrows. He was staring at the screen as though he might challenge it to a duel.

He'd probably win. Winning is his thing.

"Trudy, are you all right?" my stepfather asked in his melodic Spanish accent.

I'd only had my current name for a year at this point, and already it sounded much more normal than my birth name. Trudy just sounded all sorts of wrong at this point. "The name's Drusilla."

"Mr. Ross told me you were in the hospital. I can see you're hurt. Tell me what happened."

"I had a little accident on a scooter. One of those Vespa things. They're unbalanced crap."

There was a long pause. "I don't believe you."

My stomach muscles clenched and I felt the familiar wash of adrenaline down my spine. Exactly how much did Roberto know and, if he knew, why was he playing with me like this?

And then it dawned on me: of course I would have lied to the lawyer. Roberto would expect me to lie to Nathaniel. The lawyer would have expected me to lie and would have told the Vespa story as though it were a lie. I had the best lawyer on the planet.

"You can look up Vespa safety ratings online, Roberto."

"What happened, Trudy?"

"My name's Drusilla. If you can't remember a simple name, Roberto, perhaps you ought to look into getting tested for Alzheimer's. Which would be a terrible development for a CEO, right?"

My stepfather is an extraordinarily wealthy man and head of one of the largest investment banks in the world. He managed that feat on his own, well before he married my mother. His sigh was both dramatic and melodic. "Drusilla. Tell me what happened."

"Oh, all right," I said. "I was riding on the back of a motorcycle with a friend—"

"Who?"

"Uh...Raven. I think."

"Raven. Is that her given name?"

"His stage name. Maybe. Wasn't what I liked about him best, if you know what I mean. Anyhow, we weren't going very fast and we took a little tumble. That's it."

"Were you drinking?"

"Yes, but I wasn't driving."

"And this other person?"

"Took off. No idea what happened to him."

I waited to see if Roberto would take it. After all, going off drunk on a motorcycle was exactly the kind of thing he expected me to do. Hell, it was the kind of thing I had done all the time as a teenager in Manhattan and London. I hadn't done it in years, though. Not for a very long time.

"Mr. Ross will take care of it," Roberto said. I would have pumped my fist in the air but I was on camera. "However, this won't happen again."

"Oh, come on, Roberto. I didn't ask for this trouble."

"And yet miraculously you keep finding it. Perhaps you enjoy bad situations."

Rolling my eyes seemed like a better video chat choice than flipping him off. Though I was sorely tempted.

"Enough about your issues," he said. "How are things going with your project?"

Ah yes. The project. The project to get me out of Los Angeles and home to New York.

Eleven years ago I murdered someone. I'd had a very good reason to do it, but murder is still a huge and horrible thing. My mother, who'd washed her hands of dealing with me when I was fifteen, refused to so much as answer the phone when I called for help. When my father found out what I'd done, he sent someone to track me down and kill me. After all, I'd cost him a lot of money when I killed his business partner, and money is all that man cares about.

Not surprisingly, I got scared, and Stevie and I went into hiding for eleven years. I'd had very good training from my bodyguard, who was former Special Forces. I knew how to hide.

My mother, not knowing whether I was alive or dead after I vanished, had me declared dead privately and with no tabloid fanfare. Then she hired actresses to play me in public. It's not hard to arrange that sort of farce when you have more money than Croesus. And when all of Croesus's money was at stake. From what Stevie had been able to piece together, my being dead put the issue of the vast fortune I was supposed to inherit under a huge cloud. Having actresses pretend to be me pushed the day of reckoning for what would happen to all the money off until my thirtieth birthday.

It also complicated my simply being able to show up and get my money without my family's approval. Not only would I have to prove I was who I said I was, but they could fight me every step along the way. If I revealed publicly the reason for my disappearance—the name of the person I had killed—the firestorm would be immense. No doubt my father would show up to join in the fun.

Keeping my money from possibly ending up in my father's hands has been a family priority for decades.

When my mother married my father, her grandmother Ida didn't like him one bit, because she was a wise, wise old woman who believed thirty-five-year-old men had no business marrying seventeen-year-old girls. Too bad no one listened to Great-Gramma Ida, despite her pocketbook. When I was born she announced she was leaving ninety-five percent of her fortune to me, which probably made my father ejaculate with excitement on the spot. Then she added that I wouldn't inherit until I was thirty. Ida figured thirty years was long enough for me to become my own adult. And long enough for me to learn what kind of man my father really was.

When my brother was born, Ida split the pie between the two of us. That probably really irritated my father. Now there were two people he'd have to hide his true nature from for thirty years. And, to no one's surprise, he couldn't do it. When I was five years old, he introduced me to my little sister Stevie. Her mother was our former ski instructor. That was the end of his marriage and the start of a very complicated trans-Atlantic custody arrangement.

Ida died two years after I disappeared. I wished I'd been able to say goodbye to her.

Stevie was not only the reason for my parents' divorce, but also the reason I had not yet returned to New York despite Roberto having found me. My mother hated Stevie from the moment she was born. My return to New York was going to make all hell break loose on its own. Stevie accompanying me was an absolute no-go.

The project was to get Stevie standing on her own so that I could leave her.

Roberto hadn't even told my mother he'd found me alive and well after eleven years of not knowing. The consequences of that omission on their relationship were going to be bad enough. Bringing Stevie along with? No.

"It's not going well. I think I told you last week we were going to see another psychiatrist. Complete bozo. Ten minutes in, he starts discussing medication."

"There are several medications which can assist—"

"Roberto, I don't have any concerns about why someone might want to take drugs. The more the merrier. But he didn't even know the reasons why yet. Have you ever been to a psychiatrist?"

He answered a tad too quickly. "I have not."

Ooo. Liar, liar. "Then let me tell you how this works. The first session is a get-to-know-you kind of cocktail party thing. The two of you chat, but you stay vague on the particulars until you get to know one another. The three doctors we've seen have been bozos, giving diagnoses right off the bat. And they're also expensive. Maybe I should become a therapist. There's really good money there."

"Yes, but therapists have to listen to people," Roberto said. "Your skills lie elsewhere. Which brings me to the subject of this chat. You need to start developing the expertise you're going to need in New York."

"Doing coke at parties in Tribeca?"

Roberto did not laugh at that. On the up side, he didn't get angry and end the call, either.

He finally responded with, "No. That is not what I meant. You will have family responsibilities."

"Don't we have fleets and fleets of top MBAs to handle things for us?"

"Yes. But at best they don't care about whether your properties thrive or die. They move on to their next challenge no matter what. At worst, they're amoral thieves who plan on robbing you blind."

"You're an investment banker, you ought to know."

He waited a second. "Yes."

In case I haven't mentioned this, Roberto the investment banker is the least avaricious and most normal and reasonable person in my family. More than once I used to wish he'd been my real father. My life would have improved immensely on Day One, starting with me being a different person.

"What's Chance doing?" I asked.

Chancellor was my brother, younger than me by fifteen months. Everyone talked about how close we ought to be, us being practically Irish twins and all. Everyone would have done better to discuss how we were different species created out of the same genetic material. Chance was the kid everyone hated in school: he was smart *and* he worked hard, with excellent grades and a focus on being the top at everything he did.

The last time I spoke to him was shortly before my entire life went to hell in London and my father had plans to ship me off to boarding school in Switzerland. Chance's response: "Maybe you'll learn something for once."

"Chance is doing excellent work. He has a JD/MBA from Harvard. Did you know that?"

I'd never even heard of a JD/MBA degree, although I could parse what it was from the initials. That seemed about right for that stuck-up prick. "Good for him."

"Currently he's senior vice president of sales and marketing at van der Laan."

My mother's family giant cash cow. "Then the family's taken care of."

"You really want to leave your future to your brother's care?"

Oh.

Excellent point.

Once Chance was in charge, my future would look very sketchy indeed. I would inherit my half fifteen months before he got his. Chance was both educated better than I was and had real-world business experience. I was doomed.

"You have some work to do to get ready. While you seek out help for your sister, you need to work on a few things for yourself. I have the name of someone I'd like you to work with."

"Roberto, I'm never going to be much of a reader."

"No. But you can be functional. Next."

Functional. Fuck you, Roberto.

"You need to buckle down and find someone to help your sister process past events. This should be your full-time job. You need to put everything else aside." He smiled. Maybe it was a smile. Debatable. "Including motorcycle rides from men named 'Raven.' Or this other adventure, last week, a visit to an imprisonment camp for Cambodian illegal immigrants? Did I read that correctly?"

He knew about Anne and me going to Baldwin Park. Was he following Anne's career? He must be.

Whether he was or he wasn't, I was absolutely certain now that Roberto knew the motorcycle story was bullshit. And it wouldn't be long before he found out what had happened.

"Visiting doctors is expensive, Roberto."

He nodded. "That's why you're going to start working for me, Drusilla."

"Amongst the things that are *never* happening—"

He sighed. "It's money. Of course you're going to do it."

On the one hand, I clearly needed money. Unlike most people, I admit freely that money is a great motivator in my life. Money, after all, was the main reason I'd gone with Anne to interview Courtney at a crappy motel in Koreatown. On the other hand, working for Roberto was a very bad, terrible, awful avenue to take toward even greater financial dependence on him. Money is control. Always has been, always will be.

"I want to help you out, Tru—Drusilla. You know this to be true. The sooner you can figure out a stable situation for your sister, the sooner you will return home to where you belong. And the real work can begin."

I stared directly into the tiny black hole that marked the computer's built-in camera.

He was right, of course: either I figured out how to set Stevie up to become stable and happy on her own, or Roberto would get tired of waiting and take over the problem for me. Stevie would vanish off my radar forever. He was being generous in allowing me to give it the old college try.

"What do you want me to do?" I asked.

"Nothing immoral or illegal," he said.

I shrugged. My definitions of acceptable morality and legality are adjacent but not identical to the widely accepted ones.

"Or even difficult," he continued. "This doesn't even involve falling off the back of anything."

I waved my hand in the air. "Stop telling me what it's not and start telling me what it is."

"A friend of mine—"

My face may have betrayed my doubt in that description, because Roberto nodded.

"A gentleman of my acquaintance, who I've had the pleasure to get know, is setting up a charity venture in Los Angeles. He has asked for my help. I am sending him two things: money and you."

A million possibilities ran through my head: Perhaps Roberto had a mistress. (No. My stepfather had issues, but despite being Spanish he despised men who cheated on their wives. I wouldn't believe he had a mistress if he showed me pictures of her himself.) Or maybe Roberto had a drug dealer. (Who he kept stashed away with the mistress. Not a chance.) Gambling, corporate espionage, corporate sabotage, international political spying, jewel thievery, or high-seas piracy, perhaps. Came up with a "No" on all of them.

I was all the way to the possibility of "Nazi art theft" when Roberto said, "Oh good Lord. The look on your face right now."

"Be a lot more specific about how I fit into this," I said.

"He is having trouble working out the details of a function. A party. You are good at partying. I believe you can help him work out the problems he's having. And he might be able to help you with a few problems you have."

"Let me make certain I understand. I set up a party, and you're going to pay me for this?"

My stepfather showed me a real smile. "And you're going to earn every penny. And by the way, Drusilla? Many happy returns."

"It's March, not New Year's, Roberto."

"March thirty-first, in fact. Happy birthday."

My surprise must have shown. "It's not—" Oh Hera. It was. I was turning twenty-eight years old tomorrow. That much closer to thirty. "Instead of this stupid job you want me to do, you could send me a birthday check and make up for all the years you and Mama missed."

"No," he said, and he switched off his camera.

CHAPTER FIVE

STEVIE HAD NEVER BEEN TO Anne's house in the Beachwood Canyon area before. For one thing, we lived near the Pacific Ocean, and Anne lived near the Cahuenga Pass, east of Hollywood, off the 101 freeway. In Los Angeles, this was like us living in separate states.

Also, Stevie had little need to visit Anne. She was my friend, not my sister's.

I drove up Beachwood Drive on autopilot, doing this for the forty-first hundredth time. It took me a while to notice that my sister had launched forward in her seat and was staring rapturously out the windshield.

"What's wrong?" I said.

She pointed before turning to me, the sweetest smile on her face. "The Hollywood sign," she said.

"Yeah, Anne lives right near it."

She giggled nervously. "There it is." Her voice was breathy.

At that moment I realized we'd been living in Los Angeles for two months and I hadn't yet taken her to see the Hollywood sign. My sister loves television and movies to an unholy degree. Over the past decade watching TV and movies has been her main way of dealing with humanity. And yet here we were, in the center of the galaxy for TV and movies, and I'd never taken her to see the archetypal symbol for the entire industry.

I also hadn't taken her on any studio tours, to any of the theme parks, or to an actual film set.

On the plus side, however, I had gotten us free room and board with an Oscar-winning film star who was enraptured by Stevie's cooking. That had to score me some points in her book.

Eventually it would. After all, anything was possible.

"It's no big deal," I said. "It's just a stupid sign."

"And it's there. It really looks like that."

I grunted. "Oh, all right. We can drive up closer."

She shook her head. "I can see it from here." Her face was blissful.

I reminded myself that once I had my inheritance back, I was going to own a significant portion of one of those theme parks and Stevie could go any time she felt like it. Provided I played my cards right and was allowed to keep in contact with her.

Which meant getting Roger Sabo's crap under control. And fulfilling Roberto's little task.

Anne's house sat up one of the many winding, shady side streets that branched off of Beachwood Drive toward the top. It was a tiny, whitewashed, two-story, two-bedroom house that had no garden to speak of but did have a garage, so it was the kind of house that had everything the modern Angeleno needed. Her parents (who, like everyone else in town, worked in film and television production) had helped her buy it a few years before.

I parked on the driveway, on the right side. Her white VW convertible, as always, was parked on the left side. She never parked in the garage, because she had already filled her garage with too much junk to ever open the door again.

One upside of being itinerant was that Stevie and I had trained ourselves to carry the bare minimum with us, which often meant one box that had papers in it and nothing else.

We knocked on the front door and after a couple of seconds I turned the handle and went in. Eventually Anne was going to learn basic home safety, although keeping her doors locked hadn't kept me out of her house in the past.

"It's your neighborhood burglary squad," I called.

"Only steal the bad stuff! I'm upstairs," Anne yelled.

Stevie looked around inside. There was a small entrance foyer that led off to the living room on one side, the kitchen on the other, and the stairs up to the bedrooms. The kitchen had a breakfast nook, a sliding glass door to the side patio, and a small bathroom. It was tiny and fussy, with mirrors on the walls to make the place seem bigger and a tiny Oriental rug over the tile floor in the foyer and a standing Tiffany lamp stuck awkwardly by the coat closet that held three coats.

But Anne had the entire place to herself. Lucky woman. I could only fantasize about what living by myself would be like. After years of living with Stevie in close quarters, I indulged those fantasies a lot.

Stevie's attention was caught by something in the living room —over the fireplace hung the framed poster from Colin's magic show in Las Vegas. I had given the poster to Anne on our first meeting, a sort of "Surprise, your murdered boyfriend turns out to be married, but don't worry, the marriage wasn't for real!" kind of peace offering.

After the wild ride Colin's murder sent us on together, I was amazed she kept the poster.

She'd put it in a better frame than I had, in fact. Quality.

Anne came bouncing down the stairs, her short brown hair wet and her face freshly scrubbed. She looked a lot perkier than she had this morning. I guess she hadn't met with any lawyers or gotten any familial ultimatums in the meantime. Lucky girl.

"Hey, you guys!"

"You're always so friendly," Stevie said.

Anne blinked in surprise. "Thanks, Stevie. I think. And now for something you've probably been waiting for." She reached into the pocket of her denim shorts and pulled out several bills folded together. "Here you go."

I took the money from her and spread it out. Five fifty-dollar bills. "That's more than we agreed on."

"What happened yesterday was a little more than we agreed on, too. It's my way of saying thanks."

I never turn down extra money, especially if I didn't have to do anything extra to earn it. "You're most definitely welcome."

My accountant plucked the bills out of my hand.

"Stevie, give that back."

The beautiful green paper disappeared somewhere into her voluminous ankle-length skirt. "You'll only spend it."

I made the "gimme" gesture. "That's generally how one uses money, yes."

Anne watched us like a tennis match.

"We're not usually like this," I said to her.

"What? It's exactly like you guys. Now, let's get started with today's meeting. What's the news?"

I eyed my sister, wondering how to frisk her and find the money. "Sabo's still charging us with assault. And there's a little extra cherry on top: Courtney's siding with him. She's signed an affidavit saying we started it."

"Oh my God," Anne said.

Stevie stared at me. At which point it dawned on me that I had forgotten to share that tidbit with her. "She's signed it already? But...didn't you say he hit her, too?"

"Psychology is a strange and terrible thing."

Anne pushed her glasses up her nose. "I was going to offer coffee, but maybe it's time to move straight to the bourbon."

"Keep the bourbon on hold for me until I'm allowed to drink."

"Do you have any tea?" Stevie asked.

Anne had a box of Lipton tea in the cupboard, which Stevie sniffed at and decided she could accept the suffering it entailed. While my sister puttered around the kitchen in an attempt to brew something palatable with less than optimal ingredients, Anne and I sat at the kitchen table with our two glasses of non-alcoholic lemonade and her laptop, the little white apple on the back glowing at me.

"What are we going to do?" Her hand gripped the glass so tightly the blood drained out of her fingers. "This is really scaring the shit out of me. No one's going to hire me if people accuse me of assaulting them."

I nodded. "Let's remain hopeful that reason will prevail, but in the meantime Nathaniel is working on it."

"Nathaniel?"

"My lawyer."

"Oh, right." She finished her drink. "How do you afford that guy anyhow?" she muttered.

Anne was staring off into the distance as she said that, so maybe she didn't even hear her own words. But I did. And Stevie did. My sister glanced at me from her position at the stove and I could tell we were thinking the same thing: Damn. Or however Stevie might phrase it. *Oh, botheration*, perhaps, seeing as how *bugger* was too obscene for her. Anne had noticed Nathaniel Ross was a little out of my financial league. That wasn't good. Curious journalists tended to cause problems for people who had things they wanted to hide. Time to move the conversation to less dangerous topics.

"There's something decidedly odd about this entire situation. Roger Sabo keeps getting into trouble and then he keeps getting right out of it."

"You said you think he's a CI."

"Do you have anyone at the PD who can find out whether he is or not?"

She raised her eyebrows. "I was kinda hoping you could get Samuel to tell you."

"Samuel?"

That was enough to shake Anne out of her doldrums and smirk at me. "Detective Gruen? Isn't his name Samuel?"

Oh, right. I never thought of him as being a Samuel. In the heat of passion I'd probably still call him Detective. I spent a few seconds imagining that situation, decided I really needed to find out for sure, the sooner the better. Then I shook my head. "He doesn't want to tell me anything. Not surprisingly. "

Stevie joined us at the table and dragged one of the coasters over to put under her mug of tea. On a table made of Formica or vinyl or something that couldn't hold a mark if you wanted it to. "Explain to me about these charges."

"We have to convince Roger and Courtney to drop them."

My sister nodded slowly. "And do you have a specific plan yet?"

Anne laughed. "Are you kidding? How are we going to do that?"

I had the feeling Anne wasn't going to like my idea. I also had a sneaking suspicion I wasn't going to let her feelings interfere with what I chose to do. "We have to make their lives difficult in order to convince them they're better off dropping them."

"Whoa!" Anne said. "What do you mean by 'make their lives difficult'?"

"All I want is them to leave me alone. Us, I mean. Leave us alone. Beyond that, I don't give a good goddamn what they do with their bodies or their lives or their time."

Anne looked at me, shocked at my callousness. "He's hitting her."

"And she doesn't want to be saved from him" My voice got a little loud and beside me, Stevie flinched.

"What the hell, Drusilla. She's twenty-two? Maybe twenty-three?"

I pointed at my sister. "So's she. Color me not impressed. Courtney's old enough to take care of herself." Given the number of times daily I doubted whether Stevie could take care of herself, perhaps my certainty was misplaced. However, I was well aware of what I'd been capable of at twenty-two, so it was possible. "Right now the person I'm concerned with is me. Us. Let's approach this problem as though you and I matter, then worry about her. If

Courtney wants help to get out of this relationship with Roger Sabo, then fabulous, I'm all for it. But my primary goal right now is to help us."

Her mouth opened and I was sure that one of Anne's patented contrarian discussions was on the way. But then all of the air went out of her and she deflated. "Okay. So what do we do?"

"We make their lives difficult, they back off, and then we leave them alone."

"And nothing else, right?" Anne said.

"What else would there be?"

"I've seen when you get angry at people," she said.

"Isn't that the whole reason you brought me with you to that interview in the first place?"

The three of us sat there silently for a moment.

I sat up straighter. My back told me it didn't appreciate the extra strain. "We need this lawsuit gone, Anne."

"Okay. So where do we start?"

I opened my mouth as though I were about to contribute something fantastic, and then like always I turned to Stevie. "What do you suggest?"

"What do we know about Roger Sabo?"

"He's a creep, and he leads a charmed life."

Anne typed on her computer. "What else?"

Stevie raised her hand, as though we were sitting in class and she wanted to add to the conversation. She'd never sat in a classroom, though, so that was behavior she would have learned from television. "This morning I did a few basic web searches on him. There's almost no information on him. Every mention originated with *Girls Becoming Stars*."

"Like he only existed for the show," Anne said.

"Like he came out of nowhere," I added. "Roger Sabo's not his real name."

That happens to be a trick Stevie and I are familiar with.

Anne nodded. "Okay, well, there's an investigator we sometimes use at the magazine who can look into that."

"*People* magazine uses investigators?"

She shook her head. "Sometimes, but this guy works for the other one."

Like I can keep track of who Anne writes for on a weekly basis. Given the differing types of assignments she was getting, it was impossible for me to guess.

"He can look into Roger's background. Find out why he keeps getting away with murder. He probably has contacts at the LAPD."

"It's fairly clear Sabo has contacts at the LAPD."

Anne shook her head. "No, the investigator. He's a former cop."

Stevie raised her hand again. "I did quite a bit of reading about this show, and I have to say I don't understand the premise."

Anne shrugged. "What's to understand?"

"There were these eight young women who came to Los Angeles to find work—"

"See, you're already showing that you have a different point of view. They came to become megastars. They were the prettiest girls in their hometown, singers, models, whatever, and they wanted to hit the big time. Only they discovered that everyone in Los Angeles was the prettiest, most glamorous person in their hometown, and they're all waiting tables at the Daily Grill. I watched the second episode last week or something and it's all about a couple of them being told by casting agents they need to lose twenty pounds if they want to get sent on auditions. They're already stick thin, and they have to lose twenty more."

"There's pretty, and then there's L.A. pretty," I said.

"Exactly. The show found these eight however they find the guinea pigs for these reality shows and they brought them to L.A. and showed them on the grind for finding work in the entertainment business. And they were on TV for their first job, so that was a huge step above everyone else who'd just arrived in town and had to lose twenty pounds." Anne clicked something on her computer. "It was clear by the end of season one that most of them had lost the weight."

"How old were they when this started?"

"Oh, I know this one," Stevie said. "According to the press release, they ranged between eighteen and twenty."

Anne clicked her tongue. "Which means anywhere between seventeen and twenty-four. Everyone lies about their ages around here."

My sister read the screen of the laptop. "We know why Courtney was on the show. What did Roger do on it?"

"He was an assistant producer," Anne said. "And now there's this reunion show being planned. I guess he wants in on it."

"How is an assistant producer different from a regular producer?" I asked.

"Oh my God," Anne said. "There are so many kinds of producers. There's line producers and executive producers and producers who are just the managers of one of the stars of the show. This is going to take a while."

I waved my hand in the air, telling her to continue.

"You're certain they didn't know one another beforehand?" Stevie asked.

Anne nodded while she typed. "That's a good point. I already have an interview set up with one of the producers...executive producers. That's what you think of when you hear the word 'producer.' His name's Micah Schlegel. We can find out what we can about what Roger and Courtney were up to when the show was in production."

"How many producers does one show need?"

"Do you not know about the kinds of producers there are?"

I shook my head. "Not unless that's important."

She shook her head.

"You were supposed to do this interview with Courtney. Did you get any contact information for any of the other girls on the show? Maybe one of them kept in contact with her?"

Damn, Anne could type like a maniac. She could give Stevie a run for her money. "That is a great idea."

"When did this show go off the air?" Stevie said.

Anne clicked a few things, her face lighted with the strange pale glow from the screen. "Almost two years ago exactly."

"What has Courtney been doing since then?"

Anne clicked on something. "I don't know. She just moved back to L.A. about a week ago."

"Moved back from where?" Stevie asked.

"Broken Arrow, Oklahoma," I said. "You should hear that girl's accent, Stevie, honestly, it's to die for."

"I gather I'm hearing it *right now*," my sister said. The furrow was back at the top of her nose.

Oops. Just thinking about all those rich vowels that poured out of Courtney's mouth, I'd changed my accent. Probably shouldn't have done that in front of a civilian.

In fact, Anne had noticed my little switch and was staring at me. "Man, you're really good with accents. You totally sounded like you were from there."

"Mimicry. Like a parlor trick." I needed to change the subject and get Anne to stop thinking about me and accents. "Why did she go back to Oklahoma? The show had *just* ended. Wouldn't that be the time to strike in Hollywood? While the iron was hot and she still had some fame?"

Anne stared off into space, contemplating my question and forgetting her own. "Maybe she was burned out?"

"Two years ago she would have been twenty-one. Or something like that."

Anne shrugged. "But she'd already been on the show for two years. And reality TV can chew you up and spit you out." She shook her head. "Television's gotten crazy. All of my cousins are thinking of getting the hell out and going into investment banking, to get some stability in their lives."

I pointed to Stevie. "Find out what Courtney was doing back in Oklahoma." To Anne I said, "You find out what she's been doing here since she came back."

"And what are you going to be doing, while we're doing all of this?" Anne asked.

"Yesterday Courtney signs an affidavit saying we assaulted Roger and her. This morning she calls you, says she wants to talk to me. Why would she do that?"

We all looked at one another. Anne shrugged.

"Exactly," I said. "After you find out some of these things, I'm going to have myself a nice long chat with Courtney."

Stevie shook her head. "That is a terrible idea."

"You think everything I do is a terrible idea."

She waited until a few seconds had passed before nodding in agreement.

"You are so mean to me, Stevie. Anne, give me Courtney's number."

Chapter Six

AS SOON AS I TOLD Courtney who was calling, she burst into tears and cried her way through saying she was sorry, *oh my God* she was sorry, but there was nothing she could do that would help me. She had to side with Roger.

If that were true and she had no choice, she wouldn't have called me. She either wanted me to tell her everything was all right, or she wanted something from me.

In the absence of all other data, begin with the expectation that people want something from you. Which was fine. After all, I wanted something from her: to drop her affidavit. As a bonus, if she could help cause trouble for Roger, so much the better.

"Let's calm down, love. I can't talk to you like this. Take a few deep breaths. Breathe in...hold it...breathe out."

She actually did it. And she did become remarkably calmer after two breaths.

"Is there a color that makes you feel calmer?"

"Well…blue's my favorite color."

"Blue's *perfect*. Okay. Just feel that color flow through your entire body."

Within a few seconds she was relaxed and the tears were done.

"Wow, that was amazing," she said.

The next step was to get her to start saying, "Yes." Saying "Yes" would make it easier for her to agree with me about a lot of things. It's an old trick, but it works. "Is Roger with you right now?" I asked.

"No," she said.

"Are you alone? Now, Courtney, I know you're far from home and far from your family. You feel alone, don't you?"

"Well…." She didn't agree, because maybe that would feel too disloyal to Roger.

"No, he ain't up yet."

"Okay, so it's just us?" When she murmured, "Yes," I responded, "Does he sometimes make you feel uneasy?"

"Yes."

"Courtney, you're between Roger and me on this issue. And it's hard, because you want to support your friends. My family has a saying, though. 'Don't borrow trouble.' Have you ever heard that?"

"We say that, too!" she said.

"If you had your family here, what would they tell you? They would tell you not to get involved in this, wouldn't they?"

"Yes, but—"

"But you don't want to tell them about what's happened, because you're afraid to tell them about Roger?"

She let out the kind of sigh that signified she was letting go. "Yes."

"Okay. I think you might be happier if you get permission to leave this situation from someone who's not me and not Roger. Is there anyone in this area who you trust? Someone who makes you feel as secure as you do with your family?"

She was quiet so long the only way I knew she was still there was her breathing.

"Maybe you have someone you trust to help you figure your way out of this?"

"Well, there is one person."

Fabulous, I thought.

"Will you come with me?" she asked.

"Of course I will." I high-fived Stevie, who'd sat next to me during the phone call, knitting.

And that was how I ended up meeting Courtney in a church parking lot in Tarzana.

⁂

When Courtney told me where to meet her in Tarzana, Stevie looked up the address, and then checked the address of where Courtney had worked when she was on the show. All of the girls on the show had had some kind of "day job" to show how they were supporting themselves while waiting for their big break, and Courtney had worked as a receptionist at a place that did financial counseling for people with credit troubles. On my way to my meet with Courtney, I took a roundabout detour by a small one-story strip mall in Panorama City, north of Van Nuys.

Panorama City was melodically named but not quite as easy on the eyes. Every street seemed to be four or six lanes wide, and every business had gigantic signs to catch the eye of the passing driver. More Hispanic, less business park development than other nearby areas of the Valley. I was glad for Stevie's exact directions on how to get to the strip mall, because there was one on every block of the Valley, it seemed, and there were so many names packed onto the signs by the curb that, even if I could have read them, I couldn't have read them all in the time it took to drive by them. This one had twenty shops crammed into a large L-formation, including a gyros shop, a beauty salon, and a *lavandería*. The storefront catty-cornered from the gyros shop had a white plastic sign with black plastic letters and a simple, unadorned cross on it. According to Stevie, that sign should read Hitchcock Christian Financial Counseling. I stared at the letters until they rearranged themselves into the word Hitchcock.

I got a feeling for the neighborhood, and then I headed to Tarzana.

Most people hear the name "Tarzana" and think the place was named after the character Tarzan. And then there are the people who think the character was named after the place. In fact, both came from the same source: author Edgar Rice Burroughs had a ranch named Tarzana, where he wrote about his famous character. One little-remembered characteristic of the whole suburb was that it was originally designed to be an all-white community, where it would be against the law to sell property to anyone who wasn't Caucasian.

Tarzana was much whiter than Panorama City, that was for certain. It was one of the suburbs on Ventura Boulevard, which served as the main artery through the San Fernando Valley; six to eight lanes wide, full of cars, with every conceivable business (and probably a few no one had conceived of yet) on it.

The signs on buildings on Ventura Boulevard were large, as they were everywhere in Los Angeles (have to catch the driver's eye!), but the signs in Tarzana were more uniform in their size and branding then they were in Panorama City. There was almost no graffiti, which always surprised me driving around a giant city like Los Angeles—London and Paris and New York had more graffiti in central areas than Los Angeles did. The building fronts were white and gray. The groups of people waiting for buses were different. Signs for the L.A. Opera hung from the lampposts.

Courtney had asked me to meet her at Tarzana First Christian Church. The building itself was large, in the middle of the block. The triangular facade that faced Lindley Avenue was huge, and the facade's only decoration, a simple, unadorned cross, was probably ten meters high. The church's walls were white and plain and three stories tall.

The parking lot was huge, too. Perhaps a hundred parking spaces, which meant they had lots of parishioners. And best of all, there was only one way in and one way out, both from Lindley. It wasn't hard to imagine civil, happy parishioners politely flowing toward the exit in their sedans and minivans.

One way in and one way out made it very easy for me to watch both the entrance and the exit from where I was parked in the shade of a California Black Walnut tree, at the corner of the parking lot.

The only other cars in the parking lot were far away from the church, on the side of the parking lot next to the First Christian Day Care and Preschool. I could see a small playground with swings, a sand pit, and lots of two- and three-year-olds running around yelling their heads off.

I wondered how many of the little kids on that playground would grow up to appear on shows like *Girls Becoming Stars*. Or would think there was anything the tiniest bit glamorous about the lives those girls led.

A light blue hatchback pulled into the parking lot by the large IN arrow. It had Oklahoma plates and one person visible inside: Courtney. She parked in the center of the parking lot, as I'd asked her to. All of the windows on the car were up. Mine were down. She got out and looked around.

She was wearing a crop top and low-riding shorts. Her hipbones were perfectly outlined in the afternoon sun. When she turned, her top moved and I could see the light shadows marking her ribs. In that hotel room I hadn't really seen how thin she was, but now I could, and the verdict was she was skeletal. My estimate that she weighed a hundred pounds had come about because the stated goal of many actresses was to weigh no more than 100 pounds, no matter how tall they were. Looking at her now, I was willing to bet that Courtney fell on the wrong side of that number. A light breeze startled her as she stood there, perched on her five-inch-high espadrilles. Adding five inches to her height only made her look bonier and less substantial, but that was the look so many girls pursued. And it was the one they needed, quite frankly, for the business they were in.

I let her stand there for thirty seconds before opening the door of my car. If anyone had been crouched down in her car, waiting, the heat would have driven them out by now.

"Courtney!" I said, and she whirled around. She had good balance on those shoes.

I waited in the shade. She came to me.

"Well, don't you look the vision of comfort in this weather," she said.

"All an illusion," I assured her.

She looked up at the church. "I love coming here."

"I wouldn't have guessed."

She smiled. She was going to need to visit a cosmetic dentist to give her the smile TV demanded: veneers, whitening, perfect formation. Her teeth were too discolored now. "Well, not the church so much. But there." She nodded at the preschool. "I worked at a preschool back home. Little kids are just the best. Come on."

We walked over to the cyclone fence between the parking lot and the outdoors play area where the kids ran around screaming. There was a big multicolored play structure, a giant sandbox, and a wall where the kids drew chalk art. The sandbox had six toddlers crawling around, bashing shovels at the sand and dumping as much of it outside of the box as they did in it.

How did the preschool keep the sand clean of debris from passing cats, I wondered.

Courtney crouched by the side of the sandbox. She made exaggerated hand waves at them. "Hi," she said, over and over. "Hi, there."

One little girl, her blonde hair tied up in a multitude of hair bands, waddled over to the fence. She had big brown eyes and a smile with a couple of tiny teeth poking through.

Courtney stuck her fingers through the links to pet the little girl's hands. "Hey there," she said, her smile wide.

I wouldn't have guessed Courtney liked little children.

One of the teachers, a young woman who wore her light brown hair pulled back in a ponytail and rubber-soled shoes designed for playing in sandboxes, walked over and picked up the little girl. The toddler giggled and immediately started fussing with the teacher's t-shirt.

"Courtney," the teacher said. "You can't keep coming by here."

That surprised me more. Courtney had come to the preschool multiple times? According to Anne, she'd only been back in Los Angeles a week.

"Don't pay me any mind. I had to stop by the church today. Just taking a looksee at all the adorable kids." Courtney stood up and turned away from the teacher. "Let's go, Drusilla."

I gave a perfunctory smile to the teacher, who wore a worried expression as she stood at the fence, waiting for us to leave.

Courtney and I walked away from the preschool and headed toward the church. More importantly, we walked into the shade from that walnut tree.

"Did you know that everyone who works at that preschool is a member of this congregation?" she said.

"That's nice, Courtney, but we have other things to discuss right now."

"It's a really great community."

"I'm not much of a churchgoer, honestly. We need to talk about you dropping your affidavit."

"I can't." She shook her head. "I'm sorry, but I can't."

And yet she had asked to meet me and showed up at the appointed time, alone. No one would come all the way to Tarzana if they didn't have to. So she was still open to being talked into it.

"I look forward to talking to your friend," I reminded her.

"He can help us figure this out," she said.

"Who is he?" I asked.

"You'll meet him. He's real smart. He knows lots of things and can help us out. And maybe...maybe he can help you out. You need money, right?"

I wondered for a moment if I had said something in the motel room about needing money. But a simple rule to keep in mind is that everybody needs money. It's the basic motivator for getting up in the morning.

"How much money?" I asked. My voice cracked.

"Well, he can help you out, depending on your circumstances." She sounded so matter-of-fact. She sounded almost practiced.

Like she was giving me a pitch.

Who had talked whom into this get-together, exactly?

"Where can we find your friend?"

I assumed she was going to point across the street. Instead, she smiled and said, "He's a couple of blocks from here."

"I'll drive," I said.

CHAPTER SEVEN

COURTNEY DIRECTED ME TO A bland, featureless office building a block off of Ventura, the kind of building with interchangeable tenants. That was one of the things that drove me the most crazy about Los Angeles: because it had grown so fast after World War II, so much of the architecture of anything built post-war was simply disposable. Any given building looked like the one next door and the one across the street and all of them were probably pre-made at some lot fifty miles away.

We parked in the subterranean garage. Commercial offices didn't work in strip malls like retail did in this area. This was an office building, with a door into a lobby and a stairwell with skylights in the central atrium. The plaque on the door Courtney led me to was well-designed and classy, but it bore one major superficial resemblance to the place I'd just visited in Panorama City: the initials down the side read HCFC. Hitchcock

Commercial First Construction.

There were lots of reasons to do that, the very least of which would be they could share stationery. The more cynical part of me said they could share things like books, too, but I couldn't see how a construction business and a financial counseling office would serve one another.

Courtney swayed on those high heels over to the door. The massive, carved door with the twisted metal handle clearly showed off the design aesthetic of the company, because that door didn't fit in with the rest of the building's architecture at all. The door probably weighed more than Courtney did, but she pulled it open easily and sauntered through the doorway with an air that she belonged there. I followed behind and watched the faces of the people working inside. There were four standard-issue gunmetal-gray desks in the main room, all behind a movable partition; one desk was up front with a receptionist, and the other three had guys in short-sleeved shirts working phones. On the movable partition were posters depicting some real-estate developments. I assumed they were projects Hitchcock Commercial was working on.

Everyone looked up, saw Courtney, and went back to what they were doing. I managed to catch instantaneous reactions, flashed across the faces of the men and one woman looking up, and the only thing I could characterize them as was "not welcoming." No one smiled, none of the guys' eyes lighted up. Whoever Courtney was in this place, she wasn't one of the gang.

"Hi y'all!" she said, as though she were. "Is he around?"

No one answered. The receptionist kept right on talking to whoever was on the phone.

Courtney tapped the desk in front of her. "Hey there, Mary. Is Mr. H here?"

The receptionist held up an index finger in a gesture meaning, "Wait a moment." Mary gave off the distinct impression she wanted to hold up a different finger but was restraining herself. Still talking, she typed something on her computer.

A door at the back of the office opened and a medium-height, slender man walked out. Late twenties, with smooth skin, blond hair, a pleasant, roundish face and glasses that magnified the size of his blue eyes. He wore a short-sleeved button-down shirt and a wedding ring.

"Hey, Courtney," he said. He wasn't any happier to see her than the guys in the front office had been.

She moved toward the door he'd come through, like she was going to walk through without a care. "Is he back there?" she said idly.

He stood in her way. "Look, we've talked about this. You can't just keep dropping in."

"Mr. H told me I could come by any time I felt a pressing need to." Courtney turned toward me. "I'd like to introduce him to my friend over here."

The man glanced at me, disinterested. "You need to call ahead of time, Courtney. We're running a business here."

"Come on, now, Jonathan, what's he doing that he can't take a little break from?"

Jonathan, he of the short-sleeved button-down shirt, lost some of the general pleasantness in his face and glared at Courtney, letting his annoyance show. "He's working. We work in this office."

She reached out to touch his arm and he backed away. Jonathan did not care for Courtney one bit. "Why don't you go back to your numbers and your spreadsheets? I can walk on back and tell him I'm here myself."

Jonathan put his hand on the door. "Go home, Courtney. Set up an appointment. I'll tell him you want to talk to him."

"I'll do what I like."

"Come on, man," one of the guys seated at the front desks said. "We're on the phone."

I knew two things: this wasn't the first time Courtney had pulled this stunt, and despite how much she disrupted the office and annoyed the employees, she was allowed to do it without consequences.

Courtney grunted and reached for the door handle again.

Before her hand could connect or Jonathan could stop her, the door opened, revealing three middle-aged men, chatting cordially as they walked. The one in front nearly walked into Courtney before saying, "Hello there! I'll be with you in a moment," in a jovial, impersonal manner. The other two gave Courtney a thorough look-over before walking around her and continuing their conversation.

Courtney gave Jonathan a smile and walked through the open doorway.

The man who'd nearly careened into Courtney was clearly the one in charge of this office. He had a head of thick steel-gray-and-white hair, a paunch, and a tiny little cross on the lapel of his shirt. The people who advertise their beliefs openly tend to be the ones who are most concerned that you believe them. I was already a mite suspicious of what we were doing here, and between the cross and his fake joviality, I was prepared not to believe a word the man said.

The three men walked past me and all three of them gave me a once-over as well. No one stopped to tell me they'd be ready to talk to me in a moment, so I walked over to Jonathan.

Jonathan pinched the bridge of his nose under his glasses. "Go ahead, go on back."

I smiled politely. "I apologize for the interruption. To be honest, I'm not even sure why we're here."

He couldn't keep himself from snorting at that. He knew why.

"Does she come here a lot?"

He shook his head. "Why don't you head back to Greg's office and you can wait for him."

Just then, the man himself, Greg Hitchcock, passed me on his way back toward his office. As he walked by, he trailed his hand along my back. Some men have no respect for personal boundaries. Given that this was the man Courtney so desperately wanted me to talk to, snapping his wrist and maybe each of his fingers could wait until after I found out why Courtney wanted to involve him in our little dispute.

"Be with you in a minute," Hitchcock said to me, and he gave me one of those winks men think are so charming but come off as sleazy. "Let me go see what Miss Cleary wants. Jonathan, why don't you get our guest here a cup of coffee or something like that?"

Jonathan pasted a tight expression on his face, akin to a smile but much more tense. "May I get you something?" he asked. "Water? Coffee?"

"Certainly." I wasn't thirsty. If getting a glass of water would prolong our conversation so that I could find out a little more about Courtney and her business here, then I would get the glass of water. "Do you have somewhere I can sit down while I wait?"

"Sure." He wasn't happy about it, though.

Jonathan led me through the doorway into the hallway that led straight back. The hallway had four doors on it, plus one at the end with the familiar blue circle indicating that it was a bathroom. He led me into the first office, which was apparently his workplace. On the desk was a large computer screen and a keyboard, plus lots of extremely neat piles of paper. To one side of the computer screen was a photo of him, a woman, and a baby girl.

It took me a second to recognize the preschool teacher we had just talked to.

The bookcase behind the desk chair was packed with books, all of them upright and in good condition. There was a watercolor of Jesus with his heart glowing and an inspirational poster that had a cross radiating light and text in some kind of italic font—way too difficult for me to decipher.

"We haven't been introduced. My name is Drusilla Thorne."

"Jonathan Ricciardi." He shook my hand firmly and didn't linger on the touch for a second longer than needed.

"I'm sorry to have disturbed your work day. It can be hard to get back into the flow."

He opened a refrigerator cube and took out a small water bottle for me. "No trouble," he lied, not very well.

"Are you the office manager?"

He sat in the desk chair and glanced at the computer screen. "I'm the accountant," he said.

"Is that your wife?" I pointed to the picture of the preschool teacher.

He looked at the photo on his desk with great pride. "Her name's Alison. And my daughter, Hailey. She's eighteen months now."

Hailey. The little girl Courtney had focused on at the preschool. "She's beautiful. Looks just like you."

He looked down and fidgeted with a pen on his desk. "Thanks."

He was embarrassed at my compliment. I wanted to take a photo of his blush to remember the moment. A nice man who wanted to do his job and not cause waves. I wondered how he managed to qualify for residency within the Greater Los Angeles area with a personality like that.

"Is this place affiliated with the financial counseling office?" I said.

Jonathan shook his head. "No." He emphasized the denial hard. "No, they are two separate entities. Greg started that service with some people from the church. But it's not part of the church and we have nothing to do with it here."

"The church. Tarzana First Christian?"

"Oh. You know it?"

"I've been there before," I said. "Are you a member there, too?"

"Yes, I am. That's how I originally met Greg."

"That worked out nicely," I said, and we both laughed. "Have you been here long?"

Jonathan looked off into the distance, then shook his head. "Going on six years."

Six years. The longest I'd ever been in one place in my life was probably three or four, and my only excuse for that was that I'd been a child who had no say in the matter. "Well, congratulations. Seems like this business is doing very well."

He blushed again and said, "Thank you," before glancing up, startled.

Courtney's hand curled over my shoulder. "Dru, come on with me a moment. I want you to meet my friend Mr. H. Hey, Jonathan, I saw Alison and Hailey over at the school. They seem to be doing real well. That girl is growing like a weed. Such a sweet young lady."

He nodded at her without responding. His mouth had set into a firm line. Instead of the mention of his wife and daughter making him more amenable, it was making him more upset.

I picked up the unopened bottle in front of me and stood up. "Thank you for the water, Mr. Ricciardi."

Courtney was all smiles as she put her arm around my shoulder in the hallway. "Let's introduce you to Mr. H."

"And why do I want to meet him?"

"He's a real good man, Drusilla. He can help you out."

I stopped her in the hallway. I towered over Courtney—she was only about five centimeters taller than Stevie, which put me at about fifteen taller than her. She was also about as thin as my last few alibis, with no muscle on her at all. I backed her up against the wall. "Let's be clear about something, Courtney. The only help I require at the moment is your asshole boyfriend dropping the assault charges against me. To that end, I want you to withdraw your affidavit. I'm going to talk to your Mr. Hitchcock, and after I do so, you're going to follow through on your part. Or am I mistaken about what we're doing here?"

She pushed away from me. "I need your help, Drusilla. You need my help. We're sisters, when all is said and done."

"The only person on this planet I love unequivocally is my actual sister. You aren't her. You and I are nowhere close to being said and done. Don't push it."

She opened the door with the biggest nameplate on it.

When we walked into his office, Greg Hitchcock was leaning way back in his desk chair, phone tucked between his chin and his shoulder. He grinned like he'd just heard the world's stupidest joke and couldn't wait to repeat it. "That's a ten-four, Mikey. I'll see you on Tuesday at eight a.m. sharp. No handicap from me. Not after what you shot last time. Okay." He hung up and sighed heavily, like arranging a golf date was the hardest thing he had to do all day.

Then he leaned forward on the desk, clasped his hands together, his big, scratched, dulled wedding ring out front, and said, "Now what can I do for you ladies?"

Courtney had come back here to talk to him for several minutes, and he claimed not to know why I was there.

"My friend Drusilla here is going through a tough time," Courtney said. "I thought maybe you could help her out."

"Well, if we can help her out, I'd love to. What seems to be the trouble, young lady?"

He started rubbing the cross on his collar. He either had a nervous tic or he was trying to subliminally reinforce his Christian credentials. If my guard wasn't already up, that would have done it.

As the old saying goes, 'Whenever someone starts telling you what a good Christian they are, hold on tight to your wallet.'

"Like everyone else, I find myself slightly short of income."

"Well. That's probably a tough situation for a glamorous young lady like yourself."

He kept calling me "young lady." True, I was much younger than he was. But much like his pointing out the cross, his use of the term seemed to be more for my benefit than his.

Time to play along. "I don't know what skills I have you might find useful."

"We could always use a receptionist over at the Financial Counseling service. Can you answer phones?"

"And how much does that pay?"

He mentioned the hourly figure. Slightly above minimum wage. I smiled politely. While I had taken plenty of jobs for much less money, I also hadn't been paying income tax on any of it. This money was for a real office job, with a W2 and everything. It was ridiculous to think anyone near an urban center in the US was supposed to live on that small an amount of money. I wondered how much the firms with my family's name on them paid junior-level employees. As little as they could get away with, undoubtedly.

It was time to push my luck. "I'm in a real fix, Mr. Hitchcock. Courtney says you might have some work."

Courtney put her hand on Hitchcock's shoulder. "Greg is willing to help you with that."

Now he was Greg. Fascinating.

"Maybe I could drive you home and we could discuss it," Hitchcock said. "Where do you live, Drusilla?"

"Pacific Palisades."

Hitchcock blinked in surprise. No one making minimum wage lived in Pacific Palisades. Or anywhere near Pacific Palisades. His gaze slid over to Courtney in a silent question. When he looked back at me, he licked his lips. "I guess driving over here would be a big commute for you."

The cost of gas weekly would easily eat up whatever money I earned.

"I thought you lived near Century City," Courtney said.

"That's where my lawyer works," I said.

"Lawyer?" Hitchcock asked. His voice dropped in register.

At that, Hitchcock glanced at Courtney. His friendliness seemed to have vanished.

"Why do you need a lawyer?" Hitchcock said.

"Do you know why Courtney and I have become acquainted, Mr. Hitchcock? No? I would have thought Courtney might have mentioned something. I had an altercation with Courtney's friend Roger yesterday. Do you know Roger?"

Hitchcock looked puzzled for a second and then shook his head. "Who's that?"

"Roger has got Courtney involved in an assault case. I would be the person who was assaulted."

"I didn't want to say anything, but you poor girl. What happened?"

"It's no big deal," Courtney said.

"You're not going to drop that affidavit, are you?" I said.

"What affidavit?" Hitchcock said.

I shook my head. "I'm done here. See you in court."

Jonathan looked up from his spreadsheet as I walked by. I didn't stop to chat.

CHAPTER EIGHT

WHEN I RETURNED TO THE house in Pacific Palisades, I had a thumping headache, a definite desire to drink myself stupid, and more questions than I'd started the day with.

I left a message for Anne, telling her that Courtney was a pain in the ass and I had learned absolutely nothing.

Stevie came into the kitchen, fresh from gardening. She wore a huge wide-brimmed hat, her khakis were covered in mud, and she had a giant smile on her face. "You're back!" she said. "How did things go?"

"My nefarious plot to force Courtney to drop her affidavit has not gone well."

She pushed past me to rummage in the hall closet and came up with the canister vacuum cleaner that was in the house when we first moved in.

"Tell me about it as we get to work."

"Get to work doing what?"

She led me out the kitchen door. "It's Tuesday."

I didn't work an office job and I didn't watch television regularly. I often had no idea which day of the week it was. "And this is relevant because...?"

"We clean out your car on Tuesdays."

To the best of my knowledge, I'd never cleaned out my car, on a Tuesday or on any other day. Good to know Stevie had a system, though.

As we walked through the kitchen and outside into the garage, I told her about my visit to Greg Hitchcock's office. Clearly Courtney had remained close to her on-screen boss from the show.

"I did a bit of reading about him after our powwow with Anne yesterday," Stevie said. "He's done exceptionally well in the building business. He has projects all over Los Angeles."

"The economy's turning around," I said.

"He seems to have expanded right during the crunch. He moved to Los Angeles ten years ago and his business has tripled every two or three years. Including in a recession."

"How is that possible?" I asked.

"There must be quite a need for commercial real estate in greater Los Angeles," my sister said.

"Where are they putting it?" I asked.

In the garage she already had a bucket in the garage's laundry sink, along with a few sponges and two pairs of rubber gloves.

She put the pink set on and held out the yellow gloves. "Here's a pair of marigolds," she said.

"You seem to be doing fine without my help," I told her. "Also, I'm in pain. Before we get started, could I have a Vicodin or something?"

She sighed as she plugged the vacuum into the wall. Then she opened the passenger door and made a face. "Oh, for goodness' sake, Dru," she said. "You bought another purse?"

"I haven't bought anything in weeks. You keep taking my money."

She pulled off her gloves and laid them on the roof of the car before leaning inside. She stood up again, holding a very cute clutch purse made out of needlepoint. It had a unicorn on the side and a set of keys in an attached keyring. "It's not really your thing, is it?"

I stood up. "That's not mine. That's Courtney's. She must have left it when we drove together."

Stevie unzipped the purse and glanced inside.

"Her driver's license, ten dollars, some change, a motel room key, a phone number, and a library card."

"Courtney Cleary has a library card?" I asked.

"Drusilla, be kind."

"Why?" When Stevie made her disappointed face at me, I sighed. "If I must. Let me see it."

My sister's fingers remained firmly attached to the purse and its contents.

I lifted my hand, palm out, and swore solemnly that the ten dollars would remain exactly where it was until such time as Courtney decided how to spend it. Only then did Stevie hand it over.

It was definitely a cute little purse. The keyring had three keys on it: two house keys and a car key. The driver's license was from California, not Oklahoma, and it showed her big bright blue eyes and the big bright hair. The motel key was one of those electronic cards with no identifying information on it. The purse had nothing unusual or hidden in it.

I handed everything back to Stevie and called Courtney.

Courtney picked up on the first ring.

"Where are you?" I asked.

"You really pulled a fast one today," Courtney said. "I'm going to amend my affidavit to say that you're causing problems for me. You are *harassing* me."

No way had she come up with that idea on her own. Who had given it to her? Roger, or her good friend Mr. Hitchcock?

"Courtney!" I said sharply.

"Drusilla, you have nothing to say to me that I care one iota about."

"I have your keyring and your wallet. If you ever want to drive your car again, you're going to meet me."

"Oh, goshdarnit. Really?"

"I really, really have them, and if you really, really want them back, we're going to have to meet. And we are going to discuss that affidavit of yours again, only for realsies this time."

My sister was glaring at me over the roof of the car.

Only then did I realize I had slipped into using her Oklahoma accent. Again. For Zeus's sake, when we lived in Texas I didn't have this much trouble avoiding taking on extra accents.

Oh, I told myself, the happiness I'd feel when this woman was out of my life.

Turns out I was wrong about that, too.

⁂

Courtney wasn't at the construction office in Tarzana. She was in the motel she was staying at. Only she was at a new place. Even in Los Angeles, if you have one incident where somebody assaults somebody else and the cops have to intervene, you're probably not going to be especially popular with your motel's management. She had moved to a small motel in North Hollywood that made Mason's look like the Ritz-Carlton. North Hollywood, despite the name, was not near Hollywood. Hollywood was in the Los Angeles basin. North Hollywood was over the ridge in the San Fernando Valley. It wasn't one of the prettier areas of Los Angeles. The sooner I was out of there, the better.

The Motornight Motel didn't have bushes out front that could serve as either a hiding place or decoration. It was downright scary looking. The driveway to the front of the hotel had cracked asphalt, with weeds pushing through. The soda machine was for an off-brand, with some logo I didn't recognize. The front doors of the motel rooms faced the cement-block wall of the building next door. The back of the motel faced a narrow side road that would have been called an alley in a proper city. All the windows had grates on them.

I called Stevie. "This is either a hooker hangout or an addict breeding ground."

"Please be careful," my sister said.

"I don't see anyone around," I said. "Not even another car in the car park."

"How did she get there if she doesn't have the keys to her car?" Stevie asked.

Good point.

I was not going to limit my options by parking in the one-lane wedge between the motel and the building next door. I parked on the giant six-lane boulevard nearby. Then I took a long walk around the block the motel sat on, noticing who was around. I didn't see Courtney's hatchback, and I didn't see anyone sitting in a car who resembled Roger Sabo. Which didn't mean he wasn't there. He could very well be waiting for me inside the room—after all, I had no idea what kind of car he drove.

The windows on the back of the motel were large and had an AC unit wedged into each one. The security grate was next to it, but there was a gap between the two. One room's window had its shades open and it was easy to peer in and see some details of the room: one single overhead light fixture, a mirror mounted on the wall (no frame), and the occupant.

Courtney had the curtain open. Seriously? In this neighborhood? In this motel?

I could have walked straight up to her window and knocked on it, but instead I walked back to the narrow front entrance, continuing to look out for Roger Sabo. All the rooms of the motel were painted a darling shade of faded orange. I knocked on the door with the number Courtney had given me, and then stood on the side of the door that would open, so that anyone inside would be facing toward the opposite corner. If Courtney wasn't the person opening the door, I wanted a few seconds of warning.

She looked around for a second before seeing me there. "Well, come on in then."

"Who else is here, Courtney?"

"No one."

"I want you to open the door all the way and show me that there's no one else in there."

"Who would be here?"

"Your friend Roger."

"He owes me better than this."

"You talked to him earlier today."

She gaped at me for a moment, her mouth hanging open with

this weird twisty curve to it. "We had a fight. Which is why I'm here."

A lucky guess. Make enough of them, and people only remember the times you were right. "You forget. I'm psychic. Who else is here?"

She didn't seem to see the contradiction between me being psychic and not knowing who else was there. "Nobody. Come on in."

I followed her in. I checked the bathroom, including pulling the shower curtain back. I checked the closet, which had Courtney's suitcase and a small rectangular bag with a fat and happy cartoon bear on it. Both the bathroom and the closet were empty of Roger, though, which was all I needed. The main room was tiny and dirty. Everything was an even worse shade of orange than the door, even the things that hadn't started that way, such as the carpeting, the curtains, and the bathroom floor. The bed was one I wouldn't have sat on, let alone slept in. And she was the one with the curtains open.

Not too far away was a giant, noisy, smelly boulevard. Right outside was a sidewalk anyone could pass by on. Why on Earth did Courtney keep the curtains open, when people walking by a cheap motel would have a direct view of her room? There's simply no telling with some people.

On the bureau was a small plastic sandwich bag with some yellowish powder in it. High odds that was meth. I wasn't surprised to see Courtney used it. One thing Anne had told me was that meth was extremely popular with actresses and models, because one of the best known side effects of the drug was that the user lost interest in eating. In a business where staying skinny was the primary measure of a woman's value, a drug that could help with that was the Holy Grail, no matter the side effects.

She saw where I was looking. "You want some?"

"Absolutely not." I didn't even want to be in the room with it.

The noise of a motorcycle revving in the parking lot shook the room's window.

"Let's get this over with."

"Where's my purse and keys?" she demanded.

I'd forgotten them in the car. Talk first, then I'd go get them. "Why do you even want to be involved in Roger's lawsuit anyhow?" I asked.

The motorcycle whined, then stopped, then became louder again.

"You'd better be a sound sleeper, or you're not going to get any sleep tonight," I said.

"Aren't you sweet to be thinking of my needs?"

"Thinking of mine, actually. Could you close the curtains?"

She grunted at me and turned to pull the curtains closed.

The motorcycle stopped outside Courtney's window.

Its rider was all in black: black leather pants, a black leather jacket with chrome zippers, and a black helmet, its black face visor in the down position. Which seemed odd, given that it was dusk. Who rode around with the visor down at night?

For that matter, who rode their cycle on a sidewalk?

The motorcyclist raised his hand.

It took me a moment to realize the hand had a gun in it. And it was aimed right in the gap between the security grate and the AC unit.

"Down!" I yelled. I hit the floor as the window exploded. I rolled over and wedged myself up against the side of the bed and kept my eyes shut to avoid flying glass.

If I counted right, the gun fired five times.

Somewhere between the crown of my head and the window I heard Courtney land with a thump on the carpeting. She made a gurgling noise.

From my position on the side of the bed, all I could see was Courtney's hair. I reached through and picked up the corner of the bedspread. She was lying on the carpet, her face turned away from me. The back of her head was a bloody, twisted mess.

"Courtney?" I said.

She didn't respond.

"Courtney!"

Nothing. No movement. No more noises.

No more gunshots, either, so that was a positive note.

A series of rapid blows on the door to the motel room yanked my attention away from Courtney to the door behind me. I could see the In Case Of Fire instructions shake in their little plastic holder on the door. "Who's in there?" yelled the man's voice.

I couldn't tell who it was. Maybe had a Hispanic accent, but I couldn't concentrate on the sound long enough to figure it out.

Through the window I heard someone shouting and the screech of tires on asphalt. And in the room the AC unit was making a loud sputtering noise.

The door into the room bowed under the blows from outside.

Courtney still wasn't making a sound. From the looks of what was left of her head, she wouldn't be, ever again.

I pulled my phone out of my pocket and dialed 911. Through the open motel window, I could hear sirens off in the distance, but in this part of Los Angeles they might simply be background noise.

The 911 system put me on hold.

Holy Hera. I really needed them to answer, now.

The only way out of the room was through that door, where someone was wailing on it something fierce. Might be someone to help. Might be someone to finish the job. Or maybe I could go the other way, through the broken window, but right now I didn't feel like risking it.

The hammering on the door intensified. The In Case Of Fire announcement kept pulsing in response to the blows. The white plastic Do Not Disturb sign kept flapping up and down, keeping time. From my position behind the bed I stared at the stupid, meaningless icon printed at the bottom of it, a drawing of a cat wearing a top hat while snoozing on top of a motel. I knew I would have to tell them where I was and for the life of me, I couldn't remember. Somewhere in North Hollywood, in a horrible, dirty little motel. I did not want to die in a terrible motel.

"Nine one one," said the operator.

"There's been a shooting." I added extra waver to my voice to indicate anxiety. My past experience with violence sometimes renders me a little too calm in these situations.

"What's your location?"

I looked at the cat wearing a top hat.

"The Motornight Motel," I said. "Something like that. It's on Lankershim. I think. I can't even remember."

"Are you somewhere safe?"

"No, dammit, someone has been shooting at me! And someone's trying to break in to this room! And I think someone's dead."

Through the window a crowd of people had started gathering. Maybe they were pointing at Courtney. I didn't want to know.

"Which room are you in?"

"It'll be obvious."

"Is anyone hurt?"

"Someone got shot. She's bleeding."

"Can you get somewhere safe?"

The bathroom looked like the safest bet. Yet another door to get through, smaller, easier to defend. On the other hand, I'd be cornered if anyone came looking for me with a vengeance or a handgun. None of this boded well for the quality of my life expectancy at the moment.

"Yes," I said.

"Stay there until the police arrive."

I went into the bathroom, which was tiny and ancient. There was a simple sink counter, with no shelves underneath it. Two plastic cups for drinking. A toilet. A pair of thin bath towels. The shower was a small plastic corner unit, separated from the rest of the room with a plastic shower curtain.

A curtain that ran around a metal rod.

I yanked the shower curtain off the rod, tugging as hard as I could to loosen where the rod was bolted into the wall. My arms ached with every pull. The bolts moved, which said something about the age of the plaster on the walls. When the shower curtain was free, I jabbed the metal rings into the top edge of the crappy, low-rent bathroom mirror and opened the bathroom door long enough to drape part of it across the jamb. Then I closed the door again and spread the plastic curtain across the doorway. Anybody coming through that door was going to be confused for a moment by running into a sheet of plastic.

After that was secure, I grabbed the curtain rod and hung from it with my full weight, my shoulders aching and my bruised stomach muscles vibrating under the strain, feeling as though they were peeling apart, strand by strand. The rod bowed slightly but didn't bend or yank out of the wall.

"C'mon, dammit," I muttered. I would allow myself to cry after I had completely failed.

I held on and kicked my feet out to the toilet, gripping on to the sides of the bowl with my shoes.

The added force pulled the rod out of the wall and I crashed down to the floor, the metal rod missing my face by a few centimeters. The slam against the floor shot through my body like a bolt of pure white pain.

If the person coming through that door didn't succeed in killing me, I absolutely was going to take a few days holiday and not move a muscle.

But now I had a metal rod in my hands, and I could wait for whoever was coming through that door.

Waiting there gave me time to consider what the hell had just happened.

The best case scenario—and I couldn't believe those words came to my mind as I waited—was that this had been a case of mistaken identity and the shooter meant to get someone else. North Hollywood undoubtedly had its share of violence and drug trafficking, so maybe we'd drawn the short straw. Los Angeles had fewer murders these days, not *no* murders.

If Roger was the killer, he had had plenty of time to get to me during my walk around the block. And of course, he'd have had plenty of opportunities to kill Courtney whenever he wanted.

I kept seeing the two of us standing in the room, nowhere near one another, and no one could confuse one of us for the other. So if the shooter had meant to kill one of us, Courtney definitely the target.

I wedged the metal rod between the door and the base of the

toilet, banging it a few times with my hand to make sure it was firmly stuck in place.

How did a minor celebrity from a stupid reality TV show end up as the target of someone with a gun?

I sat back in the shower stall and waited to find out.

CHAPTER NINE

HOW LONG HAD I BEEN in that bathroom? I had no idea.

Through the door I could hear voices, banging, police sirens in the distance. They got louder. I assumed they were headed to the motel.

My spot was in the shower. I stayed there.

Someone rattled the doorknob on the bathroom and yelled, "Who's in there? Who's in there, goddammit?"

I didn't recognize the voice. Maybe the motel manager. Maybe a cop. I didn't say anything.

The door to the bathroom bowed inward a few times, like someone was trying to bang it open. My improvised barrier held despite the cheap construction of the components, but the door to the bathroom was right across from the wall of the closet, meaning someone trying to bust down the door in here couldn't get a running start.

My cell phone vibrated against my hip. When I pulled it out, I licked my lips and discovered my tongue was dry. I'd been waiting to react for so long—somewhere between ten minutes and two hours.

I couldn't concentrate hard enough to resolve the various letters into words, but the pattern of words on the screen was easy enough to figure out with a glance: *Det. Samuel Gruen.*

"Hello?" I said.

"Are you in the bathroom?" he said.

"Yes."

"Are you hurt?"

I did a body scan. I'd probably bruised myself getting the shower rod and my side hurt like hell, but other than that.... "No, I'm all right."

"Can you open the door?"

"Yes."

"Then open the door."

A quick series of tugs on the metal shower rod told me I'd done a better job barricading the door than I expected. My upper body still hurt from the fall I'd taken getting the shower rod out of the wall, so I swung my legs around and kicked the metal bar as hard as I could. It took a number of sharp, vicious jabs before it finally gave way—and my body lurched forward at the same time.

Ow.

The metal rod clanged as it rolled under the sink counter. When I stood, I was shakier than I'd expected myself to be. It took two hands gripped on the doorknob and a thorough pull to get the door unstuck. The plastic shower curtain had created a tight seal around the frame. Nice.

Detective Gruen was right outside the door, his face a mixture of concern and suspicion. He had his jacket drawn back, ready to grab a weapon. Once I had opened the door, he pushed it open all the way, checking out the rest of the bathroom.

"Is Courtney dead?" I asked quietly.

"Yes," he said. His hand gripped my arm and he led me out of the bathroom, into the tiny hallway of the motel room. A pair of techs in blue windbreakers with large easy-to-read yellow letters spelling out LAPD on the back were bent over the spot where Courtney had been lying face-down. Gruen directed me out the door, to where a passel of cops were holding back lookie-loos. I hoped no one took my picture and posted it on the Internet as a possible suspect.

Gruen led me down the walkway, past the cement pool area, to the front of the motel. There was an ambulance waiting there, the rotating red flashers lighting up the fronts of all the nearby buildings and the sides of parked cars.

"You hurt?" he asked.

"You already asked me that."

"Maybe the endorphins have worn off," he said.

The paramedic, a pudgy Hispanic woman wearing latex gloves, used a flashlight to check my vision.

"She's been hurt recently," Gruen told her.

I pulled up my shirt so the woman could check my bandage. "Seems okay," she said. "A little bleeding." She dabbed some kind of ointment on it.

"You were there when it happened?" Gruen asked.

"I have to call Ross."

"You don't have to call your lawyer for this."

"Trust me when I say, I absolutely do, yes."

"You were inside the room, right? Well, the shooter was outside the room. What's the problem?"

Cops. They're so cute when they're deliberately overlooking the obvious. I was present when a homicide occurred. He could tell me anything he wanted to right now, perfectly legally. He wasn't the one who filed charges, after all.

I ignored him and took my phone out.

Gruen was doing his job. I also reminded myself that he didn't necessarily need me to help him. What I needed right then was Nathaniel to show up and do his job, which was to protect me from Gruen doing his.

"You didn't call him while you were in there?" Gruen asked.

My laugh surprised even me. "I didn't even think of it. I was mostly waiting for someone to burst through the door and kill me."

"Are you okay?" he asked.

I was a million miles from okay. I nodded and said, "Just shaken up."

As I hit the auto-dial for Nathaniel's cell phone, I wasn't thinking about Courtney or about the fact that someone out there had decided murder was the best solution to whatever their problems were. No, all I could think about was that getting involved in another murder was exactly the sort of leverage Roberto needed to stop listening to any of my objections and yank me out of Los Angeles.

⟡

As soon as Nathaniel arrived, he separated me from the paramedics and Detective Gruen and brought me over to his Mercedes sedan. Again in the passenger seat, for the second time that week. Nathaniel was not only my lawyer, but he had a lucrative second gig going as my chauffeur. I ran my hands over the seats, feeling the smooth, tough surface of the leather. The leather of the seats in my mother's car had been softer, more like lambskin than this. If I remembered the seats correctly. Were they specially made seats, or did I have a faulty memory?

Nathaniel got into the driver's seat before using his fingertips to turn my head so I had to look at him. He stared into my eyes, as though he could diagnose a concussion by looking at it.

"How are you?" he asked.

Practically speaking, I was fine. The adrenaline was fading. My muscles were loosening from their clenched, ready position. The sudden shock of Courtney's murder was draining away. "Fine. I wasn't hurt."

"Jesus, Dru, someone got murdered in front of you. How are you?"

Not exactly the first time that's happened to me, I thought. The better part of valor decreed I refrain from saying that aloud. Perhaps my immediate downcast gaze got the point across. I turned away from him and went back to staring through the front windshield at the ambulance's flashing lights. "I didn't get shot or hit by the glass. I'm okay."

Ross shook his head.

I cleared my throat and looked up again. "The detective wants me to tell him what happened. He says it's obvious I wasn't the perpetrator."

"Were you in the room?" Nathaniel asked. He waited for me to nod. "Were there drugs in the room? You were angry at her, weren't you? Wasn't she present at an assault you were involved in? Didn't she sign an affidavit saying you caused it? Did you want to get back at her for that? What about the restraining order? Do you know how to fire a weapon? Did you try to help Courtney once she'd been shot or did you let her bleed out? Did you see who did fire the gun? Was it a man or woman? Are you certain of that? Is there any reason you might want to aid the perpetrator and hinder their investigation?"

It wasn't hard to figure out where he was going with those questions.

"The only response to these questions is invoking your fifth amendment rights. We're not doing that. It's great to hear they're sure you didn't pull the trigger. No, you're not talking to the cops. Don't say a goddamn thing."

Don't say a goddamn thing.

I put my hand over his on the steering wheel. He pulled away from me like I had leprosy. It showed good sense on his part. I understood that. "That goes for you, too."

"What?"

"Please don't say anything about this."

"Drusilla, I'm your lawyer. I don't say things."

"To Roberto. Don't say anything to Roberto."

Nathaniel was silent, the lights outside flashing off his blond hair. "You know I can't promise that."

"Please. For a while. A couple of days. Give the police two or three days to find who did this, and it'll wrap up, and he doesn't need to know."

His brown eyes were in shadow and I couldn't read them at all. "He's going to find out. Better coming from me."

"He will make me leave Los Angeles and leave Stevie. And Zeus knows she's not ready for that."

"Why do you do that?"

"What? Why do I dance to his tune? Same reason we all do."

"No. The whole Zeus thing. Sometimes you say Hades. Once I think you said Freya. It's weird."

Of all the things Nathaniel could have asked about at that moment. It certainly derailed my earnest pleading. I had to think about where that habit had started from. "My sister likes to think we're High Church Anglicans. The sort of people who wouldn't take the Lord's name in vain. So I take other names in vain. Doing it all the time makes it easier not to do it in front of her. Because normally I'm about thirty seconds from a full-on Tourette's explosion."

He had to smother the laugh that was trying to sneak out. "Your sister's a weird one."

And there it was. My best shot for getting Nathaniel to understand what I was up against with my family, with Stevie, with my whole damned life. I grabbed him by the arm. "Yes, she is, Nathaniel. She is. And it's clear I've helped do that to her. I know that. But Roberto wants me to leave her and I can't. Not yet. She's not ready to be on her own. If he finds out I'm involved in another murder I will disappear tomorrow."

The lawyer stared at me from under his dark blond eyebrows. He propped his arm over the back of my seat and leaned in. Not sexy. Felt comforting, actually. Sweat and maybe the remnants of his morning soap or cologne. "I'm not a wizard," he said. "The best I can do is keep your name out of the paper. That's if and only if the PD doesn't pressure you to talk by leaking your name. Unofficially, of course."

I made a mental note to talk to a detective about that possibility. "You can't tell Roberto."

"I don't take money from clients and then not do what I've agreed to do."

"Is your agreement to report on me, or to keep me out of trouble?"

"This is not a discussion we're having."

This was absolutely a discussion we were having. That we needed to have. Might not be one he wanted to have, might not be one I ever expected to have, but we were having it. And it was only fair that Nathaniel understand the constraints I was operating under.

"You know my real name, don't you?"

He shook his head. "No."

Was he kidding? He was smart and he had enough information—Oh. Right. I was speaking to a lawyer, and he had answered the precise question I had asked. Nathaniel Ross's careful word parsing he made me smile. "Let me phrase it this way. You're fairly certain you have guessed what my real name is, aren't you?"

He chuckled, probably recognizing the game. "Yeah. I think so."

"Then you know, when all is said and done, I will be a valuable ally for you."

"Well, since you want to discuss this, let me be clear. Right here and now, Roberto Montesinos is a valuable client for me. You're just a pain in the ass who keeps getting into trouble."

"Yes. But you don't have any really important information about Roberto that gives you leverage on him."

"I don't have any—"

"When I was sixteen, I killed a man."

Nathaniel swore under his breath. "Shut up. Right now. Not another word."

"I can't prove that to you, though, because the official cause of death was heart attack brought on by pneumonia. Lots of important people swore in front of Parliament or wherever they swear these kinds of things that he died from natural causes. He was an important man. I'll save you having to do a Google search. His name was Peter Quaid. Ever heard of him?"

The sound of Nathaniel sucking in his breath was answer enough.

Peter Quaid might have been dead for eleven years, but the name was still famous. Billionaire media mogul, opening up the airwaves on satellite, a name that was shorthand for the brave new world of instantaneous media everywhere. He'd definitely been charming and telegenic. If the news reports Stevie and I couldn't avoid were accurate, millions of people were shocked and saddened when he died in his mid-forties, at the height of his empire-building. A heart attack can get anyone, any time. The commentators on Quaid's channels and competitors' channels mourned.

Nathaniel rocked his head against the seat rest. "Jesus Christ. Why are you telling me this?"

"Maybe he did die of natural causes. Perhaps it was a heart attack. If so, it was brought on by my application of a cricket bat to the back of his head six or seven times. I lost count after four."

He held his index finger up. "Shut. Up. Now."

I batted his hand away and leaned in closer. Now I could see the reflection of street lamps in his eyes. "He was on top of Stevie at the time. She was eleven years old."

He did not blink. Good man.

"I will do anything to protect my little sister. I have done things to protect her. You don't want to know how I got us out of London that day. Everything I did that day I would do again if I had to."

His mouth opened and closed a couple of times, as though he kept thinking of things he wanted to ask and then realized he was better off not knowing the answer to. Finally he shook his head and sank away from me. "What the hell? Did your father know what this man did?"

I snorted with laughter. "Know about it? He arranged it. My father made a lot of money from having a close relationship with Peter Quaid. They were finishing up a multi-billion-dollar deal to merge their companies. A deal where Stevie was the signing bonus. Because Quaid had already got tired of me. At sixteen, I was too old."

Nathaniel, the criminal defense lawyer, stared at me. He must have heard worse over the years. People can survive some terrible life situations. I'd at least had a roof over my head and food whenever I'd wanted it, which was obvious as I'd spent most of my adolescence kind of pudgy. It's when I finally started growing that Quaid started looking for a replacement.

"My father wants me dead. He even sent someone to kill me. It's why I've been hiding. If Roberto takes me back to New York and leaves Stevie on her own, how long do you think it will take for him to make her pay for what I did?"

He didn't answer me. What was he going to say? Instead, we sat in his fancy Mercedes sedan not saying a word. The night was so noisy, with the sounds of people milling about on the street and cars whizzing by on the boulevard. People only whiz by when it's late at night. During the day, the traffic usually crawls.

When I decided he had thought long enough about what I'd said, I reached over and put my hand on his. He didn't pull it away this time. I leaned toward him, which was more about making him aware of me than needing to whisper. Then I whispered.

"I need you to help me. I will do anything you ask me to. Now, or in the future."

When he snorted, he breathed too rapidly. I was making him nervous. Good. "You really shouldn't give open-ended blank checks."

"I do if I need to. I do if I'm willing and able to pay up. Which I absolutely am. I do what I have to do when I have to. And I don't agonize over it or regret it for even ten seconds. What I need right now is time. Time to figure out what I can do with Stevie to protect her. If you have any ideas, fabulous. Let's hear them. But right now, if I go back to New York, she's as good as dead."

He tapped his thumbs on the steering wheel. Probably looking for the best angle for this situation, or maybe wondering how he could fire Roberto and me as his clients. Maybe he was picturing the gigantic stretch of Malibu beachfront real estate he was going to buy with the money he could make off my family.

He pushed the button that started the car. "My father always spells God with the 'o' left out. He says it shows respect to the creator. Shows awareness that you're not even worthy to write the name."

"Religious beliefs are weird."

"That they are. I will call you tomorrow."

I opened the passenger-side door. "Fair enough."

"What are you doing?"

"I need to drive my car home, Nathaniel. No one survives for long in Los Angeles without a car."

"I'll follow you," he said.

"Make sure you charge for every minute of drive time."

Once in my car, I stared at the wheel. It was hard to remember what I was supposed to do next. This key in my hand—why? Oh, that's right, to begin driving the car.

In the space between my seat and the center console, a few metal zipper teeth peeked out at me.

Courtney's purse and keys. I still had them.

A glance in the rear-view mirror told me Nathaniel was ready to shadow me home.

Well...fuck.

I opened my door and signaled to him. He got out of his car and walked over. "What is it?"

I pointed into my car. "The whole reason I came here to talk to Courtney. I forgot to bring them in."

Nathaniel looked at me. "You are a piece of work." He went to his car, undoubtedly to get an envelope to store them in before handing them over to the police.

CHAPTER TEN

STEVIE GAVE ME HOT CHOCOLATE to wash down the Vicodin tablet before bed instead of the G&T I asked her for. Then she asked if I wanted her to sleep in the same room as me, so I wouldn't feel alone. I told her that wasn't necessary because I was fine.

Instead, I lay awake for hours, staring at the ceiling and burping chocolate-scented acid.

After an hour or two of bad dreams involving blood and people pointing at me, I sat in bed and stared out the window at the sunrise. For the first time in a long time, staying in bed felt superior to doing any other activity. Good things happened in beds, and very, very bad things seemed to happen out of them.

I'd gone with Anne on that interview to help her out, and I ended up in a fight and with an assault charge against me. I'd talked to Courtney to straighten out what happened during the interview, and now Courtney was dead. I could only imagine what would happen if I ever ran into Roger Sabo again.

Maybe Courtney's murder had been random. There had been fewer than three hundred murders in the past year in Los Angeles—the news constantly bleated about how L.A. was now the safest big city in the nation—and some percentage of those had to have been random. Gang-related, or drug-related, or whatever. Perhaps a bullet meant for a drug dealer hitting a passerby instead.

Courtney's murder wasn't a random drive-by, no matter how much meth she snorted. She had been well-lighted in the motel room's window. The murderer could have been after me, but when I was standing anywhere near Courtney, it was quite clear which one of us was which. Her murder had been deliberate.

The obvious question was: Did Roger kill Courtney? If he did, why did he wait until I was with her? And if he didn't pull the trigger, how had the killer known where she would be and when? The murderer could have been following me to get to Courtney, of course, but how would anyone have known that I'd be talking to her? The killer would have had to get that information out of Stevie, and she wouldn't have said a thing to anyone.

And that man she'd wanted me to talk to, Greg Hitchcock. Could he have murdered her? It had happened right after they talked.

Courtney had been the target. I couldn't for the life of me imagine why.

Not my problem, I told myself. The city of Los Angeles retained the services of well-armed, good-looking men (and probably women, too, though I hadn't met any yet and wasn't planning to) to find the answers to those questions, and my job was just to stay the hell away from it.

The house was quiet. Which meant Stevie was outside in the garden, poking at green things, or in the main house, cooking. My phone was on the kitchen table with a sticky note stuck on top of it. The note had an arrow on it, pointing to the front door of the guest house.

I checked the phone: three calls from Anne, one from Nathaniel. A couple of others I didn't recognize, which meant they could wait.

Sabo was my main problem at the moment. Courtney's death changed nothing when it came to the problem he presented me with, so that was what I had to focus on today.

On the front door of the guest house was another sticky note with an arrow. My sister had a gentle way of guiding me to where I needed to go, and she was telling me to head outside. Perhaps she had been struck by the need to make lots of French toast for breakfast.

As I walked into the garden, though, Stevie and Anne walked through the gate on the side of Gary's house, heading toward me. Anne's hands rolled forward constantly as she explained something to Stevie, and my sister kept nodding.

"Hey!" Anne waved at me, as though I hadn't seen them coming my way. "Did you hear?"

She sounded concerned and upset. But not at me. Which meant that her news probably concerned Courtney's murder.

"Just put my feet on the floor. What happened?"

"Courtney was shot and killed last night," she said.

Since her opening line wasn't, "Tell me everything you know about what happened last night," she didn't know I'd been with Courtney when it happened.

Stevie rubbed her fingers on her collarbone, confirming my

suspicion. If I wanted to pretend I had no idea what Anne was talking about, I was in the clear.

I could tell Anne not only did I know that but why, or pretend that I had no idea. With option one, the conversation was going to rapidly turn into an interview. And that was too risky.

I slowed to a stop by the line of chaise longues by the pool.

Anne nodded furiously. "Last night. In her hotel room. Somebody shot her."

Stevie curled her fingers at me, which meant, *react to that news*. So my mouth dropped open and a few moments of silence went by. "That's horrible. Do they know who did it?"

She shook her head. "The cops have a witness they want to talk to."

That would be me, I thought.

"You saw her yesterday, right?" Anne asked. "How did that go? What happened? Have the police talked to you?"

"Are you working on a story about this?"

She pulled her cell phone out and glanced at the screen, which was covered in notifications. "You bet I am. This was a shitty little human interest story on Monday morning and now it's about a murder. Just a second." She walked away from us, phone to her ear.

Stevie took my hand in hers and pulled me back toward Gary's house. I turned the handle on the French door and my shoulder ached so hard I let Stevie pull the door open. "Let's get you some breakfast," she said. *Sotto voce*, she added, "She called your phone so many times in a row I decided it was best to answer it. She was on her way over, so I let her in the front gate. What are you going to tell her?"

I looked out at Anne, chattering away into her phone. "Do what I always do. Stall. What are you up to today?"

She pointed toward the library. "Working in there. On a project. Come find me afterwards?"

"Be good. Try to spend at least fifteen minutes outside today."

Stevie gave me a thumbs-up and disappeared through the butler's pantry, heading toward the east wing of the house.

In the kitchen, Anne plopped down on the stool next to mine.

"We're going to talk to Micah Schlegel today," Anne said.

"Why do we want to do that?"

"He's one of the producers from *Girls Becoming Stars*. We already had an interview scheduled to talk about the *GBS* reunion. He might know some stuff about Courtney and Sabo we could use for this assault charge. On the way you can tell me everything that happened with Courtney yesterday. Maybe there's something there."

And my job was to prevent Anne from figuring that out.

"Let me grab my things and we'll chat," I said.

※

On the drive to Micah Schlegel's office in Studio City, I told Anne about my chat with Courtney and how extremely familiar she was with the owner of the office she'd worked in. She'd wanted me to talk to him for some reason. Then, he'd offered me a part-time job.

"That was awfully Christian of him," Anne said. "That's it? She didn't talk to you about the lawsuit?"

"Never figured out what she wanted," I said. "Now I don't know what to do."

"Did anything happen that might tell you why someone wanted to kill her?"

I shook my head. I wanted to stop thinking about Courtney

Cleary. "Explain to me who this person is we're going to talk to."

"His name's Micah Schlegel. He produces reality TV shows."

"How do they differ from regular TV shows?" I asked.

Anne glanced over at me. "Seriously, you live in LA?"

She spent the drive over the Sepulveda Pass and into the San Fernando Valley explaining the economics of reality TV shows. The successful ones made a lot of money but had no lasting power, because no one watched reruns, and the unsuccessful ones didn't cost that much to produce, so churning through a lot of crap to find the ones that worked was economically viable. On the other hand, a standard TV sitcom or drama might take hundreds of thousands or even millions of dollars to produce one episode and then get canceled right away, because the real money was in surviving a few years and reaching syndication. Lots of places were choosing short-term money over the long-term.

A show like *Girls Becoming Stars* could burst onto the scene, be incredibly popular for two years, and then flame out, and that would be considered an unqualified success. The producers made some money with almost no investment and then were on to their next project.

"Leaving the stars of the show high and dry and wondering what just happened."

"Exactly," Anne said. "Gotta feed the beast. And you get so used to the money and the perks and then it all vanishes."

"And you end up dead in North Hollywood."

"Can you imagine?" Anne said.

Studio City was named after its origins in the early days of the movie business, when the undeveloped area was used as studio lots. Westerns were filmed there. I myself never particularly enjoyed Westerns. Good vs. Evil? Cattle vs. Sheep? Everything the main characters were fighting over was eventually going to give way to whoever owned the railroads, so all those poor bastards did was distract everybody from the real issues, which was who owned the land.

My unique perspective on the opening of the West may have been colored by the fact that one of my great-great-grandfathers was a railroad tycoon who married a silver heiress and bought up cheap what these poor ranchers and farmers had been killing themselves to own and work on.

It was tough to imagine movie cowboys riding around modern day Studio City. Despite the name, the place had zero glamour, although it was one of the wealthier areas of the San Fernando Valley. Ventura Boulevard looked much the same here as it did in Tarzana: lots of tall palm trees, garish billboards, and oversized store signage competing for drivers' attention. There were some pedestrians, but the cliché about Los Angeles being designed for drivers was triply true in the San Fernando Valley. The Valley really came into its own post-World War II and the layout was absolutely designed for autos: wide lanes, large radiuses on sidewalk corners to make turning easier, and every ten feet another driveway.

The buildings on the block near Schlegel's office held dentists' offices, doctors' offices, TV producers' offices, realtors' offices. Every single one of them had flat, featureless architecture and looked like every other building for miles, designed to be torn down and replaced with something else in a decade or two. Schlegel's building was at least a decade past its expiration date, but the office itself was in fine shape.

Except for the piles of paper everywhere. That was kind of horrifying.

"Don't step on that!" the guy on the phone yelled at me. He

was pointing at the pile that was leaning against the wall for support. My foot had almost made contact with it, because the paper had blended in with the white wall behind it.

I raised a hand in apology. And carefully scanned the room for further minefields.

"Micah Schlegel?" Anne said.

The guy on the phone waved us back from him, still focused on his call. *I'll get to you, stop pushing me.*

Schlegel was a young guy, maybe the same age I was, twenty-seven or twenty-eight. His brown hair was wild and curly, sticking out in all directions, and he wore glasses with wire rims. I had a stereotype of TV producer as a more the older, cigar-chomping type, but in today's TV environment, that guy wouldn't have enough energy to keep up with the pace. Schlegel wore a t-shirt and jeans and he kept talking into the phone a million miles a minute.

Also in the office were two other desks, against the far wall. One had another guy with headphones on, typing as fast as he could, and the other had a young woman, answering an actual landline phone and scribbling things on a piece of paper. That summed up Los Angeles: everyone was on the phone all the time. All three voices echoed around the small room, hardly dampened by the carpeting or the baffles created by the towers of paper. But none of them seemed at all disconcerted by the noise made by the others.

I would be a bad fit for this office.

"Shit!" Schlegel yelled. "Mariah! Scott Thomason over at Fox wants a meet. Set it up."

The woman at the desk, who I assumed was Mariah, lifted her middle finger and waved it at him. But she scribbled something down.

Schlegel pointed at me. "You Anne da Silva?"

Anne took a step forward. "I'm Anne." She stuck her hand out. "Hi."

"Either of you want coffee? I want coffee. Jesus. Today's crazy. Need to get out of here. Come on, let's go."

The three of us walked over to a nearby Starbucks. Anne bought a small coffee, Schlegel ordered a gigantic milkshake-type drink with whipped cream sliding off of it in cascading waves, and I kept my moral superiority by having nothing. Stevie kept me on a tight budget, which makes moral superiority easy.

Schlegel was being slammed with interview requests since the news about Courtney's murder had broken. "I can't believe it," he kept saying. "I just talked to her, you know, yesterday. And I don't have time for this, you know? I'm trying to get all this stuff done and she's dead."

A pair of guys at the table next to ours swiveled around when they heard Schlegel say that. I lifted my eyebrows at them and they turned back around.

"You're working a lot?" Anne said.

"Eighty hours a week," he said.

"What's the show?"

"This is for the reunion show," he said. "You work eighty hours a week developing projects, calling people, putting shit together. When the show's actually in production you work a hundred hours a week."

"You've had shows on the air. Doesn't that count for something?" I asked.

"No one has it made in this town," he said. "No one! And everyone always thinks, 'Oh, all I gotta do is get my one break and I'll have it made!' But that's bullshit. You always have to hustle for your next job. Always."

Gary had taught me much the same lesson. He had a matched set of those statues everyone in town wanted, owned the sobriquet "Legendary," had millions of dollars in the bank, and still took starring roles in big-budget horror flicks just to keep working. He had to keep his name out there, because in less than a year executives would say, "Sir Gareth who?" And if he didn't take the money, someone else would.

"So what's your story?" Schlegel asked me. "You an actress?"

I shook my head. "Personal assistant." I pointed at Anne.

"Huh." That answer gave him nothing he could use for his own advancement or to promise me some. He lost interest in me and I worked on a sculpture using a couple of plastic straws snagged from the condiments counter.

"So let me tell you this flat out," Schlegel said. "I'm not going to talk much about Courtney. I know that's why you called, but I'm not talking about her."

"Grieving?" I said.

"The police?" Anne said.

"PR." Schlegel shook his head. "The publicity from this is gold. Right now I need this."

Anne pushed her phone closer to him. "Let's talk about the reunion show. Are all of the girls going to be on it?"

He made a dismissive noise. "Man, Courtney wasn't even going to be on it until a week ago."

Anne and I looked at one another. So much for him not talking about Courtney. She leaned forward. "What changed?"

Schlegel shook his head. "We have to put this together kind of fast, you know? Some of the girls don't live in Los Angeles anymore, and some have moved on to other things, if you know what I mean."

The smug expression on his face when he said that made me want to put one of my straw sculptures up his nose.

"But mostly we want the girls who are doing interesting things now. You know. Who have a story."

I cut Anne off before she could ask her next question. "You keep saying 'a story.' I have the feeling you're using the word differently than the rest of us do."

"You know. This one's working as a model, this one's got, you know, kids, this one's still going to auditions and really focused on the dream, you know? Everybody's got a story. We're not going to have time to repeat stories, so we have to pick the interesting ones."

"Why wasn't Courtney going to be on the show?"

Schlegel shrugged. "Well. You know, she's nice and all. But I asked her to maybe come up with a different angle on things, you know?"

"Oklahoma wasn't a good story?" I said.

Schlegel pointed at me. "Exactly!"

"What changed?"

"She told me she had a great angle. Nobody else had this."

"And you're not going to tell us what it was."

He shook his head. "You know how much this is worth in terms of ratings now?"

"Even though it might be why she was murdered?" I said.

"Wow. You think?" he said.

I wanted to give Anne the signal that meant *You create a distraction and I'll strangle him*, but at the last moment I remembered only Stevie would understand what that gesture meant. And she never created the distraction, no matter how much the person deserved strangling.

"Who else is going to be on the reunion show?" Anne asked.

Schlegel rattled off the names of several other girls who they were looking to include on the reunion show.

"Will Roger Sabo be working on it?" Anne asked.

Schlegel made a face. "That asshole. Jesus, I hope not. You guys know him?"

"He brags about his time on your show quite a bit," I said.

"He was useless. Well, there was one thing he was really good at."

"Scoring drugs?"

"Okay, *two* things he was really good at."

Anne and I exchanged a glance before I smiled. "What was the second thing?"

"Did you ever watch the show?" he asked me. When I didn't respond, he looked at Anne. "You did, right? 'Kay. So one of the problems the girls had was how they were going to support themselves while doing the auditions, making the rounds, what have you."

I looked at Anne. "Didn't the show pay them a salary?"

Anne shook her head. "These shows set them up with a 'normal life.'" She made quote marks in the air. "The girls hold down jobs, they go to auditions...."

"And somehow in between everything else they become stars."

Schlegel nodded. "Right. That's the show. Shows have stories, too. Well, Sabo finds us a place that does a sponsorship on the show and hires some of the girls for, like, answering the phones."

I watched Anne nod, like that made any sense. She kept paying attention, so perhaps what he'd said sounded like English to her. I interrupted him. "What's a sponsorship? They bought commercials?"

Anne shook her head at me. "No. In order to finance these shows, there are product placement ads. What sodas the girls drink. What cars they drive. In return, the show features that brand heavily, with the logo front and center on the screen."

Schlegel nodded. "The one Sabo brought us was Hitchcock Christian Financial Counseling."

That was the first fascinating thing Schlegel had said all day. Because Hitchcock had definitely acted like he had no damn idea who Roger Sabo was when I mentioned the little sleaze's name.

Anne said, "Roger Sabo, the drug dealer, brought you a Christian organization?"

Schlegel sucked a wad of whipped cream off his straw and stared at me to see if I was watching. "It was a minor deal, but it worked pretty good. You know, it was good enough for him to score a producer title. Well, *assistant* producer. And it showed a couple of the girls as being wholesome Christians, which, given the rest of the things they were doing—"

"Which girls went to work at this Christian office?" I asked.

"The down home girls, the ones from Oklahoma and Texas."

"Courtney Cleary and who?" I asked.

"And Randi Narvaez. The one from Dallas."

The one from Dallas. Every girl was a type, who fit into a slot. A slot defined by her story. TV liked its types and its easy stories.

"Is Randi going to be on the reunion show?" I asked.

Schlegel nodded. "She is now."

"Now?"

"You know. Since Courtney... Randi and Courtney worked together. We have to have her now."

"But you weren't going to have her before."

He shook his head. "Randi's story was okay. Nothing special.

She's doing under-fives. Mostly no dialogue, which is, you know..." He tilted his head to the side.

Could this Randi woman have guessed she was not going to be on the reunion special? Would that be a big enough incentive to kill Courtney?

This town was making me suspicious of everyone's motives at all times.

Anne started scribbling on a notepad. "What did the girls have to do at this office?"

"They would sometimes answer the phones. Shit, did you ever watch this show? Even with our amazing, miracle-working editors, it was clear they were useless."

"These jobs...were bogus?" Anne asked.

"You gonna put that in there?" he said.

She pushed her glasses up her nose and leaned toward him, co-conspirators in the behind-the-scenes details. "I just want to get a feel for how this worked behind the scenes."

Schlegel nodded. "They didn't do any typing. They didn't take messages. They called home on the phones. We had to cover their long-distance charges, for Christ's sake. I don't think a single one of them did anything if the cameras weren't rolling."

"Where can I sign up for that sort of work?" I asked.

Anne kicked me under the table. "Why would the employers go along with this?"

Schlegel laughed. "You're kidding, right?"

She shrugged. "I should ask anyhow."

"Well, you can't put this in. Or you can't put that I said it. But they went along with it because it was great publicity. Their companies got named over and over again on a show everyone was watching. Who wouldn't want some of that, you know?"

Anne might have been working on a story, but I was there to learn everything I could about Roger Sabo to get him off my back. I leaned over to Anne and whispered, "Were Courtney and Roger together during the show?"

Anne glanced at her notepad, as if checking what I'd said, and repeated the question to Schlegel.

"Yeah. Not exclusively. Roger was kind of popular around the shoot, if you know what I mean."

"Because of the drugs?" Anne asked.

Schlegel nodded. "Sabo was the connection. Everyone else's sources kept getting busted."

Anne made a notation. "What kind of drugs?"

Schlegel shrugged. "Anything you wanted. He had the best stuff. Some of the girls spent a lot of money with him." He shrugged. "But you know, the girls...they need to watch their weight, right?"

"Cocaine?" Anne said.

Schlegel screwed up his mouth, like he was asking himself, *Which turnip truck did this chick fall off of?* "Meth. Smoke a little meth, stay skinny."

Meth. The stuff in Courtney's motel room. Her teeth hadn't been too pretty, either.

"Isn't meth worse for you than cocaine?" I asked.

"Yeah. But it's cheaper. And you can go for days without eating, you know what I'm saying?"

Anne looked down at her notes. "You said everyone else you knew got busted. Was that before or after Sabo joined the team?"

"After. Definitely after. There was a one-to-one correlation there. Maybe he was defending his turf, you know?"

Anne and I glanced at one another. That definitely scored one point for the theory he was a confidential informant. If Roger Sabo could pick off his competition like that, he was a player. We were going to have a lot more trouble with him than I had imagined.

Also made me wonder if maybe Courtney had caused trouble for Sabo and he had to defend his territory.

I shook my head. I was not going to think about Courtney's murder. The detectives of the LAPD were on the case and it was none of my business.

Roger Sabo, on the other hand—I needed to deal with him, in a hurry.

Chapter Eleven

SCHLEGEL HEADED BACK TO HIS office and we walked back to Anne's car. She turned on the AC and put the recording of the conversation on the car's stereo so she could make sure the sound had come through. She nodded, satisfied, and took the headphones off. Then she stared at her phone for a few seconds and stuck each earbud of the headphones back in her ears. "*Of course*," she said suddenly, violently. She pulled off the headphones again. "I am such a moron."

"I never contradict a person on their self-assessment, but do tell. What about your phone made you come to this conclusion?"

She held up the phone. "I taped it. I taped the entire interview with Courtney."

"And this is interesting and important why?"

"Everyone present knew I was doing the interview. Are you surprised to hear I was recording it?"

I shrugged. "No."

She shook the phone in my face. "We have a recording of who started the fight, stupid. And it's not like anyone can claim they didn't know they were being recorded. It's why we were all there in the first place."

I wasted no time taking my own phone out and calling Nathaniel Ross.

"It's iffy," he told me. "Probably won't be allowed."

"Will it put enough pressure on Roger to drop these assault charges?" I asked.

"Have Anne email me the recording. When you're alone, call me. I need to talk to you about last night."

"Done." I hung up.

"Now what," Anne said.

I called Stevie. "Here's a name for you. Randi Narvaez. She was another girl on this show and she and Courtney spent a lot of time together. Much of it at Hitchcock Financial. Can you find where she is?"

We drove back to Pacific Palisades and discussed Courtney and the show.

"Why did she come back?" Anne said. "I could kill Schlegel for not telling us."

"Yes, but telling us would ruin the publicity for his big reveal," I said.

After a long pause, Anne said, "I shouldn't have said that. I wouldn't do that."

"What?"

"Kill him."

"It's only a figure of speech."

"It's a *terrible* figure of speech," Anne said.

Anne's journey through being morose was a waste of everyone's time, including mine. "Courtney came back a week ago. Why was she living out of motels? Even a crap apartment has to be cheaper than a series of motels."

"A good Christian girl from Oklahoma wanted to be a star so bad she'd do meth."

"Your first mistake is to think that someone's religious beliefs have any effect on their actual behaviors," I said. "People simply are who they are."

When we arrived at Gary's house, Stevie handed each of us a small cup of espresso. Anne sipped hers, while I slugged mine back.

"Ow," Anne said.

"Least of my aches and pains right now." I handed my dirty cup to Stevie. "What have you found out?"

Stevie plucked Anne's cup out of her hand. "Randi Narvaez has been working in movies and TV for the past several years. Small roles. Many without speaking parts. I tracked down her manager's information. When I called, he said she wasn't taking phone calls from anyone, due to recent circumstances."

"She's holding out for a big interview," Anne said.

"You could call her," I said. "Or we can get her attention even faster. Is Gary home?"

Stevie nodded. "Outside. Why?"

I ignored her and headed through the butler's pantry to the French doors that led out to the outdoor living room. Anne followed close behind me.

Gary was stretched out on the sofa, enjoying the heat while keeping out of the sun. He was smoking one of his Cuban cigars and paging through a script. He gave me a mild wave when I came barreling through the doorway, and then looked concerned when I stopped to talk to him.

"I have a favor to ask," I said.

"I hardly know the day has begun if I haven't got one of your ridiculous requests. What is it?"

"Can you bring someone to the set for a possible walk-on?"

He shook his head. "Casting's set."

"I didn't say you had to cast her. Just have her show up as a possible."

He took a puff on his cigar, inhaled, and held it, staring at me the whole time. Then he blew the smoke out and put the cigar in the ashtray. "Is this concerning...." He lazily made a circle around his forehead.

He meant my injuries. "Yes," I said. "It's about that."

"Is this person the one who tried to kill you *this time*?" he asked, as though only mildly interested in the answer.

"No," I said.

Since moving into Gary's house, I'd nearly gotten killed here twice, by two different people, on the same night. Looking a little worse for wear had probably set off a few alarms for him. Albeit, not the same alarms as he'd had installed after the last time.

After a moment, he shrugged. "Certainly. When do you need to speak to this person?"

"Are you going to the set today?" I asked.

He shook his head. "Tomorrow."

"Then one more thing."

He picked up the cigar again.

"Can you have whoever's in charge of casting send the request?"

He chuckled silently as he took another drag on the cigar. He puffed out a few smoke rings. "You're unbelievable sometimes."

"That's why you love me."

He made a face at that. "This girl. Is she good-looking?"

I glanced at Anne, who nodded. "Very," she said.

"Ooo, I like her better and better. Can I meet her?"

I made a face. "Gary, darling, do you want to make me jealous?"

"Depends. Will I get a laugh out of it?"

"You're horrible. Stop smoking. It'll kill you."

When we returned to the kitchen, Stevie was stirring a giant bowl of what I suspected was brownie batter. Anne picked up her purse and keys off the kitchen counter. "What is your relationship with him?" Anne asked me.

"What do you mean?"

"You live with him...except you don't. You live in the guest house, with Stevie. He tells everyone you're his girlfriend, but...you're not. Is he gay?"

I shook my head. "Not gay. Despite being a British actor."

"So what's the story?"

"It's not important, Anne."

"It's so weird. Just always makes me wonder what else you're not saying."

When she left, I locked the front door behind her and returned to the kitchen.

"She's suspicious you're not telling her something," Stevie said.

"She's not even an investigative journalist. She does puff pieces on celebrities, for the love of Zeus."

Stevie nodded. "She's smart and she's very curious. Which is a good combination for her."

"Yes. And it's terrible for us."

My sister thought about that, and then she nodded.

I didn't need new friends. I needed no friends.

Chapter Twelve

GARY'S MOVIE WAS CURRENTLY SHOOTING what he described as "the endless house party scene." The production was working out of a house up in Point Dume, taken over for two weeks to film one sequence of the movie. Instead of enjoying a mansion on its own strip of beachfront property, there were forty people standing around wearing some version of the t-shirt/jeans/headset combination. All of the trailers for the production were crammed in at the end of the street. We had to park at a nearby lot, and a golf cart was sent around to pick us up.

To pick Gary up. I was simply along for the ride.

The golf cart driver, named Pete, shook Gary's hand vigorously. "Good to see you again, sir." All I rated was a quick "Ma'am."

As we bumped along the unpaved path to the main house where the shooting was centered, nearly every single crew member turned and waved to Gary, who waved back. For such a strange, solitary man, he was a ridiculously popular figure on movie sets. Not only because he was a star, but because unlike many actors on movie sets he actually talked to the people working on them. He waved at the security guards standing on the perimeter. He smiled at the crew members. He remembered names. If he worked with someone more than once, he remembered their kids' names. He opened doors for the women instead of expecting them to be held open for him. As long as people were polite, he didn't mind signing autographs or posing for pictures.

It's when anyone—crew members, other actors, fans—mistook Gary's social defenses for overtures of actual friendship that the problems started. He would tense up and fold in on himself, not leaving his trailer, his house, his bedroom.

The entire golf cart ride I either had my hand on Gary's forearm or our fingers entwined. The protective circle around Gary went through me.

When we got off the cart, near the makeup trailer, I whispered, "Show me how happy you are I'm here," in his ear and he laughed like I'd just told a dirty joke.

Did I mention he's a great actor?

A guy with short blond hair, wearing one of those headsets and clutching a clipboard, came running up to him. "Gary!" he said, proving in one word he was one of the smart ones who took the star at his word about what name he preferred. He looked at me. "Drusilla, right? Hey. Good to have you back here again."

I kissed his cheek. "Eddie. How are Maisie and Ginny?"

Always ask after a person's kids. The spouses can and do change. Barring a disaster, the children don't.

"They've started walking. In opposite directions. My wife's

going nuts."

I laughed. "Oh, hey. Do you know where I can find Ofelia?"

"She's out front, I think." Then he opened the makeup trailer's door and said to Gary, "Let's go over your schedule for the morning."

And just like that, Gary was taken care of, and I was on my own until the next time we had to do the lovey-dovey thing.

Time to find Randi.

Ofelia was the extremely organized person in charge of keeping casting straight for the movie. She was young and very efficient, always with her list of things to take care of and her hair in the straight, even ponytail tied back with a perfectly symmetrical bow. We had met just before filming started and chatted. She asked me if I wanted a walk-on role, and I demurred. At this moment she was at the crafts services table, going over a clipboard's worth of information with a PA wearing a headset. On a chair near her was a very bored, very beautiful young woman with long black hair and dark eyes. She was small and slight, with the same proportion of oversized head to tiny, waifish body that Courtney had. She and Courtney had probably offered a fantastic contrast on *Girls Becoming Stars*: the blonde and blue-eyed waif, and the dark and brown-eyed siren.

I walked over. "Ofelia, hi." We kissed on the cheek, because that's what two people who have a passing acquaintance do on movie sets. "I'm looking for Randi Narvaez."

"That's me!" said the beautiful woman. "How you doin'?"

"I don't know what Gary was talking about," Ofelia said. "We don't have—"

"It's okay, I'll talk to her," I said. "Randi? Walk with me a moment."

I steered her toward the set, which was on the back patio, overlooking the Malibu coast. The cameraman had the video feed working and the grips were double-checking the lighting. Gary's double, a man about the same height, with the same color skin and a similar hair pattern, was standing under the lights.

"Who are you?" Randi asked. "I was told Sir Gareth Macfadyen called and asked for me directly." Her Texan accent had faded, or she'd worked on reducing it. The faint twang brought back memories of when Stevie and I had briefly lived in Texas. That living arrangement had ended badly.

Remembering Texas made me remember Courtney getting shot. I faltered, forgetting what I was about to say.

"Gary and I live together. I asked him to call."

She eyed me and took a step back. "Look, I don't know who you think you are or who you think I am, but I am not interested in any of your games."

"I needed to speak to you. You've heard about what happened to Courtney Cleary, right?"

"Oh, no," she said, her voice getting very angry. "I'm not talking to you about her."

The contrast between Randi's voice—which definitely showed her anger—and her complete lack of facial expression was surprising. She was twenty-four or twenty-five and already used Botox. Lots of the younger actresses and models did, in order to keep any forehead wrinkles from forming. In ten years, films and TV would have no actresses able to form facial expressions. But the women would look the same for decades.

"I need to talk to you. I had a run-in with Courtney and her boyfriend Roger Sabo."

"Her boyfriend?" Randi snorted. Loudly.

"Well, they were certainly together when Roger decided to beat me up." I lifted the sweep of hair to display my cut.

"Wow." She leaned closer to me. "Did Roger kill her? I always thought he might."

Oh, thank you, Zeus above. Randi knew something about Roger, something that might help me immensely with getting that son of a bitch off my back.

"Why did you think that?" I asked.

"I could tell you a few things about Courtney and Roger." She paused, as if trying to remember a particular incident. "And why would I tell you one damn thing about that asshole?" Randi asked.

Whenever someone asks you a question, assume they're not being rhetorical and they're actually asking for information. The same goes with sarcasm: take the words at face value and respond accordingly. It saves everyone getting into fist fights.

"What would make you tell me anything about Roger, Randi?"

"Am I actually here about a part on this movie or what?"

"No," I said. "But you have met Ofelia Delasante, and now she knows your name. And you're on this set. What do you want?"

Her eyes flicked to her right and then back again. It was a quick, involuntary movement.

I turned around to see what she was looking at.

The crew were making last-minute adjustments to the lighting and placement of furniture. It seemed amazing that that much gaffer's tape could be on the floor and that many lighting scrims could be positioned around the room without some of it showing up on screen. Lots of beautiful people wearing cocktail attire stood off to the sides, waiting for the call.

The main thing happening to the right side of the scene before us was the sight of Gary listening carefully to everything a wild-haired guy wearing a Mariners ball cap and Metallica t-shirt and ripped jeans had to say. Wild Hair was the director, probably. A man who was maybe thirty and had done some commercials and music videos was telling Gary how to act.

Gary's best acting job on the movie was going to be pretending this kid had anything to tell him about his craft.

Who was dating whom was a popular story in Hollywood.

"You know he's my boyfriend, right?" I asked.

"How serious are you two?" Randi asked.

I thought about what Micah Schlegel had said: everybody's got a story. Randi wasn't accepting any phone calls—until word got to her that Sir Gareth Macfadyen wanted to talk to her on a movie set. When she figured out there was no role, she hadn't stormed off. Instead, she stayed to talk to me. Gary's girlfriend.

Randi wanted the Story of the Girl who was Dating a Bona Fide Movie Star. Actually working in movies was not as high on her priority list, it seemed.

"We're flexible with our arrangement," I said.

"I don't do three-ways," she said.

I took a moment to imagine a three-way involving Gary and me and just about anyone else, and it ended much the same as whenever I imagined Gary and me dating for real: my mental movie machine broke down, unable to form the picture.

I also didn't believe Randi about what she would and wouldn't do, but that was neither here nor there. "Neither do I. However, I will introduce you to him. Possibly even convince him to have dinner with you."

"Why?"

"You tell me whatever you know about Roger Sabo and

Courtney Cleary. Especially Roger. In as much detail as you can manage."

Something akin to glee flitted across Randi's face. "More than happy to talk after dinner."

I smiled, no glee whatsoever. "You need to make this worth my while to even broach the topic with my...beloved."

Every single fiber in Randi's body radiated annoyance. "Okay. So Roger was a producer on the show—"

"Mostly because of his drug-dealing skills. Well ahead of you there. What else?"

She clicked her tongue a couple of times. "Do you know Greg Hitchcock?"

"The construction bloke? You and Courtney worked for him, right?"

"Still do, sometimes. You want to know a few things about Greg?" Her drawl got lazier by the syllable.

Hm, interesting. But not germane to the topic under discussion. "Not unless it has something to do with Roger Sabo."

"Well, this certainly did. The second I heard Courtney got murdered, I immediately thought of Roger and Greg. Both of them might be kind of angry at her. Roger had quite the temper on him to begin with." She pointed at my hairline. "I'm guessing you know that."

"What about them, Randi?"

"I never did understand why Courtney came back to Los Angeles," she said. "Not when she was making such good money from both Roger and Greg staying put in Oklahoma. But of course she wanted to be here."

"Are you telling me both of them were paying her off?" I asked.

"You didn't know that, huh? I'll tell you the rest. Tomorrow." She smiled.

If the Hollywood actress thing didn't work out, perhaps she had a career in writing suspense.

Well. Time to put up. I consoled myself that in this situation everyone won: I would get my information, Randi would get her moment having dinner with a famous man, and Gary might get laid, which normally put him in a good mood.

Stevie would be disappointed that I had done it, though. But she had her methods and I had mine.

As I approached him, Gary didn't even stop the conversation he was in with one of the gaffers to wrap his hand around my waist and let his fingers rest on my ass. Then he looked at me and said, "You'll need to leave the set soon, darling."

The gaffer moved away to give us a modicum of privacy, in the middle of the chaos of a film shoot.

I put my hand up to his face but was careful not to make contact with his skin, lest I mess up his makeup. We leaned toward one another simultaneously, as though having an intimate moment. Since nearly everyone working on the movie was standing in the room at that moment, everyone saw us in action. Gary could sell our fake relationship so hard that sometimes I wondered if he was actually coming on to me. He was, after all, a professional.

"Randi wants a date with you," I said quietly.

"A date?"

"You know. Dinner. Chitchat. Possible pap photos."

"Possible?"

Randi wasn't going to be the Girl Who Dated Important People if there wasn't photographic evidence. "Okay, yes. Definitely photos. Think of it this way. You'll be the stud cheating on his twenty-eight-year-old girlfriend with someone even younger."

He groaned. "Anything else?"

"That part I leave up to you, tiger."

The guy with a different ball cap on wandered by and said, "We need to clear the set."

"Five minutes," Gary told him. To me he said, "Is this important?"

Was this important? Most likely, anything Randi had to say I could find out some other way, but getting her to tell me directly would simply be faster.

I crossed my fingers over my heart. "You don't have to do anything except have dinner with her. Enjoy."

He made a moue, leaving no doubts of his feelings about this setup. "The thing about women half my age is they don't know anything, so they're really dull. Not counting Stevie, she knows a lot of things, she's extremely interesting. But most of them..." He shook his head.

I interlaced my fingers with his. "They can have their upsides, darling."

"You'll save me if things go wrong, won't you?"

"That's what I'm here for, Gary. You light up the bat signal, I come running."

Thankfully, that had only happened once, with a woman who had turned out to be a crazy stalker. It was nice, proving my usefulness to him with a bare minimum of effort.

He kissed me on the cheek, his lips barely making contact with my skin. "Fabulous."

One crook of my fingers at Randi and she came running over to us. I left them to discuss where they'd be having dinner that night.

CHAPTER THIRTEEN

MY STEPFATHER ROBERTO HAD ASKED me to talk to Dr. Anson Villiers about the nonprofit foundation Villiers was setting up to help at-risk youth in Los Angeles. Roberto was going to lend his company's name and donate money. I made a call to Villiers's phone number, which turned out to be in Beverly Hills, to set up an appointment to see him later that day. Then I asked Stevie to find out who this fellow was.

"Why?" she asked.

"Because I need to go talk to him."

"Why?"

"Because he's starting a nonprofit charity thing that I'm going to help with."

She narrowed her eyes. "Why?"

"Could we do the Socratic method another time? Do your keyboard tippy-tapping thing and tell me who this person is."

Anson Villiers turned out to be a psychiatrist who worked in Beverly Hills. I wasn't sure which part surprised me the most: that Roberto was acquainted with a psychiatrist, that said psychiatrist would be in Beverly Hills instead of on the Upper East Side, or that Anson Villiers was black.

Damn. My prejudices and expectations were intact, it seemed.

Stevie read to me what her web search had turned up. "He publishes a lot of work on the long-term effects of learning disabilities on at-risk youth, particularly minorities."

In addition to being a corporate good deed, Roberto undoubtedly saw the irony in asking me to help out. "Let me guess. The long-term effects are...bad."

"You needn't be so cynical. If his office is in Beverly Hills, he could spend his days doing nothing but listening to the problems of extremely rich people, without doing any of this."

"Extremely rich people have problems, too," I said.

"They tend to have more resources, though."

After a half minute of silence, I said, "Oh...shut up."

"Why are you meeting with him? Is he a possibility for..."

"I didn't even know he was a therapist until twenty seconds ago. I wasn't planning on talking to him about referrals, but that's a good idea. He might have some recommendations for us. Don't burn down the house while I'm gone."

Silly advice, really. Of the two of us, I was far more likely to do that.

Villiers's office was in a medical building on Roxbury Drive, a stone building built during the sixties with a tiny, slightly scary elevator. Four flights of stairs was almost no work and I felt as though I'd been sitting in a car for most of my natural life recently.

When I got to the top of the four flights, I remembered that I had recently been in a fight that had landed me in the hospital, and perhaps the athletic heroics could wait for a while.

The waiting room for Office 421 was a tiny square parked between two internal doors: one to Villiers's and one to another office. I ran my fingers over the nameplate on each door to be sure which one I should wait for to open.

Villiers opened the door to the waiting room at three after the hour. He was a middle-aged black man, with light brown skin and prominent freckles across his nose and cheeks, and a slight graying of his hair. He wore a polo shirt and khakis and looked like he'd be at home on the patio at a country club. "Drusilla?" he asked, his hand out. We shook. "Come on in. Sorry to keep you waiting, got a crisis phone call from a client."

His office was tiny but still fit a three-seat sofa, an armchair facing the sofa, two side tables (each with a box of tissues on it), two bookcases, and a desk with a computer on it. There wasn't a lot of room between any two objects. There was a second door by one of the bookcases.

"What's that?" I said.

"How patients leave. So they don't run into their friends and neighbors walking out."

Smart. "Like I said on the phone, I'm here to discuss a nonprofit you're setting up."

He hitched up the knees of his trousers before sitting in the armchair. "What do you know about it?"

"That you're setting up a nonprofit."

That made the doctor laugh. Always start by making people laugh. It relaxes them.

"Rob—Mr. Montesinos said you were having a problem with one aspect of it and maybe I could help. He wasn't any more specific about it than that. So I have no idea what I'm doing here."

Dr. Villiers laughed again. He had a very deep laugh. He probably didn't laugh a lot during sessions in this room. "Yes, I am setting up a foundation that works with children of disadvantaged groups in Los Angeles on issues of literacy and learning disorders. Montesinos Investment Bank is donating money as well as having some employees volunteering time, for which I'm very grateful."

Villiers was trying to sell me on how happy he was with my stepfather's involvement. Obviously he expected I was going to report back. Which I would.

"We're having a fundraiser."

"You just said you've got money from the bank."

"Which we use to advertise the nonprofit and get more funding."

I nodded. "Takes money to make money."

"Exactly. We also want involvement from the community for the community. Even if they are in completely different sections of the city. So, we have a private fundraiser planned for this weekend to schmooze potential board members and donators. Everything's lined up and ready to go, and..."

I waited for him to continue. When he didn't go on, it dawned on me that he was waiting for me to guess. To see if I was as clever as Roberto had advertised, perhaps?

He would already have the venue for the party lined up. The catering. The guest list, obviously.

"The entertainment backed out," I said.

Villiers nodded. "Yup. Exactly." He picked a brochure off his desk and handed it to me. Slickly laid out, four colors, on heavy card stock. From the photos, this was an invitation to the party. On one page was a photo of a sweaty, smiling young woman standing with a microphone in her hand, her multicolored hair flying out in many directions behind her.

"This is her?" I ran my finger over the caption beneath the picture. E-R-I-C-A R-

"We're supposed to have Erica Rose. Do you know her?"

I shook my head.

"Up-and-coming tween pop star. She's in a sitcom called *The Kids Are Dancing* on Nickelodeon. She's had a Top Hundred single."

"I don't listen to the radio."

Villiers leaned forward, his elbows resting on his knees, and gazed at me for a moment. He had very thick black lashes. "You can't read," he said.

His assessment was so fast and surprising I blinked. "What?"

"Right where your finger is, under your finger, there's a caption. It says, Erica Rose, star of KidTV's hit *Yellow and Green*."

I looked down at the words under Erica Rose's picture.

"You can't read," the doctor said. "You were running your fingers over the letters."

Well, the man was right, after all. "Is that important?"

"Makes it difficult to get things done in our modern world."

"Are we here to talk about your problems or mine, Doctor?"

"Have you seen anyone about this?"

I laughed. I hadn't discussed this problem with anyone in years. "Some of the best doctors in the world. Most of them thought I was faking. So did half of my teachers. They said I just didn't want to study."

"Is that true?"

"Studying is a lot harder if it takes you an hour to read a page. So, yes, true." I smiled. "I found other ways to occupy my time."

He didn't find that at all sexy or intriguing. "Interesting." He stared at me like I was a case study for the taking.

Maybe I was. Perhaps Roberto had set this meeting up deliberately, wanting me to meet someone who specialized in the psychological effects of my particular little problem. Did Villiers really have something he needed me to work on, or was this meeting about me?

I don't like being someone's case study. Tends to end badly for all involved.

"If we're here to discuss me, we're done, Doctor."

He clapped his hands together. "Okay. Erica Rose, all of a sudden, is not returning my phone calls. Roberto wants you to fix this."

"How old is she?"

"Sixteen."

Terrible age. Sixteen-year-olds make awful life choices. "Sounds to me like she's a stuck-up brat who doesn't understand the importance of sticking to agreements."

Villiers handed me a piece of paper with a name and a phone number on it. "Her phone number. Could you talk to her and find out what the problem really is?"

"When is this party?"

"Saturday."

I folded up the paper and tucked it in my pocket. "I'll talk to her and get back to you ASAP."

"Would you like to talk to someone about this issue?" Villiers asked.

"I'll consult my schedule," I said. "Most days I'm busy."

CHAPTER FOURTEEN

ALL NIGHT LONG I DREAMED of watching Courtney die over and over while the cops stood around and didn't pay attention. Roger Sabo and I sat on the bed in the motel room together, and he kept taking cannabis cigarettes from one of the nearby cops and passing them to me, saying, "You see how it is."

My mouth felt cottony when I woke up, and I reminded myself to cut down on dream-smoking. I couldn't figure out why Courtney's death was affecting me so much. After all, I'd seen people die, up close and violently, starting with the man I killed, followed by the man I had let die (he was there to kill me, so I wasn't motivated to save him from a long plunge into a frozen lake), followed by my first husband, David, who'd been killed in cold blood right in front of me. Since then there had been... I began counting on my fingers and when I raised my left hand for the second go-round I stopped counting.

Time to go find Stevie and get her to make everything all better. My body felt recovered enough that I could dress in something slightly dressier than the sweats and t-shirt combo I'd been wearing non-stop for a few days, so I put on the blouse with three-quarter sleeves (hid most of the bruise on one arm) and my linen Capris. I changed the belt from the stiff leather thing to the spongier fabric one though, in a concession to my stomach muscles.

The guest house was empty. I walked outside and found the garden was deserted. Stevie must have gone over with Gary's medication.

The back door to Gary's house was unlocked, as always. I poked my head inside and yelled, "Anybody home?"

"In here!" yelled a female voice.

A female voice that was decidedly not Stevie's.

Gary and Randi were in the breakfast nook, which was a large and airy room off the kitchen that jutted out into the garden. Three walls made of glass, with stained glass running around the top of the panes. Gary sat facing out to the garden, looking deep in thought about something, wearing his big old dark blue bathrobe. Randi sat on the chair next to his, her dainty feet with their fancy pedicures in his lap and one hand draped on his shoulder. She wore a satin zebra-striped robe and kept whispering things at him. The clear glass teapot was on the table, next to a plate holding the last few slices of Stevie's most recent baking adventure.

I put the smile on my face first. It's the easiest way to put yourself in a good mood—put a smile on, and your brain interprets this as meaning you must be happy. Function follows form. You say fewer mean and cutting things that way. At least, that's the theory, and I love theories of behavior.

"Good morning!" I said as brightly as I could manage. "Aren't you two just the picture of a leisurely morning repast."

"Would you care for a cuppa?" Gary asked. One of his hands idly stroked Randi's foot and played with her toes.

"Tea? No, thanks. Just popping by to see how things were going."

Randi rested her head on Gary's shoulder. "Just fine."

Gary seemed on the happy side of placid, which was good. If he was happy, then everything was great and I should just get over this sick feeling in the bottom of my stomach that I'd made a huge mistake letting this hook-up happen. "Are you due on set today?" I asked him.

"No, thank God."

Randi leaned over and put her hand over his.

"Have you seen Stevie?" I asked.

"Oh, yes. She told me to tell you she'll be in the library."

"Did she stop in here to talk to you?" My oblique way of asking about his medications in front of a virtual stranger.

He gazed at me a moment before nodding.

I patted him on the arm. "You get started with the day, darling. Wear something comfortable. It's going to be hot."

"It's Los Angeles, it's always hot. That's why we live here."

I kissed him on the cheek. "The kind of hot where you can't even move. You should go for a swim."

"Oh," Randi said. "That sounds great. Is your pool heated?"

I could tell by the look on Gary's face that he was baffled by Randi inviting herself along for his swim.

He looked at me. "Do we still have guest suits in the cabana?" he asked me.

I guess he had had himself a very good time with Randi last night. Well, that was fine. For the moment. The second Randi made Gary unhappy she would be out of our lives so fast everyone's heads would spin. "Should have," I said.

She stood up. "Well, let's swim."

I stood in her way. "Gary, go ahead and start getting your laps in. Just need a few moments with Randi."

We sat back down at the table. I snagged Gary's plate of cake and dragged it over.

"Courtney and Roger," I said.

"So where do you sleep when he has other women here?"

"And lastly Greg Hitchcock," I said. "Anything you know about Greg would be much appreciated."

"None of your stuff is in his bedroom."

"We don't like to mix our things. Also, it's none of your business. I talked to Greg the other day. He acted like he didn't know who Roger Sabo was, but then it turns out he really, really does."

"Does he ever," Randi said. "You wanted to know why both of them were paying Courtney off, right?"

I nodded.

She shook her head and let a gleeful grin cross her mouth. "I don't know." She sat back. "I honestly have no idea."

Son of a bitch.

I counted backward from seven hundred and forty-three by twos, to calm myself down and avoid wiping that smile off her face the hard way. When I got to seven hundred and seventeen, I said, "Tell me everything you do know then. How do you know they were paying her off?"

"She told me. She had it good back in Oklahoma. You can get a big place with California money. You know how much a two-bedroom apartment costs there? And there's only one little bitty thing wrong with it."

"It's in Oklahoma," I said.

"You got it. God, I wish she'd just stayed there."

"Why?"

Randi rolled her eyes. I didn't know people literally did that, but there she was, giving me the well-known sign that meant *Duh*. "She was annoying. Did you ever meet her? Everything was always about her."

"Narcissists often find that a difficult trait in others."

She laughed and nodded. "I know, right? Anyhow, everything out of her mouth was about her, her career, her money, her family."

"Did you see her in the week since she came back to Los Angeles?"

She nodded. "She was with Roger. God, he's so creepy. All they could talk about was the reunion special and how they were going to be the focus of it. I was like, Roger, you ain't no girl."

This woman had to know something I could use to pressure Sabo. Perhaps she didn't know anything about everyone's favorite drug dealer. Maybe she knew something about Hitchcock. "You know about Greg, though, right? You worked for him. How did you end up there?"

"You don't know anything about it, do you?"

"We had a deal, Randi. Roger Sabo tried to kill me the other day. He probably killed Courtney. All I want to know is why. Maybe you know something that can help me. Why did you go work in a financial counseling office? You don't seem like the financial counseling type."

She laughed.

Which surprised me. I'd been expecting her to take that as an insult. But she laughed.

"No one there's trained to be a financial counselor."

"That doesn't sound like a very effective way to run that office."

She made a noise. "Look. They'd get people from the church to volunteer and work with people. Do you know who goes into places like that? People who need help. Any kind of help. Money help. Greg's a good guy. He helped them." She grinned.

Something about that grin told me she was remembering something, so I asked, "Did he help you?"

She laughed. "No, not like those people. It was great working for Greg. He was...nice."

"How was he nice?"

"He'd loan me money. Never asked for it back."

No one who's smart about their finances loans money without asking for it back. Unless it's not really a loan.

"Did you have to sleep with Hitchcock a lot?" I asked.

She made a raspberry noise again. "Come on. Hardly involved sleeping. It was no big deal. Plus, whenever I needed a pick-me-up he had one."

Okay, that was interesting. "Hitchcock keeps drugs around?"

"Don't look like that. He doesn't use. Sometimes people just need something to get through their day, you know? He'd have stuff."

I opened my mouth to ask, "Where did he get it?" when the obvious answer occurred to me. "Did you ever buy from Roger directly?"

"I avoided the fuck out of Roger as much as I could. He's a creep. Courtney was all over him and I said, 'Trust me, he's all yours, hon.'"

Hitchcock was running a semi-functional financial counseling group, paying his young office workers for sex, and keeping drugs around, maybe even right in the office. I wondered what I could get out of Randi if I really pressed her on some issues.

"Why isn't Hitchcock paying you off the way he's paying Courtney?"

Randi smiled at me. "Who says he's not?"

Talk about holding out on me. "Is he?"

"I've told you everything I'm going to tell you. Okay? We're even now."

"Randi. Darling. Honey. Tell me what's going on, or, trust me, you're not going swimming today."

She stood up and stared at me. "None of your things are in Gary's closet. You don't have anything he wants. I do. That's how it works. *Darling. Honey.*" Then she waved toward the pool area, toward someone I couldn't see. "This is a nice house. Gary said I could make myself at home. So I'll see you around, Drusie."

The library was everyone's favorite place in Gary's mansion. Most visitors were awed by how gorgeous and overdone it was. The library created thrills with its pretentiousness and theatricality: the curved staircase up to the second floor of books, the floor-to-ceiling views out toward the Pacific, and the comfortable sofas and chairs for enjoying an intellectual chat about some book everyone swore they enjoyed.

No one who ever came here had ever read a book in their lives unless it was assigned by a producer.

Gary liked the library because visitors were so awestruck by it they transferred their high opinions of it from the room to him. I liked it because those comfortable sofas and chairs were wonderful for curling up on and having a nap, especially in the late afternoon sun as it came in over the Pacific. Stevie liked it because it was a library with lots of books in it. The library was genuinely her favorite room in the house.

When I joined her, she was not enjoying one of the books. She was working on whatever project had consumed her the past several days. Normally, the Oriental rug near Gary's desk had a set of four armchairs on it, all of them massive wooden things with enormous carved armrests and a delicate paisley print, that sat like points of the compass on the rug. Stevie had pushed the armchairs off to the side and the entire area was covered in piles of folders. Papers and scraps were arranged in towers of varying heights and structural integrity. On the bit of parquet flooring between the rug and one of the sofas facing the windows were smaller, neater piles, each one marked by a small card that had one word on it written in black marker.

"What are you doing?" I asked.

Stevie scanned the paper in her hand and then put it, neatly, in one of the labeled piles. "Organizing. Gary asked me to organize his papers. He's been avoiding it for a while."

"Several years, by the look of it."

She would be in here for days, happily pushing paper around. The whole world was out there, waiting to be explored. She had a cushion on the floor to sit on. She wouldn't see anything out the windows while she worked.

Stevie dropped the pages she was holding and rocked backward onto her haunches. Her mouth was open and she let out a huge sigh. "I forgot to make you coffee."

"What?"

"That's why you're here. Because you've had no coffee." She

stood up and wiped her hands on her skirt.

"Sit down. No, not on the floor. On a chair. I am not here because I need coffee. I do need coffee, but that is not why I am here. I just finished a very depressing conversation with Randi."

At the mention of Gary's hook-up Stevie looked very morose. "Oh."

"Don't you start getting all weepy. She told me the most dismal story about Greg Hitchcock's financial operation." I gave Stevie the short version of what Randi had told me. "I'm not even certain I have enough of a connection between Hitchcock and Sabo. She did, however, give Greg Hitchcock a hell of a motive to kill Courtney."

"You're assuming Courtney knew everything Randi does."

"I'm assuming Courtney brought me into Hitchcock's office so I could 'be nice' to him. I'm nice to him, he's happy, maybe she tells Sabo to back off. She certainly thought she had the upper hand."

She closed her eyes and looked away for a moment. Then she took a large breath and let it out slowly before turning back. "If Hitchcock killed Courtney because of what she knew about his activities, then Randi would be in an even deeper spot of trouble. But she doesn't seem very concerned about her own safety."

I screamed in frustration and punched the cushion of the chair I was sitting on. "None of this helps me with Roger Sabo."

"Leave him be, Drusilla. Stay away from him."

"Sabo has already put me in a bind with...my friend in New York." I slapped my hands together and stood up. "Speaking of whom. Let me get what he needs me to do out of the way and be done worrying about him. Tell me about Erica Rose."

Nothing makes my sister happier than expounding on research. "Erica Rose's father is named Chris McClanahan. He's also her manager, and he has quite the checkered history." She pulled up a couple of pages that were lying off to the side. "He also worked in the construction industry, in Simi Valley." She pulled out one in particular. "And, in what I am hoping is a gigantic coincidence, he was acquainted with Mr. Greg Hitchcock."

She laid the paper down in front of me. It was a newspaper picture of a line of middle-aged white men, in suits and ties, standing in front of a giant seal, with a headline below it. Except here Greg Hitchcock's hair was mostly dark brown, with the beginnings of gray appearing. And he was younger, and thinner, and his jawline hadn't filled out quite so much.

No matter how suspicious I was of coincidences, finding a story about Greg Hitchcock while looking for information about Chris McClanahan seemed to be an actual matter of random chance. It happened both of them worked in the construction industry, and at one point they'd known one another. Everywhere is a small town, when you get right down to it.

I flapped the paper up and down. "What is this?" I asked.

"Chamber of Commerce awards dinner, honoring construction industry excellence. This was fifteen years ago. I haven't found any other ties between the two of them. A year after Mr. McClanahan went to prison—"

Prison? I held my hand up. "Whoa. What? I think you skipped something."

"Oh, right, sorry. About a decade ago Mr. McClanahan was arrested and convicted of drugs trafficking. His workers smuggled in methamphetamine from Mexico and distributed it off construction sites. He served five years, released five years ago, on probation. He can't work in any licensed industries."

"Really? Then the music industry is an awesome fit. Not

especially concerned with people's legal histories. Or moral ones. Or—"

"His daughter is doing quite well for someone who's just starting out."

I couldn't get over the coincidence of a man I was looking into for Roberto also knowing a man I was looking into for my own problems. Did Roberto somehow orchestrate this? "When did Hitchcock move to Los Angeles?"

"About eight years ago. Mr. McClanahan was already serving time."

"Back in Simi Valley...did they compete for contracts, or—"

She shook her head. "Mr. McClanahan did residential construction, particularly these instant developments that spring up overnight. Mr. Hitchcock has always worked in commercial. From what I've been able to gather, there's not a lot of overlap between those."

There had to be some link. McClanahan had been arrested, I had gotten into trouble with the police... "Who arrested McClanahan?"

She glanced at one of the papers in the stack, although if she'd read it once, she knew the answer. So charming of Stevie to act like she needed to refresh her memory. She flashed the page at me. It showed a smiling young man in full uniform, posed shaking hands with his lieutenant. "Officer Broderick Tennyson. He got a commendation."

I glanced at the paper, which showed a young uniformed cop. I didn't recognize the name, so he probably wasn't one of the cops I'd had the pleasure of meeting during my short time in Los Angeles, particularly the night Courtney died. And, as Stevie had said, he worked in Simi Valley. I wasn't exactly sure where Simi

Valley was, but it wasn't Los Angeles.

"Okay, skip it. Chris McClanahan plays tough. He has a daughter who is probably supporting the family. He's clearly comfortable with playing hardball." I looked at my sister. "I'm okay with that."

"Be careful."

"Erica Rose and her father are no problem. I'll call you after I'm done in Tarzana."

She nodded.

CHAPTER FIFTEEN

RANDI'S COMMENTS ABOUT THE FINANCIAL counseling office had piqued my interest about what kind of place it was. Since I had an appointment in the San Fernando Valley later anyhow, I could hit both of the places on the agenda, and maybe take care of all the problems on my plate. Greg Hitchcock claimed to be big on helping people, and I needed help with Roger Sabo. In order to nudge him along the path of maximal aid, I needed to know everything there was about him. And it was strange that a man who clearly did so well in construction—Stevie's research revealed he had a booming business that had weathered the recent economic downturn with few problems—would do such a half-assed job with his financial counseling center. Sure, maybe he enjoyed chasing the secretaries around the desk once in a while, but there were easier ways to do that than setting up an entire office for it.

I parked at the strip mall in Panorama City and went into the gyros shop. It had a giant (if slightly discolored) window that looked out at Hitchcock Christian Financial Counseling. I bought a soda and sat at the counter to watch who went in and how they looked coming out.

The big glass front window of the financial counseling office had a curtain pulled over half of it, to prevent people from seeing inside. The logo and other words that been painted on the inside of the window had been seriously scratched up by people waiting on the inside, using their thumbnails or car keys to carve graffiti into the paint, or simply peel the paint off.

Even before someone got in the door of the financial counseling office, the place gave off a vibration that it was run-down and shabby, and you were too for going there. I tried to imagine the mindset of someone heading into this place to sort their finances. They had to be at a place in their life where assistance from this operation looked good, which meant things had to be bad.

One of the things that had baffled me when we moved to Los Angeles were these signs that seemed to be stapled to every telephone pole. Stevie told me most of them were about weight loss —people were selling herbal formulas that were supposed to help with weight loss as part of a multilevel marketing scheme. The sellers had to buy a whole bunch of this product and then sell it to other people. Except you didn't start making money until you got more people to sell the product, and then you got a teeny little bit of every sale they made. Which led to even more of these signs going up on telephone poles.

The only people who made money were the ones running the herbal supplement company.

The people selling the supplements were the types of clients walking through this door, looking for a way out of their mess.

I sat there for an hour and four people went in, three of them Hispanic women. Two had long thick black hair and the third one had bleached her hair. It had come out red. Two of the women were pudgy and one was stick thin. One of the women had two kids with her, a baby strapped to her chest with a Baby Bjorn and a little boy barely able to walk on his short little legs. The man was young, wiry, wearing very baggy jeans and a white hoodie that was now some shade of tan. Not one of them had dressed up for their financial appointments, dressing in jeans or jean shorts or denim cutoffs.

Even with my relatively casual outfit, there was no way I could go in there without standing out like a sore thumb. My skin was so pale I made white people feel ethnic. If there was something illegal going on inside, when I walked in everyone was going to shut down faster than a glass factory during a riot.

Several people exited while I sat and watched. The man in the hoodie came out five minutes after he went in. A couple of women I hadn't seen before left. A Caucasian man, with a mustache that screamed used car dealer, walked out. He was wearing a shirt and tie and stripped off his suit jacket as soon as he left the financial counseling services office. He headed straight into the gyros shop, where he checked me out openly.

I ignored him. Openly.

He took his sandwich and drink and walked over to my table. "Mind if I join you?" he said, in the process of sitting down. He had a Southern California accent. He'd been here a while, maybe his whole life.

I rated the likelihood that anyone was going to get together and talk about my accent. "Could I even stop you?" I asked, speaking pure Angeleno.

"What brings a pretty lady like you here?"

"Do you work at the financial place?" I asked.

His chewing slowed down, and then he swallowed and smiled. "Yeah. Yeah, I do. My name's Dan. What's yours?"

"You work there? What do you do?"

"We help people who've run into financial difficulties. You know, overrunning your credit card or borrowing too much money. What'd you say your name was?"

"And you can really help?"

"We sure can. You want to come next door and talk about it?"

The woman with the bleached red hair left.

"Yeah, I got some problems with money I owe? My friend told me to talk to Mr. H if I ever ran into problems."

"Who's your friend?" Dan asked.

"Randi Narvaez? You know her?"

His eyes didn't even widen. He'd never heard the name. Fame is so very fleeting. "Nope. But if she's a friend of yours I'm sure she's the best."

"She's real good friends with Mr. Hitchcock."

"I didn't get your name," Dan said.

"Brittany," I said.

"Why don't we talk about where you are in this process, Brittany? You have some unsecured debts? Maybe some credit cards?"

"Credit cards, my car loan, this doctor who took out my wisdom teeth—" I yanked the side of one cheek back, like I was going to show him where the teeth had been cut out. "And now I need to get veneers, you know, to make my head shots better? For auditions? And when you don't have the money..." I shrugged.

"Well, we can totally help you with that," Dan said. "We have helped a lot of our clients reduce what they owe to just a fraction of the original amount."

"Yeah, well, I don't have a lot of money, *obviously*," I said.

"We charge only a small percentage of the total amount you end up saving," Dan assured me. He wrapped up the second half of his gyro wrap and wiped his mouth with a napkin. He still had sauce in his mustache. "Why don't you come next door with me and we can run some numbers?"

He'd already told me two things about Hitchcock Financial and both things were clear indicators the entire operation was a scam. "Great!"

Dan held the door open for me at the gyros place and at the financial counseling office like we were on a date.

The interior of Hitchcock Christian Financial looked pretty much the way I expected it would: a lot of plastic and a lot of linoleum. The stale air in the waiting area smelled of sweat and spices and something sweet, like spilled soda. Everyone working behind the front desk was Caucasian, everyone sitting in the orange plastic chairs was Hispanic. Two of the women I'd seen, including the one with the two little kids, were still waiting. The one with the kids was talking to the woman next to her about *Señor Hache*. Two middle-aged men and one man in his early twenties. Everyone waiting had headphones on or around their necks.

Behind the front desk were eight cubicles, curtained on all sides with heavy gray drapes.

The receptionist was a woman in her sixties, her hair dyed slightly too dark for her skin tone, wearing a polyester scoop-neck blouse and jeans. She also wore a headset, had a fan on her desk, and was ignoring the woman who was trying to talk to her in halting English. The receptionist did a double-take when I walked in with Dan. Perhaps I didn't look like their usual customer.

Dan pushed open the gate by the receptionist's desk. "Hey, Linda, I'm going to talk to her right now. Let me get her started on some forms."

Linda picked up a clipboard with a cracked ballpoint pen attached by a chain and handed it to Dan.

He held open the wooden gate for me. "Right through here."

I followed him to the first curtained cubicle on the left. "Randi didn't say I'd have to fill out any forms," I said.

"Okay, so let's just talk."

"Is Mr. Hitchcock coming by?"

Dan smiled tightly. I was his, not Hitchcock's. "No, he's not coming in here today."

"Randi said I had to talk to him."

"Well, why don't you just talk to me for a couple of minutes."

We talked for five minutes. I whined a lot, he kept trying to get me to fill out the forms. Finally I burst into tears and ran out, calling him "mean."

I hoped no one got a good look at my completely dry eyes.

Nevertheless, I went back to my car, which was broiling, and waited. I needed to talk to one of the women who were in there, and if I got lucky she'd be someone who'd visited more than once. I had the feeling the financial counseling office wasn't just a way to skim a little money off a lot of desperate people.

The young woman with the two kids came out. The toddler, a little boy, was crying. The woman, who was twenty-two at the most, yanked him by the arm hard and pulled him along with her. I grabbed a handful of tissues out of the box in my car and ran to intercept them.

"*Perdóname, señora, por favor,*" I said. "*Para su niño.*"

My Spanish is Castilian and not Mexican or Guatemalan or any of the other dialects popular in Los Angeles. They're practically different languages, and when you start lisping everything, you stand out like the stranger you are.

She was going to be suspicious of me. If I was right about the financial counseling office, she was right to be.

"May I talk to you?" I asked her.

"What about?"

"There's a McDonald's on the next block," I said. "Can I buy the three of you some lunch?"

She shrugged and we walked over to the Golden Arches. I bought her and her son three burgers and a large fries, which cost all the money I had on me. The little boy looked at her for permission before digging in. She ruffled his hair and he started inhaling the food so fast I thought he might choke.

"Slow down," I told him. "It's not going anywhere."

He kept his gaze on me, as though I might snatch it away at any moment. I tried smiling. It didn't help.

"I wanted to ask you about the financial office place."

Her walls went up hard. She glared at me and leaned back. "What about it?"

"Is that your first time there?"

She shook her head.

"Have they helped you?"

"Yeah, Mister H helped me." *Señor Hache. Mister H.* Something about the way she said it told me it was the standard way they referred to him. She grunted a laugh and it was not a happy sound. "I didn't want to come back, you know?" She curved her arm around the boy, who was still staring. "But this one had to go to the doctor's and I need the money."

"They give you money. Mister H gives you money."

She stared at me, chewing on a couple of fries. "Hey, no offense, but I don't know you."

"I'm not a cop."

"You can say you're not."

"Look, I don't know your name. I don't want to know your name. But a friend of Mister H's is causing me a lot of problems." My injuries had made my point for me a couple of times this week, so what was one more? I lifted up the edge of my blouse, careful to turn so as not to show the little boy. "I need to make him go away."

She shook her head. "Mister H never hits. You're nice to him, he's nice to you."

Not hard to guess what "being nice" entailed.

"No. Mr. Hitch—Mister H didn't do this. These marks were given me by a man by the name of Roger Sabo. You know him?"

After a couple of seconds' hesitation, she nodded.

I paused, trying to tamp down my eagerness. I had to tread very lightly now and get her to give me something.

"How do you know him?" I asked.

"He hangs around the construction site."

"What's that?"

"Mister H is working on this big building. The guys who are working on it, they get tired, you know."

"Where is it?"

She gave me the address. Just off Ventura Boulevard in Woodland Hills. Closer to Tarzana than Panorama City, that was for sure.

"Roger is selling his supplies there?"

She nodded. "The construction workers are there all the time. Sometimes Mister H asks a couple of us to stop by."

"And he helps you pay off your bills."

She nodded. The toddler reached over for her French fries and she pushed his hand away. "You've had enough, José."

The baby woke up and started crying. She jostled him roughly, trying to get him to stop.

"Do yourself a favor," I said. "Don't go to the construction site for the next week."

"I got doctor's bills, lady," she said. "Thanks for the lunch."

I left the three of them there and walked back to my car. I couldn't decide whether I was surprised or not. Whenever men had money they liked to use the power of it, particularly with women. Everywhere, every time. I didn't see why Los Angeles, a city built on a transient population with big dreams and few opportunities, would be any different. I wanted to forget it, forget the images she'd left with me.

On the other hand, the woman's story would allow me to pressure Hitchcock to help me with Roger Sabo, so it wasn't like the entire day had been a loss.

Now to take care of Roberto's little errand.

CHAPTER SIXTEEN

SEVERAL MILES NORTH OF PANORAMA City was the upscale suburb of Sherman Oaks. Right in the middle, placed near the freeway, was the Fashion Square Mall. A large enclosed mall that followed the template of all modern shopping malls, with all the usual stores lining its corridors, like Macy's and Bloomie's and bath shops and high-priced denim shops.

Every large, cylindrical kiosk I passed had posters of a grinning Erica Rose, wearing a polka-dotted tank top and a short skirt with orange tights and her red hair splayed out behind her, leaping into the air and strumming a pink guitar. I sent a picture of it to Stevie, who called me back to say the poster was advertising both Erica Rose's TV show and her live appearance here at the mall.

Which was the reason I was there, of course.

I stopped in the jean shop to watch a bunch of teenagers take stacks of jeans into the changing room, casually dropping the ones they didn't like in piles on the floor. One girl picked up a pair of jeans and her friend immediately looked over at them. "Size *four*! Guys, she wears size four!" The girl dropped the pants like they were on fire. She was thin, approaching emaciated, but she wasn't *L.A. thin*, and around here that's all that counted.

The critic picked up a different pair and said, "Oh my God, these are so cute, I have to try them on right now." She was already wearing a pair of designer jeans, but what was one more? My first reaction was that I wanted to slap her, but in reality I wanted to slap myself. One time, when I was fifteen, I'd whined incessantly about only having ten pairs of my favorite jeans. Each of which had cost over $300. And needed its own special pair of shoes to go with it. And my mother had given in and let me go on a much-needed shopping trip, because I had *nothing to wear*.

The Fashion Square also had a large area in the center, open to both floors, where promotions could be held. Today's promotion was a midday concert by TV star Erica Rose. She was going to do a couple of songs and sign pictures.

I arrived at the mall fifteen minutes before Erica Rose was supposed to take the stage and I settled myself by a pillar where I had a view of the stage and of the crowd.

Problem one: there was no crowd. It was the middle of the week, after school, and a teenaged tween star was going to perform. I didn't see many of the middle schoolers I assumed she appealed to. College-aged teenagers, moms with babies in strollers, and other people who had the freedom to be out shopping in the middle of the week were here. But no tweeners.

Problem two: Erica Rose wasn't setting up, doing sound checks, double-checking that the stage was set up correctly. There could only be two reasons for that: she was running late, or she didn't waste her time worrying about what she was going to sound like because the entire thing was a farce anyhow. Either reason pointed toward her being both manufactured and unprofessional.

Five minutes after I started waiting, a large group—forty or fifty, it seemed like, probably one bus full—of young teenagers was herded down the hall toward the concert area. They had to dodge shoppers and one chaperone had to lean over and pull one from the clothing store she'd gone to check out.

The chaperones settled the tweens on the floor near the stage, and as they gave the kids last-minute instructions—including lots of clapping! —I counted. Forty-one. I suspected they hoped the group of ringers—what these newcomers clearly were—would spark interest from other kids in the mall to join in.

Or maybe they were there for the video crew, who came down a different corridor of the mall, following the prancing and buoyant tween star, Erica Rose, who came frolicking toward the stage. She had bright red hair teased out in a mane behind her, and she wore the same outfit as she had on the poster: green tank top, bright purple short skirt with yellow leggings. She waved gaily at everyone who stopped to watch her pass, which was most of the people in the mall, because this was Los Angeles, and there was a video crew. One girl seated on the floor near the stage popped to her feet when Erica Rose was twenty feet away, a book and pen in her hand. The left-side chaperone immediately signaled her to sit down, which she did. When Erica Rose started wending her way through her audience, the same girl popped up again and Erica Rose gave her a big hug and then signed her book.

The starlet then hopped her way up on stage to begin the show. She attached her stage mic and waved out at the audience. "Hello, Sherman Oaks!" she cried.

Well, I think that's what she said. Because she was drowned out by tremendous electronic feedback, which had everyone, including me, covering their ears.

And Erica Rose lost her smile and looked off-stage.

Mistake numero uno. You never lose your smile when something goes wrong. You continue on as though everything's perfect.

After glancing nervously off-stage, Erica Rose smiled broadly again and called out to the audience. She tried valiantly to be heard over the growing din of onlookers talking. Mistake number two: she was going to make herself hoarse trying to speak loudly. The acoustics in this mall weren't built for people to project their voices long distances; they were designed to spread sound around so the place always sounded like there was a lot going on.

Finally, the music—pre-recorded electronic dance music, with a standard 4/4 beat—started up, and Erica Rose launched into her routine. She was doing her own singing—lip syncing is a talent that not every performer has and I doubted she'd learned it yet—but it was being filtered through Autotune. I could have been the one up there singing and I would have sounded halfway decent, which was a testament to the power of software that can make someone sound like they can sing on key.

Erica Rose finished her song and bounced around the stage, waving at all the kids in the audience, most of whom were duly unimpressed. The handlers off to the sides clapped their hands over their heads and smiled gaily, indicating what the kids were supposed to do. A couple of them followed suit, and the cameramen walking through the audience immediately focused on them, which was a much bigger incentive to the other kids to get into the spirit. Clap loudly, get photographed!

The girl did another song, with much the same choreography. There was nothing wrong with Erica Rose that a few more years of polish and study wouldn't fix, but that was the problem: she wasn't still learning, she was out there front and center, trying to be a star without doing any of the work.

I suddenly thought of Courtney.

When she finished her act, Erica Rose signed more autographs and waved and smiled big. She hugged several of the girls in the audience for the cameras. As soon as the camera lights went off, though, the kids in the audience hopped up and disappeared, probably trying to spend the money they'd earned for sitting there.

Erica Rose stood on the edge of the stage area. A PA handed her a bottle of water. I zipped to her side.

"Hi, Erica Rose. My name's Drusilla Thorne."

"Who are you?" She didn't quite have the Hollywood attitude down. The first clue was that she acknowledged my existence. Her voice was strained, which meant she wasn't using proper singing technique. And she was shaking. Perhaps vibrating was a better word. Stage fright. She had done her performance and now her nerves had gone wild.

"Your performance was fantastic," I said.

She lighted up like Rockefeller Center, excited to hear those words from a complete stranger. "Did you like it?"

Well. I had Erica Rose figured all wrong. She was trying her best, I believed that. But she had a lot more work to do to be really good at not just the singing or the dancing but the performing, which was the hardest skill of all. Maybe it was even innate. It was one thing to sing, it was another to seduce the crowd into loving you.

The shaking told me she knew she wasn't there yet, and she

didn't know what to do about it.

I wanted to tell her that she was only sixteen and she had lots of other choices in life ahead of her. But right now, in this moment, she was miserable.

"I need to speak to you about an upcoming performance you have scheduled."

She tossed her red hair from side to side and grabbed a sweaty bottle of ice-cold water. "Talk to my manager."

"Who are you?" said a man standing nearby. He was in his forties, a little paunchy, male-pattern baldness. He wore a blazer over a t-shirt and jeans, but the jeans were pressed and the t-shirt was high quality, so this was his uniform, not something he'd thrown on this morning.

"Drusilla Thorne," I said, and we shook hands. "You are?"

"Chris McClanahan," he said.

"Perfect. We need to talk about the concert you're doing for the Villiers Literacy Foundation," I said.

"Listen, I'm sorry, but Erica Rose is coming down with a—"

"Save it." I leaned toward him. "I'm here from his main financial backer, Roberto Montesinos. You and I are going to talk. When and where's most convenient?"

It was no trouble throwing my stepfather's name around. After all, Roberto had known perfectly well how this was going to go once I talked to Dr. Villiers: I would play enforcer for his agenda. In case I wasn't already certain that he had me squeezed between my inheritance and the law, now I was using my unique skills for him. And even with all that, he was still the most reasonable relative I had, and he was a step-relative at that.

Chris wanted to make this issue go away. He shook his head. "Erica Rose's schedule is really crazy."

"That's fine. You simply need to open time in yours."

"Yeah? I'm kind of busy too. Fuck off."

"She will stop being busy, Mr. McClanahan." I smiled. From what I'd just seen, that wasn't even a threat: this girl was not ready for prime time.

"What are you going to do about it?"

"*Yellow and Green* is produced by Ed Rathman Productions. Rathman Productions is part of the Forrester Group. Forrester is owned by Van der Laan Entertainment. Jane van der Laan Montesinos is married to..." I waited for him to finish the sentence for me. "Roberto Montesinos. You talk to me, or Erica Rose's show ends production and she doesn't get hired by anyone in the VDL family again." Given that Stevie had explained how VDL produced most of the shows for KidsTV, I felt confident about making that promise. And if Roberto didn't want me fully representing him, he should have said something.

McClanahan grunted with frustration, which told me he hadn't been aware of at least one of the relationships I'd just mentioned. "I can't talk now," he said. "Tomorrow? Can we do this tomorrow?"

"Now is better."

He ground his teeth. "I have a meeting I can't miss today."

"The only excuse I'll accept is a meeting with your parole officer."

McClanahan stared at me. "Fuck," he muttered.

"Name and phone number. Not that I don't trust you, but I don't trust you."

He gave me the parole officer's name and phone number, which I memorized. Then I asked for a specific time the next day when we would meet. "And if you stall me again, Mr.

McClanahan, Erica Rose shouldn't show up for work on Monday."

"We'll be in Westwood tomorrow afternoon," he said.

At least Westwood wasn't the San Fernando Valley, I thought. I did not like driving into the Valley.

Which probably qualified me for official status as an Angeleno.

CHAPTER SEVENTEEN

DESPITE HOW EXHAUSTED I WAS after my failure with the McClanahans, I headed west once again to Tarzana. I picked my spot in the parking lot across the street from the building where Hitchcock Commercial First Construction had its offices, where I could watch every car that came out of the subterranean parking lot. Even as the sun headed down in the west and I had to contend with a flash of orange across the windshield as the car poked out from the side of the building, I could still see everyone's face. Sometimes having extremely good eyesight is incredibly useful. I didn't even need to use binoculars.

This exercise got trickier as it got darker. I wasn't expecting I would have to wait until after sunset.

Greg Hitchcock left in a black Cadillac SUV. It had a dent in the rear door on the driver's side. I took a moment to memorize his car, in case I ever saw it again.

The receptionist, Mary, left shortly after him. After her blue sedan left, a few other cars left, but I didn't recognize any of the drivers. After ten minutes of no cars whatsoever, I thought maybe she'd been the last one to leave and had locked the place up after the boss.

Finally, though, twenty minutes after that, my patience paid off, and one more car left the parking. A Prius, of course. Tan-colored and very sensible.

While Jonathan Ricciardi waited for his moment to join the traffic on Ventura Boulevard, I memorized details of the car. Tan Priuses were kind of thick on the ground in Los Angeles and I'd hate to end up following the wrong one.

Jonathan drove twenty minutes up Tampa Avenue to Northridge, which I had only heard of because of the 1994 earthquake. It was relatively easy to follow him from a distance, even with the turns through his neighborhood, following the bounce of his red rear lights off the nearby houses. When I turned the last corner, he had parked on the street in front of a small house with a fence around the yard. He pulled a big cardboard box out of the back of the car and kicked the door shut behind him.

The front door opened. Alison, the teacher from the preschool, had Hailey, the little girl, in her arms. Jonathan leaned over to give both of his girls a kiss as he waddled through the door with his box. The picture of suburban happiness.

My visit was really going to ruin their dinner.

I rang the doorbell and Alison answered it. She opened the door with a welcoming smile, but it dimmed. Vanished, actually. It would be fair to say seeing me made her downright unhappy.

"Hi, Alison. I need to speak to Jonathan."

"You can't just come to our house," she said. Did she

remember me from a few brief seconds outside the preschool? She must have.

Jonathan came out of the kitchen, his shirt sleeves rolled up. "Hi, what can… Hi," he said.

"I need to talk to you," I said.

He sighed, like he was giving in after a long struggle. "Yeah," he said.

"What's this about?" Alison said.

"We can't have this conversation in your office," I told him.

Jonathan took his wife's hand. "Honey, why don't you give Hailey her bath?"

"I want you out of my house in ten minutes," Alison told me. Then she stalked off through the kitchen, presumably to wherever Hailey was currently planted.

Jonathan stood there, waiting. As soon as Alison vanished into one of the rooms, I pointed at the living room. "Can we sit down?"

He looked startled. "Oh. Sure. Come on in."

The living room was small but exceptionally neat and clean. Two small sofas flanked the small square fireplace, with a coffee table between them. No TV. No toys. Every house I've been in with a toddler usually looks like a war zone, so I was duly impressed.

I took a seat on the blue sofa, near the front window. Jonathan sat across from me. His palms were plastered together but he kept twisting them, rubbing his fingers against one another. Nervous as hell about something.

"You're probably wondering why I've interrupted your evening," I said.

"I have a few guesses," he said.

"My concern is Roger Sabo."

Jonathan's unhappy grin—mirthless, rueful, and resigned—as

his shoulders slumped was not what I would have expected. So he clearly knew Roger Sabo. And he knew something bad about him.

"I have a few questions and then I'll vanish into the night."

"Don't you have to show me some kind of identification first?" he said.

"That's something cops have to do," I said.

"Actually, my guess was you're FBI, but now I'm thinking DEA," he said.

He had made such a gigantic mistake about my identity or my motivations that I laughed. "Not going to throw in the IRS for good measure?"

He shook his head. "I know all those guys already."

What did that mean? I wondered, but then one answer popped to mind: Jonathan knew the fieldwork IRS agents, not just the desk jockeys. I wondered what was in that box he'd brought home.

"You're talking to the IRS already," I said. "So you don't need me to tell you what's going on at the financial counseling office then?"

He shook his head. "No, you do not. I had nothing to do with what that's become."

"You know what Hitchcock is doing with those women?"

He squinted. "What do you mean?"

"He has money. He's dealing with women who need money. Forget it. Not my problem. I'm going to level with you, Jonathan, I'm not any kind of law enforcement person, for any agency with lots of letters in its name. I'm here because I need your help." I had shown my injuries to several people that week, but I suspected Jonathan was the wrong person to flash the side of my stomach at. I lifted my hair and pointed to the steristrips at my hairline. "Roger Sabo assaulted me."

Jonathan reached out, like he was going to comfort me. Or touch the cut. "How did this happen?"

"He has a temper and I have a bad habit of fighting back. I think he murdered Courtney. I can't prove that and frankly it's not my job to prove it. What I want is for Sabo to leave me alone. Maybe your boss can help me make that happen, and maybe you know something that I can use to pressure Hitchcock to help me."

"What makes you think I know anything?"

"Because you're the quiet, studious guy in the corner who sees everything and knows what's really going on."

Jonathan looked off into the distance for a couple of seconds at that. Then he gave me a wan, mirthless smile. "Okay. Then what makes you think I'd help you?"

"Because after what I saw at the financial counseling office today, you're in very deep shit. You helped set that place up. If you're already talking to the IRS, you know exactly what's..."

What, exactly, did he know?

Jonathan was the man who handled the money. The men who know the dollars and cents are always the ones who know what's truly going on.

He had mentioned the FBI and the DEA. He'd started with the IRS because, duh, he was a CPA and those were people he could talk to in their own language. Hitchcock getting sexual favors or Sabo doing a little drug dealing on the side at Hitchcock's construction sites—both terrible, both morally reprehensible, but in this day and age you quit your job to avoid being associated with those people, you don't run to the Feds. You talk to the Feds if you know something much, much bigger.

Money. Despite the economy having done terribly in the last few years, Hitchcock Construction was doing exceptionally good business. Except...what if it wasn't? It could be doing okay—better than okay, even — but Hitchcock had money going out the side, through the financial counseling office. A steady leak of cold, hard cash. Which had to come from somewhere.

Hitchcock. Sabo. Ricciardi. One of these men was not like the others.

"Your boss needs a steady supply of money coming in under the table. Sabo has money he can't keep in the banks." I leaned forward. "You move money around. You're laundering money for Sabo."

Jonathan deflated from the top of his head through his shoulders, slumping forward. Dammit. Sometimes I hate being right.

No, really. The only thing I ever want to be right about is who's sleeping with whom.

I waited until he looked up at me. If it's possible to gauge from appearances when a person is defeated, Jonathan was down for the count. "You didn't go to the IRS about the financial center. You went about whatever Hitchcock is doing with the construction business."

Jonathan said nothing.

The sofa I was sitting on had a few years of sun-fading baked into its fabric. His car was at least a decade old. The kitchen floor was linoleum. The accountant wasn't taking the money.

"What's their hold over you, Jonathan? Help me and I can help you."

He still had that stupid little twisted grin on his face. "I was going to leave, two years ago."

"Why didn't you?"

"The economy sucked, or maybe you don't remember that."

"Bullshit," I said. "That's not why. They have something on you. What leverage can they possibly have on a middle-class accountant in Northridge?"

He squeezed his eyes shut. "They offered me something my wife and I had been praying for." Then he opened his eyes, those clear ice-blue eyes, and he smiled. "I wouldn't change anything. I know what I'm doing"

What the hell. Just like that, I'd lost the connection. He was a million miles away now. "You have to be selfish here. Sabo is a bad guy and he hits back, believe me. Don't you want to protect your family?" I asked.

"That's what I'm doing," he said.

A quiet gasp from the doorway startled me. Alison was standing there, her hand over her mouth. She dropped it, glaring at me. "Leave my house," she demanded.

"Alison, please," he said, in a way that definitely made it sound like he wanted to tell her to be quiet, albeit politely. "Come on. Come with me." He pulled his wife down the hall and through a doorway.

Seconds later, Hailey popped out of another doorway. She was in a yellow nightgown with Beauty and the Beast on it, and she had a book in one hand. Her feet made quiet thumps as she padded down the hallway toward the kitchen. Her blonde hair was damp but drying fast, and she wore a big grin on her face.

The number one reason you have to keep a leash on toddlers all the time: they move so fast, they're gone before you think to check on them.

She headed straight for me. When she got to the sofa, she pushed the book into my hands and then clambered up on the sofa next to me. She tried to crawl onto my lap, but you never touch other people's kids without their express permission. Hell, I don't even like being touched without my express permission, which isn't that hard to come by — a person simply has to ask. I said, "Hey there, Hailey, why don't you sit next to me while we wait for your daddy, okay?"

Hailey seemed to think this was acceptable, provided I read her book to her. She looked up at me, her brown eyes seeming to take up half her face, and she nodded. Alison and Jonathan started Hailey liking books young. Smart kid. Smart parents.

The book, with thick cardboard pages and cute drawings, was the epic eight-page tale of a duck taking a bubble bath. The words were short but in large type. I ran my finger over the first sentence. "This...is..."

"Dis is Duckie!" she said, impatient with the speed of narration.

I was suddenly reminded of all the times Stevie had read the page to me instead of vice versa. At first I had thought my baby sister reading to me was pretty cool. Then I'd been angry about it. Then I'd stopped having reading time with her altogether. "Yes," I said. "This certainly is."

"Hailey!" Jonathan said. "You are supposed to be in bed, young lady." He rushed over and scooped her up, off the sofa and away from me.

She squealed with delight. "Airpwane!" she said.

"No airplane for you, missie. Time for bed."

I stood up and handed him the book. "I'll see myself out. She's adorable. How old is she?"

And then I knew. I knew what their leverage was.

"I don't want to lose her," Jonathan said.

And he was going to throw himself on the mercy of the IRS

and try to plea bargain his way out in order to keep from losing everything. Once he lost his CPA license, he was done—not a lot he could do working in the financial sector once that was gone.

I thought about Chris McClanahan, and how he was done with being licensed to work in his field too.

Alison stood at the entrance to the living room. I had to pass by her to get out their front door. "Leave my house," she said, her blue eyes glaring at me. "Leave my house and leave my daughter alone."

My daughter.

If I was right, and Hailey was the bargaining chip they had used to keep Jonathan on board, where had she come from?

When had Hailey returned to Oklahoma? Right after the show ended…about two years ago. When she would have found out she was pregnant.

Courtney…and Jonathan? No. Not possible. Even in a world where people do things they're not supposed to be capable of all the time, this was a match-up I couldn't see. Courtney certainly had enough gentleman callers. Perhaps she ended up with a baby she didn't want, and the man probably responsible for it offered it as a bribe to his accountant, who probably couldn't afford private adoption. Everybody gets what they want.

But now something had gone terribly wrong with this setup. Jonathan was talking to the government. He and his wife have a baby that's not legally theirs. And now, on top of that, the police were around, looking for answers about Courtney's murder.

Alison was also medium height, like her husband, and athletically built.

Kind of like whoever had been on the motorbike that night.

"What did Courtney do to you?" I said.

"Get out. Get out! Haven't you done enough?" Alison said, and she shut the door on me.

It was dark out by the time I finally left the Ricciardis' house. The street was mostly lighted by the living-room windows of the houses on it. I wondered how long Jonathan and Alison had lived here. Had they had Hailey yet?

I sat in my car, exhausted by my day. Hitchcock was doing something so illegal Jonathan had to tell the authorities. In fact, Jonathan was so afraid he thought I might be with the authorities, and someone would have to be extremely paranoid to think that. Even if I didn't have the story exactly correct, I could make it sound like I knew something about what Hitchcock was doing without bringing Jonathan into it. Better for Hitchcock to think I knew something Roger Sabo might have told me anyhow. Might scare him a little more.

I called Stevie to let her know I was on my way home, finally, after a full day spent chasing down the exploiters and the exploited, both on the lower rungs of society and climbing the ladder of stardom. Where exactly did Jonathan fall on that ladder? I wasn't sure.

"When are you coming home?" Stevie said.

"What's wrong?"

"I've been alone all day," she said. That surprised me. I'd left Stevie alone for days at a time in Las Vegas and she'd been very happy. But now— --

"You haven't seen Gary?" I asked.

"He's out with Randi," she pouted. "I didn't want to cook for just myself."

While Stevie's words floated over me—after the day I'd had, it was hard to concentrate on the minutiae of Gary's new relationship

—Jonathan left his house and got back into his Prius.

"Something's come up," I told my sister. "I won't be driving straight home."

I followed Jonathan down Tampa Avenue, to the point where I thought he was heading straight back to work. But then he turned and headed west.

He pulled into the strip mall where Hitchcock Christian Financial Counseling center was. He parked in front. I drove past, then came back and parked half a block away. Night in Los Angeles never means things are completely dark, and a line of shops after hours was no different. There were security lights, street lights, lights from passing cars, and the general light pollution bouncing off the night sky. Jonathan's car was empty by the time I settled into my parking space.

He walked out holding another cardboard document box. He put it in the back of his car.

And he headed back in.

Twenty minutes later, another box.

And another one.

Maybe he hadn't known what was going on at the financial counseling center.

Or maybe he thought it was something different than what I'd told him. Like, financial shenanigans he could deal with. But when I'd mentioned the women...

Interesting.

<hr />

I came home late, feeling exhausted, depressed, afraid, and achy.

I'm not especially well-equipped to feel any of those things.

My body hurt all over, and bruises from my fight with Roger Sabo on Sunday had bloomed all over my body. I'd driven more miles today than I had in a very, very long time. I hadn't eaten. My sister was unhappy because our perfect little domestic setup had gotten discombobulated and it was purely my fault.

I opened the gates to Gary's estate and took the gravel road to the back of the guest house. The motion sensor lights flicked on as I passed them. I parked by the door to the one-car garage we used and got out of my car, feeling slow, tired, and hurting all over. I stopped to stretch before opening the door into the guest house's kitchen.

Which is why I wasn't prepared for the man who rushed out of the thick twine of bougainvillea leaves that cascaded down the side of the garage. He pushed me against the side of my car and socked me in the stomach once, very hard. I careened forward and he yanked me back, hard, pressing my head against the driver's side window.

Roger Sabo.

"Leave me the fuck alone," he said.

I took a deep breath. Then I hooked my foot behind his knee and knocked him off-center, but not enough to get any serious leverage on him. He pushed my face against the glass harder.

"I should kill you right now," he said. "Stop following me. Stop asking questions. Stop talking to people about me. And don't call the police about tonight. If you do, I'll know. Do you understand?"

I nodded. And tried not to shudder as he leaned in close to my ear.

If he reached for any of my clothing I was going to fight him until one of us was dead.

"Why were you there that night? Did you bring the killer to find her?" he asked.

I stared straight ahead, at the garden hose storage reel on the side of the house.

He pushed me against the car again before he reared back and let go.

"Not a word," he said.

I stayed by the side of my car until I could move without screaming. I told myself he'd jumped me and I didn't have any warning. I told myself that if it had gotten more dangerous I would have fought. I told myself that crying was a perfectly reasonable reaction to what had just happened.

By the time I went into the house, I had calmed down. There was no use being hysterical in front of my sister. The house was dark, with the windows lighted up from the spotlights in the garden. I walked through the dark house, not surprised Stevie wasn't waiting for me. She knew better than to get anywhere near the sounds of a fight.

At the bottom of the stairs I called out, "Stevie, *alles ist ganz okay.*"

After a few seconds, the door to her room cracked open. Then she came running down the stairs.

"You're crying," she said. Which was odd. I thought I'd stopped.

"I'm okay. He didn't do anything." Well, other than increase the likelihood of internal bleeding, perhaps.

"Dru, you have to call the police."

I shook my head. "This man," I started. "Stevie, I'm a little scared."

"I'm a lot scared."

What was it going to take to get him to leave me the hell alone?

"Help me upstairs," I said.

"How did he get in?" Stevie asked.

What a good question.

The gates had still been alarmed when I arrived. How the hell had he gotten onto the property? Of course there were ways past the gates, but you'd have to know where the sensors had been installed. Sure, I knew where they were, but Gary had had a very good security system installed after the events of Colin's death.

"You haven't eaten today, have you?" she said.

My insides were still churning. "I'll eat in the morning."

CHAPTER EIGHTEEN

ROGER SABO'S LITTLE VISIT TO our house did not dissuade me from asking questions. In fact, it made it all the more clear I had to push back against this guy, and I needed to do it now. I put on a pair of stretchy capris that allowed me to move, and a short-sleeved blouse that covered most of the damage. I double-checked in the mirror to make sure nothing blue, purple, or green was showing. Putting on nicer, more form-fitting clothes did wonders for my perception of how well I was healing. Then I headed out once again, to Tarzana. I was beginning to hate the San Fernando Valley, all flat and straight-lined and stretching out like carpeting below the 405.

As soon as I walked into the offices of Hitchcock Commercial First Construction, I immediately noted all the differences between it and the financial counseling office. This office had air conditioning. None of the salesmen had pencil-thin mustaches. The receptionist was the same woman, Mary, who had been here on Tuesday, when I was here with Courtney. The chairs were comfortable and no one waiting in them was desperate.

"Is Greg here?" At this point in our relationship I felt confident we ought to be on a first-name basis.

"He's very busy today."

"He'll want to talk to me," I said. "It's about Courtney."

"Today is a bad day," she said. "Next week—"

"Mary, tell him I'm here."

The door to the construction office opened behind me, and instead of Hitchcock walking in, it was Jonathan Ricciardi. He was holding a large cardboard box, the kind that held reams of paper. I'd seen him holding a couple of those last night. I assumed this wasn't one of those.

"Hi," he said slowly, clearly surprised to see me again. He put the box down and wiggled the top off of it. Inside were flyers, and he handed me one. Whatever the rest of it said, in the center was a picture of Courtney. "The church is having a memorial service for her on Sunday. At two. If you'd like to stop by."

His request seemed so surreal after the conversation we'd had last night. "Oh, that sounds lovely. How sweet of you."

"She was a member of our congregation when she lived here in L.A. And, please, invite anyone else who knew her to come to."

"I will." I lowered the flyer. "Maybe you can help me right now."

He raised his eyebrows, waiting.

"I need to talk to Greg."

Jonathan's immediate look of alarm might have been funny, except he was clearly scared to death. I'd shown up at his house and now I'd shown up here.

"Nothing about...that," I said. "This is about his friend."

Jonathan looked at the flyers, then back at me.

"The *other* friend," I said. "Had a second run-in with him last night. Do you know where Greg is?"

He pulled out his phone and typed a few things on it. A map came up with a glowing dot on it. "He's at the construction site." He gave me the address.

"Thank you." I leaned to one side and said, "I'm out of your hair now, Mary."

I drove by the construction site—it was going to be a half-block-sized building, probably three floors tall to match the other buildings in the area, but for now it was a giant pit in the ground. Lots of men, all of them with reddish-brown skin, carrying rebar and tools and doing whatever they did. I parked a block away and walked back.

Hitchcock was standing off to one side, going over some drawings with a man I guessed was the foreman. Both were wearing yellow construction hats. The foreman was Hispanic, in his forties, holding a giant walkie-talkie. He was pointing to one area of the dig. "Jesús said the man said to dig there," he said.

"It's bullshit," Hitchcock said. "Not on the schedule."

"Call said it's real urgent."

I looked down at the giant hole as I walked toward the pair of men. There were large pipe segments in a pile, waiting to be connected to water or power. Long lines of concrete crisscrossed the bottom, with sharp red twirls of steel poking through, forming the base of the skeleton. I didn't see anything special about where the foreman was pointing.

"Hey!" Hitchcock yelled. No cross on the lapel of this work shirt. "This is a closed site—"

"Hi, Greg. Remember me? Courtney's friend?"

"You can't be on a construction site without a hat."

I smiled. "We need to have a little chat. In private."

Hitchcock's gaze flitted over to the trailer that sat on the edge of the site.

"That's okay with me," I said. "If we won't be bothered."

"Boss," said the foreman, holding up the walkie-talkie. "What do we do about this?"

"Tell Enrique and Mike to check it out. Then we keep going." Then Hitchcock pointed to me, because I was next on the agenda. "This way. Watch where you step."

As we walked around the perimeter of the site to the trailer, I saw a small area marked with the ragged remains of police tape, floating to one side in the warm breeze.

"What happened there?" I asked.

"Break-in a couple of nights ago."

"Oh? What got stolen?"

"Who cares what," Hitchcock said. "It was Monday."

Monday. The night Courtney died.

He opened the door to the trailer and waited for me to go in first. It was small, set up to act as a mobile field office, with a desk, a sofa, and a small kitchenette. Paperwork, staplers, rolling filing cabinets. As I glanced at the LAPD sticker stuck across one drawer of the desk, Hitchcock locked the door behind us.

"It's terrible what happened to Courtney," I said, sitting on the sofa. "I can't stop thinking about it."

Hitchcock sat next to me. Extremely next to me. His body up against mine. He turned toward me, put his hand on my leg. "You don't have to worry about anything. I'm very good with problems."

He smelled like onions and beer. Awesome. "My problem is

the same as Courtney's problem. Roger Sabo."

Hitchcock's eyes widened, then he smiled to cover it up. "Don't know him."

"Please let's not. You know what kind of bloke he is. I want him to leave me alone. You're going to help."

Hitchcock leaned back. "What the fuck are you talking about?"

"You are providing valuable financial services not only for the credit-challenged of the San Fernando Valley but to its drug dealers as well."

He got off the sofa and stepped backward. "Get out," he said.

"I know what's going on at Hitchcock Christian Financial, Greg. And not just the really shady credit counseling parts, either, *Señor Hache.*"

Now he moved forward. Crowding me. If he pinned me to the sofa, I wasn't going to have much leverage—he weighed at least a hundred fifteen kilos. "What do you want?"

"Exactly what I said. I'm tired of driving over the hill to the valley, so I'm going to repeat myself one more time. You tell your mate Roger to drop the assault charges against me, or I tell a lot of people what you have going on in your financial counseling office. Your choice."

"That's blackmail."

"Avoid doing bad things and that sort of thing won't happen."

He smiled and clapped his hands together twice. They made a loud slapping sound. "You don't know what you're talking about."

"Okay. If you're sure you want to do it this way. Things are about to get very messy, Greg."

"Roger should have shut you up."

"He tried. He failed. You think you can do better?"

"Look, honey, I don't know what you think you can get out of me. Money? You want money?"

I shook my head. "Tell Roger to leave me alone. That's it. That's all I want."

"You oughta be nicer to me," he said. "I can be really nice to you."

"I've heard what being nice to you entails. No thanks." The moment got ruined by loud banging on the door of the trailer.

"What is it?" Hitchcock yelled.

"You better come out here," said a man with a heavy accent.

"Not now," Hitchcock said.

"Now," said the man at the door.

Hitchcock pushed past me and yanked the door to the trailer open. The foreman standing outside paid no attention to me and whatever condition I might be in. "You gotta see this." His accented words were hard to hear over the rising wail of a police siren in the distance. Hitchcock immediately followed him, leaving the door to the trailer swinging back and forth.

I was done with what I'd come here for. I could just leave. But I was curious to see what the excitement was all about.

At the edge of the site, the foreman pointed to a gathering of construction workers in the center of the site, standing around a giant block of concrete that they had broken open. One half of the concrete lay on its side, the jagged broken piece of metal inside pointing upward. This metal was chrome and black.

It was much easier to see what was in the other half of the concrete block: a formation that looked like handlebars and a steering column.

A steering column you might find on a small motorbike. The kind I saw the night Courtney died.

"We're going to have to redo the whole area," the foreman said.

On the other side of the pit a construction worker, a thin dark-skinned Hispanic man, was throwing a fit and yelling at another of the workers. *"What did you fuckers do?"* he yelled in Spanish. *"What the fuck, man, this isn't funny."*

A couple of other guys were yelling back at him, wondering what the hell kind of game he was playing.

"Someone dumped a motorbike in the concrete?" I asked.

Hitchcock grimaced at me. "You can't be here."

"Story of my life," I whispered.

The last time I'd seen a motorbike like that had been Monday night, through the window of Courtney's motel room.

I had the distinct feeling it was the very same bike, dumped here in order to get rid of it.

Did covering something in concrete get rid of any fingerprints that might be on it?

"Okay, you need to leave now," Hitchcock said. "Did you do this? You know about this?"

"Know about what?" I asked him.

Did Hitchcock know that this motorbike had been used the night Courtney was killed? Had he used it? He was a big man, taller than me, and he would have dwarfed that little bike. The workers who were now standing around were mostly young men, tending toward the lean and muscular. Hitchcock would have had a lot to lose if Courtney talked about his operation. He could have twisted one of their arms, gotten them to do it for him. And I could believe it, too—Hitchcock clearly had no problem exploiting the lower-class and powerless—except for one thing.

His concern right now was all about the messed-up

construction site. "Esteban!" he yelled, waving one of the men toward him. He pointed toward a section of the site and called out a few commands in Spanish.

From the spot right behind the concrete block came an upwell of noisy, agitated voices. One man broke away from the group standing there. He held a burlap bag as he ran toward Hitchcock, yelling, "*It's here.*"

"Oh, shit," Hitchcock said. To the foreman he said, "Call the cops."

I wondered what they had found.

On the other side of the site, a couple of the workers dropped their tools and started running. Not to do whatever Hitchcock had said, but away. Away from the guy running the show, away from the foreman, away from me. Or someone behind me.

The foreman said, "Too late, man."

Two men were walking onto the site from the street. Not hard to guess who the workers with dodgy paperwork might be trying to avoid. One of the men had his badge visible on his belt. The other held the small leather wallet he kept his badge in open.

Detective Gruen was the one with the leather wallet, of course. He looked at me. "Going to have some questions for you."

"I need to see that," Detective Vilar said to the man holding the burlap bag.

The construction worker—couldn't have been more twenty—held it out. From the way the bottom swung, whatever was inside was small and had enough weight and solidity to form a compact weight at the bottom. Probably made of metal.

Vilar pointed to the ground and the man carefully laid it down. He pulled open the edges of the bag, enough to show the barrel of a revolver. He rapid-fired questions about it at the young man, and the worker pointed into the pit.

"We got an anonymous tip that evidence in the Cleary case could be found at this site," Gruen said. "Is this the gun you reported missing?"

"I don't know!" Hitchcock said. "They just found it."

Vilar nodded toward what was visible of the motorbike. "We're having a warrant delivered that allows us to search these premises, including the foundation you've been laying here. You need to cease operations until we can determine exactly what might be here."

"We also have questions about your relationship with Courtney Cleary," he added.

"Courtney?" Hitchcock looked down at the gun lying in the burlap sack. "Wait. You don't think…"

How amazing. Either Gruen and Vilar were some kind of supercops, or someone had phoned them with a very big tip about where the motorcycle and gun used in Courtney's killing could be found. Much as I lusted after Gruen's person, my money was on option number two.

"Do you have somewhere we could have a word with you in private?" Vilar asked.

"Yes…yes, over…" Hitchcock looked around, clearly baffled about what to do next. He waved at the motorhome sitting off to the side, where I'd just spent a moment or two.

José nodded and picked up the ring of keys attached by a chain to his jeans.

Hitchcock and his foreman headed over to the motorhome. Vilar looked at me, then at his partner.

"We could save a lot of time investigating things if we just followed your girlfriend around this city," Detective Vilar said.

"My girlfriend works for the Parks Department," Detective Gruen said, not looking anywhere near me.

I raised an eyebrow at Vilar. He gave a tiny shake of his head before following Hitchcock. Gruen stopped next to me.

"Should I call my lawyer?" I asked.

"What are you doing here?"

"I needed to talk to Hitchcock about a problem. I thought maybe he could help me." I waved my hand at the gun. "This...I had nothing to do with this."

"You weren't planning on being here today?"

"You think I would have dressed like this?" I asked.

He stopped to take in a more pronounced look at me in my tight capris and colorful blouse. I looked a wee bit healthier than I had when he'd stopped by the other day. "We need to talk."

I smiled. "Will your girlfriend be there? I'll bring my lawyer, we'll make it a couples' evening."

He stared at me.

"You know I have nothing to say, Detective."

"Is that a fact?" he said. "Even if I ask really nicely?"

"Well, can't hurt to try," I told him.

CHAPTER NINETEEN

EVERYONE NEEDS MONEY. MORE IMPORTANTLY, everyone wants money. The people who say they don't want money? Those are the ones you really have to keep an eye on. Because at the very least you want to eat well enough to be healthy, and that takes money.

It's like anyone who goes out of their way to tell you what a good Christian they are. If they have to keep telling you, they're not.

Greg Hitchcock, by any remote stretch of the imagination, had a good construction business. Construction can be cutthroat and maybe you end up working with some less-than-savory types—I did grow up in New York City, after all—but Hitchcock's firm was working steadily and by all accounts they did quality work. They weren't building with substandard concrete and low-grade steel. And they were everywhere I drove, once I knew to look for the HCFC logo on construction signs.

But for some reason he couldn't stop himself. He used money to control women who needed help. And a lot of women, if the ease with which I found one was any indicator.

And he also had some kinds of dealings with Roger Sabo, a drug dealer who had his own problems with women. Perhaps Sabo hung around Hitchcock's construction projects and sold meth to the workers who had to work obscene hours doing heavy manual work, and maybe Hitchcock got a percentage of that. But that seemed like a stupid risk to take, one that could easily bring down his legitimate business, let alone his access to an easy supply of women. Why would he do it?

It seemed strange, coincidental even, that Chris McClanahan, another construction firm owner, had gotten involved in drug trafficking, just like his acquaintance from ten years ago, Greg Hitchcock. Maybe if I were nice to McClanahan, he could explain to me how it had happened. Of course, the likelihood that I was going to be nice to him was just about nil, but a girl could dream.

"Stevie," I said, "do you still have those printouts about Chris McClanahan's arrest?"

She rocked back and forth and her fingers nervously played together. "They're in the library." She made no move toward the library.

"What's wrong?" I asked. Stevie practically lived in Gary's house most of the time: it was bigger, it had a nicer view, it had books...Randi. Had to be.

"I told Gary this morning about what happened last night."

"Stevie!" I hissed.

"It's his property. He deserves to know. And that woman started yelling at me. Started saying these horrible things. They're in the library now. I don't want to see her again."

My sister did not do well with confrontation. I reached down for her hand. "Come on."

Gary's house was quiet, except for the sounds of jazz or a light-rock station playing somewhere off in another wing. Stevie flew across the marble floor to the doors of the library, which she pulled open before dashing inside...and stopping short.

Gary and Randi were standing at the window, looking out at the Pacific. He was pointing out the landmarks that were visible. "Oh!" he said, upon seeing us. "Are you all right?"

"What do you think you're doing, bringing people like Roger to this house?" Randi said. "He's a really bad guy." She turned to Gary. "Seriously, I know this guy. He is bad news. She's probably into drugs or something."

"I didn't bring him here," I said. Why was I justifying myself to her anyhow? Who cared what Randi had to say. "Gary, have you contacted the alarm company?"

"They said the gates were opened."

"With whose code?"

"Yours," he said simply.

"That's impossible," I said. "I couldn't have done. I was gone all yesterday."

"Well, your sister was here," Randi said. She looked at the floor Stevie was working on. "This place is a mess. You gotta clean this up. You can't leave your messes all over Sir Gareth's house. You and your sister. How are you putting up with this?" she asked Gary.

"Um. Well. Stevie's doing a project for me."

Stevie grabbed the pile of papers about McClanahan and ran out of the library.

I stared at our landlord. "Stevie can stop doing this for you anytime. Just say when." I smiled, not nicely.

"Wait," Gary said.

"You don't need to be bossed around like this," Randi said, clutching his arm. "From what you've told me, this woman is dangerous." *This woman* being me.

"Is there a problem?" I asked.

"Yeah, I'd say there's one," Randi said.

Gary held his hand up and sputtered a bit, trying to find the words to start. Funny how a man so famous for speaking words found choosing them so difficult on his own. "There are some things I have been wondering about," he finally stammered.

Randi smiled. Big.

"Fabulous," I said. "Want to do this now?"

She shook her head. "Can't. We're having lunch with Tyler Faustus. You know him? No, you haven't met him."

Some Hollywood bigwig, undoubtedly.

"And then we're going away to Catalina until Sunday night. I don't want him around in case your friend Roger shows up again. So you can talk to Sir Gareth next week."

Whoa. No. That was not okay. Stevie and I were Gary's human pill-reminder alarms. He had a nasty habit of missing doses if he didn't have someone opening his mouth and shoving the medications in. "Could I talk to you for a moment?" I said. "*Alone.*"

He held up his hand. "It's fine. Away for a day."

"I count that as *two* days, Gary."

Randi nestled in closely to Gary's side. "I'll take care of him, honey. Don't you worry about him. Come on, Sir Gareth. We have to get to Santa Monica."

She remained locked to him as she pulled him out of the

library.

Stupid bastard. Old men were ridiculous when it came to young women.

Well, if that's what he wanted, far be it from me to stand in his way.

Zeus on a cloud, I'd introduced them. Stupid, stupid, *stupid*. If there's one person on earth who knows how easy it is to worm her way into someone's life lightning-fast, it's me. I just didn't think Randi was that good.

I put off any and all thoughts about what I'd have to do in the coming week about Randi, provided she didn't talk herself out of her newfound relationship by the end of a weekend away. Women who move in tend to be unpleasant about women who are still living there.

Stevie was in the guest-house kitchen, sitting at the breakfast counter. She had laid the papers she'd printed about McClanahan's arrest down the length of the counter. And she was crying.

"Sweetheart," I said, putting my arm around her shoulders. "It's okay. Everything's okay."

"He's listening to her," she said. "He asked me to sort his papers, and he didn't tell her that. He just let her say those things."

"I know. He's being a bastard. He'll get over it."

"He won't," Stevie said. "They never do."

For a girl who'd never had a relationship with a boy, she was remarkably sour on the whole idea already. We hadn't had the best examples of human relationships while we were growing up, and I'd hardly been a model of right behavior over the past decade.

"There's nothing we can do about Gary right now," I told her. "Let's look at these papers. Where are the ones about the police officer?"

Her index finger stabbed out blindly and hit a paper to her right. Stevie knew where everything was all the time.

The first time, I hadn't looked closely at the photo of Officer Broderick Tennyson shaking hands with his lieutenant, commending him on his arrest, because I didn't think it was important. But my second look showed me something different. Ten years, a man in his early twenties now in his thirties, with a couple of years of heavy drug use. It was possible, but not certain. The uniform hat, low on his forehead, obscured the view.

"Any other pictures of him?" I asked my sister.

She typed on her computer quickly. "Not much about this fellow out there," she said. "Odd, given that he was a decorated police officer. But there's this. It's old. Low resolution."

She turned her computer around and showed me the picture. I was right.

"Dammit," I said before I could stop myself. Stevie sharply inhaled, but if there was one time that had earned every swear I could think of, this was it.

Two men involved in the construction business who were also involved in drugs wasn't as much of a coincidence as I had thought. Not that my stepfather Roberto had known this when he set me on the task of helping Dr. Anson Villiers—he had asked me to do that specifically to get two pieces of information through to me.

The first was, Roberto was watching me all the time. He knew I accompanied Anne on her interviews and story gathering, so he followed Anne's career closely. He was finding out about the people and places she was going. He knew about the Baldwin Park trip, and he knew that my injuries had come from meeting Courtney Cleary and her boyfriend, Roger Sabo. I would not hide from Roberto Montesinos again.

The second thing he wanted me to know was that, when he found out Anne had that assignment, he had found out who Roger Sabo was. And when I got beaten up, he knew who'd done it. He wanted me to find out who had done it. And maybe figure out I was in over my head this time.

Because the cop who'd arrested Chris McClanahan twelve years ago, Broderick Tennyson, had changed his name. He was now known as Roger Sabo.

I had the feeling that Tennyson-Sabo's connection to two very different construction firm owners—who knew one another back in Simi Valley—wasn't a coincidence after all.

If Chris McClanahan answered one question for me he would tie together a lot of these loose ends. There was no earthly reason he'd want to answer this.

So I would offer incentives. How generous was Roberto willing to be to ensure Erica Rose performed at Dr. Villiers's nonprofit fundraiser?

He'd given me permission to speak for him, so I was figuring damn generous.

I pulled out my cell phone.

"Who is this?" Stevie asked. She blinked a few times and then turned the computer around. "You clearly know him... This is Roger Sabo, isn't it? I'll see if I can find out if he's still a police officer."

How my sister figured that out so quickly, I had no idea. If Stevie and Roberto ever went into business together, the rest of us should just swear fealty and be done with it.

"Might be tough. I think he's a very, very undercover cop," I said. Then, to the phone, "Hi Chris, it's Drusilla Thorne. We need to finish our little chat... No, *now*... Where and when?" I memorized the name he gave me. "I'll be there in half an hour." I kissed the top of Stevie's head. "I'll call you as soon as I'm done."

Chris and Erica Rose were at a photographer's studio in Westwood. I felt a little exhausted when he told me. Westwood wasn't over the hill in the San Fernando Valley, but it was on the far side of the 405. When I had money again, I would travel solely by chauffeured car and helicopter. It was a tiny office in a converted house near UCLA. A modest black wooden sign with white lettering posted in the yard out front listed the occupants. Ottofocus Photo was the third one down and had the best graphic design for its logo.

I let myself in the door in the back and a female assistant with spiky green hair and striped zebra leggings under her purple sweatshirt stopped me in the doorway. To prevent me from running pell-mell through the place, yelling, perhaps.

The photo shoot was in progress. Erica Rose was following the instructions the photographer yelled out at her: jump, wave her arms, look enthusiastic, try *really* enthusiastic this time. Instead, the teenager looked exhausted. Didn't she have to be in school? I wondered.

Chris McClanahan watched his daughter with a combination of pride and a critical eye, waving his hand at her from behind the photographer's back, telling her to move, to smile, to bend over. At one point the photographer turned and shot the world's meanest glance at him, and McClanahan didn't even notice.

Then he happened to look in my direction and swear.

The photographer looked at me to see who had possibly interrupted McClanahan's backseat driving. Then he went back to shooting Erica Rose.

"Five minutes," McClanahan said to me.

"Make it twenty-five," I said, opening the door I'd just walked through. "Or however long this is going to take."

We stood out in the parking lot behind the house. McClanahan took a soft pack of cigarettes out and lighted one. He didn't offer me one. I told myself I wouldn't have taken one anyhow. The easiest way to believe a lie is to tell it to yourself.

"Why are you here?" he said.

"Because you want to be convinced to come to the fundraiser tomorrow." And because Roberto had given me the task of making this happen. I had all sorts of incentive.

"Fuck you. We've talked about this. We're done," McClanahan said.

He didn't really think we were done, of course. You don't give directions to your location to someone you're done with. If you're talking, you still want something.

I smiled and shook my head. "You walk back in there, I assure you here and now your daughter has played her last shopping mall. Or fundraiser. Or birthday party. Or street corner. Roberto Montesinos's wife owns the company that produces your daughter's show and syndicates it. They will stop buying it. Tomorrow."

Maybe Roberto had a third thing he wanted me to figure out: I did have the power to settle this. He wanted to see how I was going to do it. This issue with Erica Rose was small potatoes compared to what I might have to deal with when I came back from the dead. He wanted to see how much work I was going to need.

"I want everyone to get something out of this. Everyone walks away happy. What is it that you need to walk away happy?"

"I've gotten the short shaft from this group since Erica Rose signed on. She needs to be respected as a professional. She's not doing this as a favor."

Translation: he wanted money.

Fine. We haggled a bit and I offered him a number in the mid four digits, in cash. Less than I'd been prepared to offer, that was for certain.

"What else do you need, Chris?"

"She's sixteen. She can't work all day and all night."

Translation: he wanted her to show up and leave almost immediately.

"She is on stage at seven o'clock and she sings four songs," I said.

"Two," he said.

She barely had the voice to do two in a row. I sighed heavily. "Three. What else?"

He paused.

He'd had a short list of demands.

"How about you, Chris? Are you being taken care of? Is there anyone you'd like to meet? Possibly discuss Erica Rose's movie career?"

His eyes widened. "Yeah," he said. "Yeah, I would. I'd like to get Erica Rose a new movie agent."

"Do you have someone in mind?"

McClanahan mentioned some name, Tony somebody-or-other. I didn't keep track of who the top agents in Hollywood were. But I was certain Roberto could find out who this person was.

"We can make that meeting happen," I said, "provided you stick to what we've agreed to here. Erica Rose shows up on time, and she does three songs. She shows up late or she leaves early, no one's going to be happy." And he wasn't going to get any of his money under the table.

He nodded. He put his hand out to shake.

"Not so fast, Chris. There's one thing you need to tell me to make me happy."

"Erica Rose will—"

"Will appear at the party she already agreed to be at. But now I've had to chase you halfway around creation to get you to agree to that. So you need to tell me something."

"Okay. What?"

"It's about your arrest."

His anger was instant. He *really* did not like talking about it. "Fuck you. No. I'm not talking about that with you."

"Chris, you did your time. Your history doesn't affect our agreement or Erica Rose's performance tomorrow night. But there's something you know that I need to know."

He stuck his index finger in my face. I didn't blink. "I got nothing with that shit anymore, do you understand me?"

I nodded. My cheek hit his index finger mid-nod. "Excellent decision on your part. I still have a question, though. It doesn't go beyond our conversation here and now." I waited until McClanahan was ready. "The bloke who arrested you. Tennyson."

If I hadn't had the mild suspicion before, the way McClanahan shook his head and gritted his teeth told me I was definitely about to ask the money question.

"You knew him before the arrest, right?"

"Fuck you, I'm not saying a word."

"You think Roberto Montesinos has a cop working for him?" I said.

"People who are too helpful make me suspicious."

I lifted up the edge of the blouse I was wearing. He stared at my stomach, with its bandage and bruises. "Broderick Tennyson did this to me a few days ago. Also, you might notice while you're looking that I'm not wearing a wire." I dropped the hem. "So could you answer my question, please? You knew him before he arrested you, right?"

"Yeah. You might say that."

"He was part of your operation."

McClanahan nodded. "Yeah."

"Tell me how it worked."

"Why? This was ten—twelve years ago. What do you care?"

"Because I think he's doing it again, Chris. He's doing it here, in Los Angeles. And I think he killed someone this week because of it. Tell me how it worked."

He told me. It was pretty simple.

The construction crews around Los Angeles were almost all Mexican or Central American immigrants. Very few of them had the right papers. Chris McClanahan had set up a smuggling operation with incoming workers: they carried in meth from Mexico and when they got to Simi Valley, they had semi-legitimate work waiting for them. McClanahan delivered the meth to Broderick Tennyson, who not only distributed the drugs but arrested McClanahan's main competition.

"How big was your construction firm?"

"We did five million in projects a year."

"And how much did you clear in meth?"

"About fifty percent of that."

Wow, I thought. Nice work if you can get it, except for the murders and the addiction and lives ruined and such. "What did it depend on?"

He shrugged. "How many guys I could get on the crew. They didn't want to keep coming in and out, and who can blame them?"

I nodded. "Did Greg Hitch—"

McClanahan exploded with anger. "That fucker? You come here and ask me about him? You know he was going to be the main witness against me, right?"

I shook my head. The stories about McClanahan's trial had been sparse. The whole thing had been put to bed rather quickly. "I didn't know that. I'm sorry. Why was he the witness?"

McClanahan seemed to finally accept he was going to stand there and talk to me until I was satisfied. "We shared crews. When guys finished their shifts for me they'd go pick up work from him and vice-versa."

"Which is how he found out about this."

McClanahan shrugged. "I told people about Tennyson's involvement and it got covered up."

Maybe Hitchcock had proposed a deal to Tennyson: they both move to L.A. and start doing this on a much bigger scale. Tennyson would go to work in Vice as an undercover cop, arresting the competition and protecting Hitchcock. And Hitchcock wasn't going to share workers with anyone this time. And how many workers did Hitchcock have going at any one time? On large-scale projects?

I wondered if Stevie could piece together how much HCFC was clearing a year in contracts. If he was doing fifty percent again importing meth—

McClanahan pulled another cigarette out of the pack. He really did not enjoy reliving his glory years. Good. Maybe he had his eyes firmly focused on the future. "We done now?" he asked.

"A limo will be at your house enough time before the fundraiser to get you and your daughter," I said. I put my hand out, and we shook. "Thank you very much, Mr. McClanahan. You've been extremely helpful."

In my car I called Anson Villiers's office and left the message that everything should be straightened out with Erica Rose. "If there are any problems, if she's late, if she behaves badly, call me immediately."

I left a message for Roberto and told him he needed to get in touch with Tony Somebody-or-other, a movie agent, to have a meeting with Erica Rose. Just a meeting. That was all I promised.

When I hung up, I stared at the phone for a moment. Should I tell Anne about what I'd just learned from Chris McClanahan? In the end I decided she ought to know. At the very least, she could start investigating it, and maybe she could make a bigger story out of it. "Ring me as soon as you can," I told her voicemail. "Not only do I have a way out of our problem with Sabo, I have a gigantic story for you." I gave her the short version on the phone, mentioning Sabo's real name.

And there's nothing that keeps a freelance journalist happier than a big story dropped in their lap.

Well, if I were a freelance journalist, that would keep me happy.

There are several reasons I wouldn't make it as a journalist, and my problems with reading comprehension were among the least important.

CHAPTER TWENTY

I LAY DOWN ON THE sofa in the library, staring up at the tin ceiling. Now that Gary and Randi weren't in here, it was quiet and relaxing again. Stevie wasn't enjoying the silence much, so I told her what I'd learned from McClanahan. "Way, way bigger than money laundering. And Courtney knew something about all of it."

"Perhaps you should call Detective Gruen with this information," she said.

I grinned. "Maybe I should, huh?"

She sighed. "That's not what I meant."

My phone buzzed with a text. Stevie glanced at it. "Anne's outside. She needs to talk to us."

My phone message about a possible story had piqued her interest. But she couldn't call first? Even I think it's a little inconsiderate to stop by someone's house without calling first. Well, unless I'm breaking in. I don't call before doing that. And since when did Anne text before she came over instead of call? "Finally. Where the hell—Hades has she been?"

Stevie did whatever tech magic she does to open the front gates of Gary's estate and we walked through his house. "Hades is not the equivalent of the Christian hell," she said. "It's more akin to —"

"Tell me all of this again, when I'm reading comparative mythologies at some university. Oh dear, you'll be waiting a very long time."

She pursed her lips and stared straight ahead.

Anne's white VW convertible was rounding the fountain as we opened the front door. But she didn't park in one of the spaces under the pine trees. She parked by the fountain and got out.

She looked mad.

To be more specific, she looked mad *at me*.

Lots of people have reason to be furious with me. Especially after what had already happened so far that day, let alone during the entire week. Anne wasn't supposed to be on the list. What had gotten under her skin?

"Anne! I've been calling you. What's going on?"

Anne didn't even come all the way around her car. She stopped at the rear bumper, pushed her glasses up her nose and glared at me. "I can't believe how stupid I am. I thought maybe I was different. You and me, we're friends. But you just think everyone's dumber than you, don't you? Well, I guess we all are."

I was about to offer her a gigantic news story. What had her back up? "What are you talk—"

"When I came here Tuesday morning, I told you about Courtney's murder. And you said later how it happened in North Hollywood."

I shook my head. "You told me—"

"I said she was murdered in her motel room. Not where. Didn't occur to me until later that you somehow knew where. All I said was 'motel.'"

"It was on the news."

"You didn't know Courtney was dead until I told you, remember?" she screamed. "*You're the witness!* I've seen the report. You witnessed Courtney's murder and you didn't say a goddamn word to me."

If the cops were releasing my name publicly, I was in trouble. Very big trouble. I skipped past worrying about Sabo. My name in the news—that would get back to Roberto in seconds. "Anne, calm down."

"Jesus Christ. What the hell happened? You go to talk to Courtney and she ends up dead. Is that supposed to be some kind of *coincidence*? Aren't you the one who's going on about how there's no such thing as a goddamn coincidence?"

"Anne. Stop."

She waved her arms in the air, like she was dispelling my words like they were bees attacking her. "No. No more. Whatever you say, you're probably just going to lie. Sometimes being with a person like that is fun. It's not fun anymore. It's crazymaking. *You're* crazymaking."

First Gary, now this.

Had everyone in my life lost their damned mind today?

"How do you dare come here and say this to me?"

"Because I don't believe anything you say anymore!" she yelled. The stone facade and brick of the courtyard made quite the echo chamber—I wouldn't be surprised to find out most of our neighbors could hear us.

"Let me finish!" I yelled back, walking down the steps. "You've said your piece, now let me say mine. You don't come here and talk to me like that and expect I'm going to take it. No, I didn't tell you I was with Courtney. I watched her die, Anne. Why in the hell would I tell you about that? The police want me to tell them what I saw. If I'm not telling them, what the fuck makes you think I would tell you?"

"Because I'm your friend."

"Funny way you have of showing it."

"Dru," Stevie said.

"Save it, Stevie. Oh, and Anne? Anything I did tell the police? It would go straight back to Roger Sabo. You want to know why? He's an undercover cop by the name of Broderick Tennyson. In addition to his other activities, such as beating up women and dealing, he's also got a massive methamphetamine operation with Greg Hitchcock. How's that for me telling you something?"

Anne's righteous indignation faltered when her interest in hearing more about those little revelations surged.

"No, no, no," she said. "I am done with your lies and your bullshit."

"Oh, no," Stevie said. "What she said just now is absolutely true."

Anne shook her head. "You seem like you're genuinely nice, but you have her as a big sister and I feel sorry for you." She walked back to the driver's side door.

"Hold up a minute, Anne," I said.

I would have told Stevie to close the gates to force her to talk, but it was too late: the VW headed out to the road.

"Dammit," I muttered.

Priorities. What was the top priority right now? I couldn't do anything about Anne's little hissy fit at the moment. I needed to know if her getting a hold of my name was because she had sources or because the LAPD was getting ready to release it publicly. Maybe I should call Nathaniel.

Or I should take Stevie up on her previous suggestion.

I handed Stevie my phone. "Text Detective Gruen."

"Drusilla, now isn't the time. Did you hear—"

"Text him and ask him how his day's been going."

"You're reacting quite poorly to Anne's visit," she said.

"Just do it."

Stevie held the phone without doing anything. "What if he doesn't respond?"

"Then I'm probably going to get arrested for something. It's a risk."

Her fingers flew over the screen of my phone. Undoubtedly she used complete sentences and proper capitalization, which I was given to understand was not normal texting style.

As we walked back into the house and returned to Gary's library, the phone buzzed. Stevie had picked the noise, which sounded like someone doing scales on a harp. Given that she was the one who had to read the texts, it seemed only fair to let her pick the noise it would make.

Stevie took much longer to read it than I knew she needed.

"What is it?" I said.

"I'm trying to figure out if this is a code or not."

"What did he say?"

"He suggests you call him."

Was that an indicator that I was about to get arrested for something? Might as well push my luck and find out exactly what Greg Hitchcock had had to say about me. Probably Gruen wouldn't give me too much of a head start if things had gone poorly.

"Ask him what's the best place to get a whiskey sour in the area."

"Is this part a code?"

"Are you hard of hearing? I have extremely good diction."

She typed furiously on the phone's screen. "Seems like a game of Chinese Whispers."

"Join the rest of humanity here in the twenty-first century. The game is called Telephone. Or Operator. Have you ever even played Telephone?"

"Only with you."

I remembered that afternoon. "Doesn't work quite the same when only two are playing." We couldn't convince the nanny to play with us. "You, of all people, calling it Chinese Whispers. For one thing, you actually speak Chinese. It doesn't sound like nonsense to you, it sounds like words and communication."

The phone beeped. "Which area?" she said.

"What does he think is nice?"

She stared at me. "Are you mad? It's not difficult. We're in the Palisades—"

I waved my hand at the phone. "Stevie. Ask him."

She typed. And waited for the buzz.

"There's a good sports bar on Cahuenga," Stevie said.

Something about Stevie of all people uttering those words made me want to cackle with laughter. Also the feeling of relief that Gruen's response most likely signaled I wasn't getting arrested anytime soon. Cahuenga. Hollywood. I wondered if he was simply in the neighborhood or if he lived near there.

"What time is it now?" I glanced at the museum-quality grandfather clock Gary had installed in the library. "Tell him to send me the address and ask if they have a Happy Hour."

My sister's thumbs flew over the screen of my phone. "Seems extremely odd to—" She held the phone up in one hand. "The two of you are arranging a date. I am facilitating a…a date. With someone you should not be dating. When you have bigger problems on your hands."

"Can't a new resident of L.A. ask someone who's lived here a while for recommendations on places to enjoy a convivial atmosphere?"

She crossed her arms, tucking my phone close to her. "This is the most bonkers thing you've done…" She drifted off, clearly running through everything we'd done in the last few days, months, years, and realized meeting Gruen for a drink had some strong competition.

"I completely agree," I said. "Going for drinks anywhere near Hollywood on a Friday afternoon? Probably sunstroke."

She shook her head. "And I helped you to do something this mindbogglingly stupid in the middle of a murder investigation."

"Yes. But you're so much better on the keyboard than I am. I have a disorder. You may have heard of it."

She muttered to herself as she brought the phone out and hit one key. "Mr. Ross will have a fit when he finds out about this."

"Mr. Ross. You're so cute. When Nathaniel finds out about what? That I had an enjoyable cocktail *by myself* at the end of the day?"

"He will stop being your lawyer. And then where will we be?"

The phone beeped.

"I suppose you want me to read you the address," she said.

"At least I'm familiar enough with the layout of the streets that you don't have to tell me how to get there," I said.

CHAPTER TWENTY-ONE

A SPORTS BAR IS DESIGNED for the people there to watch sports, preferably on screens as big as possible, and not to watch the people around them. There were three basketball games going on when I arrived. Gruen wasn't there, so I found a table in the back, near the smallest (and therefore least popular) screen. The game was visible but not directly dominant from my little perch, which was perfect. No one paid the slightest bit of attention to me, which was even more perfect. One of the nice things about television is that it magnetically draws the attention of everyone close enough to it. They only see what's on the magical glowing telly and forget to pay attention to everyone else.

Particularly the people sitting in the darker areas, because staring at a glowing screen reduces the eye's ability to focus on anything darker.

Early on I trained myself not to be drawn in by glowing

screens. This has paid off handsomely for me on multiple occasions, when I've been the only one seeing what's going on while everyone else is staring like zombies.

This goes double for these damned phones everyone enjoys, especially as they're all text based.

I propped my feet with their five-inch heels on the chair across from me. After Stevie told me where the bar was, I put on my crocheted lace dress, which clung to my curves without chafing my skin or any of my bandages, and a pair of black patent shoes. Wouldn't want to have to dress like this all the time, but there were definitely occasions. My body wasn't back into perfect shape, but you can either wait for the perfect moment or enjoy the imperfect now.

The waitress, a tall, gangly woman with long brown hair and protruding wrist bones stopped by the only other table near me that was occupied. She served beers to the two guys and replaced large, bowl-shaped margaritas for the two women, who I assumed were their dates. Once the empty goblets were balanced on her tray, she swung by my table. I ordered myself a whiskey sour. And I waited.

I pretended to watch the game on the screen and instead watched the table to my left. Everyone in their mid-twenties or trying very hard to look that way. The women were better dressed than the guys: the curvy Chinese woman was in a tight white bandage dress and spiky white heels, and the stick-thin blonde wore a casual low-cut top and a short skirt and an almost identical pair of shoes. The blond guy, who was there with the Chinese woman, wore a t-shirt and jeans, and the black-haired guy, who might have been Italian or Indian or I don't know what, was in a button-down shirt and trousers. No tie. No one in Los Angeles ever wore ties, except hipsters and lawyers like Nathaniel Ross and police detectives, which probably made them easier to spot. It was Friday afternoon; these four had cut work early and started Happy Hour.

They talked about work and how exhausted they were after a day of secretly running Los Angeles while their bosses played video poker all day. I laughed.

"This seat taken?"

The deep male voice startled me—I must have been concentrating on eavesdropping hard. Detective Gruen had his hand on the back of the chair where my feet were perched. He looked amused, probably having noticed that I'd been completely unaware of his arrival. He'd lost the sports coat and tie he'd been wearing at Hitchcock's construction site, and the top button on his dress shirt was undone, too. He was a little sweaty and a little tired and still completely gorgeous. I'd make do with the sweaty and tired.

I swung my legs down. "Please do."

He watched them move. "Nice shoes. You weren't wearing those earlier."

"They're both elegant and handy in a fight. I can break off the heel and use it as a shiv."

"They're probably not very convenient at construction sites, though."

And thus endeth the foreplay. Gruen wanted to get down to talking business before we talked anything else. Well, we had a lot to talk about.

The waitress came over with my drink and managed to set it down in front of me while keeping her back turned to me so she could face him. I understood that reaction to Gruen, but I was still going to dock her tip for that maneuver.

"What can I get you?" she asked.

He ordered a beer. "You really drink whiskey sours," he said.

I shrugged. Whiskey sours were something Drusilla drank. Every time the name changed, so did the drink. Priscilla in Montréal drank red wine, which I didn't understand at all because I don't particularly care for the stuff. Whiskey was definitely a step up.

"What brings you to Hollywood?" I asked.

"Had to drop off some paperwork."

"The curse of our time."

He nodded at that. "What's your excuse?"

"You."

Just because he was done with the foreplay didn't mean I was. Didn't hurt that it was the truth.

"Thanks," he said. "I think."

"I wouldn't have come across town to talk to Detective Vilar."

There are lots of parts of a man's body I find attractive. But like most women, I start with the eyes. His were hazel, a muddy sort of greenish-brown, and very focused. Men are encouraged to look directly at a person, whereas women aren't. I look directly into people's eyes, too. Particularly when I want to signal my interest.

Gruen was really good about keeping eye contact. I admired that about him; so many men had trouble talking to a woman. And I don't mean because they're too busy checking the woman's figure out or wondering how to ask her out or something as mundane as that. It's simply because some men don't think a woman is worth talking to. I didn't know Detective Gruen very well, but the few times we had talked made me wish there weren't such strict prohibitions against us communicating.

I had to stop meeting him over dead bodies.

"Sorry, should I not have said that?"

"We have a few things to talk about."

"Funny running into you this afternoon."

He leaned toward me. His skin smelled of sweat and salt. Since his shirt wasn't sweaty, he'd changed before coming here. "Tell me you're not poking around Courtney Cleary's death."

"Before I answer that, let me ask: is this conversation actually happening?"

He shook his head slowly. "Just two people talking."

"I've not gone anywhere near Courtney's death. That is for rather delightful men like yourself to look into. My problem is with Roger Sabo."

"Stay away from him."

"If he left me alone, I would stay home and needlepoint." I picked up my drink. "I don't needlepoint, exactly, but you get my meaning."

"You don't want to get mixed up with—"

"An undercover cop?" I said.

The look Gruen gave me was somewhere between admiration and suspicion.

"You're right, I don't. However, I have done. That isn't the least of it. Do you know about his relationship to Greg Hitchcock? You might be interested. Or does the LAPD take a cut of its members' meth-dealing empires? Could help funding shortfalls, I suppose."

"What the hell does that mean?"

I leaned toward him. If I moved a couple of inches closer, I'd be kissing him. He didn't back up. "You have to keep my name out of the papers about Courtney's murder."

"I can't promise that."

I raised my eyebrows at him. "Yes, you can."

He shrugged. "Okay. I won't unless you have a really good reason."

Fine. I'd go first. "He's not just playing a meth dealer on TV, Detective. He has the same operation going here with Hitchcock that he had going in Simi Valley with Chris McClanahan. You know that name?"

Gruen nodded.

I leaned back and Gruen's attention wandered to how I looked settling back in a comfortable position. I held my hand out, thumb and fingers an inch apart. "If this was the deal with McClanahan?" I held my arms out as far as I could without hitting other patrons. "This is the size of the deal with Hitchcock." I dropped my hands into my lap. "Don't take this the wrong way, but this is much bigger than just you handling it. Sabo is terrible, horrible, no good, very bad news. Wouldn't surprise me in the slightest if he killed Courtney." I held up my hand. "No idea whether he did or not. But he's definitely a bad actor."

"Was he there that night?"

After a second's pause, I nodded. "I saw him through the window. After Courtney was murdered. He disappeared before the police arrived?"

"You saw who did it."

"And they were fully masked."

"You need to testify he was there."

"And you know that's not happening. Ever."

Gruen leaned back in his chair, annoyed at my unwillingness to cooperate. He sucked in a huge breath before blowing it out— his version of counting backward, perhaps. His gaze flicked back to me. "What were you doing with Hitchcock today?"

"Oh, this story you are going to like." I told him about the women who went to the financial counseling office. Poor, desperate, and without means. "There were a lot of women there, Detective. Courtney took me to meet him because she thought I might be in need of his special brand of help. She knew what he was doing. He had a fantastic motive to kill her. Or have someone else do it. He wasn't the one holding the gun."

"You still haven't said what you were doing there today."

"I wanted to motivate him to tell his friend Roger to leave me alone. Then there was a crisis at the construction site. Which I had nothing to do with. The end. Are we done talking about this now?"

"What else do you want to talk about?" he asked.

I smiled. "I can think of a few things, Detective. And you're a guy, so I know you've already thought about them." That made him grin. The first time he saw me he was on the way to start investigating my husband Colin's death. Not even that will stop a man's imagination.

I put my hand on his forearm, warm and hard, and I trailed my fingernails over the fabric of his shirt. "Come on, Detective. I've been a very good citizen. In one week I've found out about two very bad things going on in your city."

"Your city, too," he said.

I thought about Gary and Randi, and Anne's fury, and Roberto's demands. "Probably not for too much longer. So if you're worried about anyone at the Parks Department getting angry..."

He laughed. "We broke up a week ago." He leaned forward, and he came so close I wondered if he was going to surprise me with a kiss. But then he whispered in my ear, "You have been nothing but trouble."

I moved my hand up to his shoulder and whispered, "Would you like to find out how much trouble I can be?"

He pulled back just enough so that our faces were close, very close. I raised my eyebrows at him. "What's it going to be, Detective?"

The waitress took that moment to stand right beside us. "Can I get you anything else?" she trilled.

"No," Gruen said. He pulled out a twenty and dropped it on the table.

That was the best "No" I'd heard in forever.

He pushed the door open and I felt a wave of the late afternoon Los Angeles heat wash over us. Hot asphalt from the streets and hot exhaust from the cars and hot grease from the bar's kitchen and hot clothes on the girls pushing their way past us and hot desperation from everyone on the make. Everyone was young and hustling and making deals and eager to brag to their friends about the awesome day they'd had. It was all bullshit and hot air and it would be just as much bullshit and hot air tomorrow, but they'd keep up their excitement all the time, every day, right up until they either scored for real or got the hell out of town.

What happened to the ones who kept at it, kept pursuing their dreams without ever grabbing the brass ring?

We stood on the small strip of concrete separating the bar from the boulevard. Friday night on the outskirts of Hollywood meant the sidewalks were beginning to fill with people on bar crawls, looking for celebrity hangouts, dressed up for chi-chi cocktail bars. I found myself not paying attention to the people coming and going. I looked at the detective, who was, as he so often was, staring directly at me. Did he look at everyone that way? I wondered. It was intense and disorienting and thrilling all at the same time.

And what did he see?

Stevie would accuse me of overthinking things, and my sister and I could safely agree on the truism that in general, I didn't think enough about things.

"Look, Drusilla—"

"Oh, shut it already." I grabbed him by the lapels of his shirt and pulled him toward me.

His lips were warm and soft and, most importantly, they were finally on mine.

That was a nice kiss. I would have smiled, but that would have thrown off our rhythm.

One thing I have learned over the years is that a man's ability to kiss and his ability to do anything else of interest are directly correlated.

As I suspected he might, Detective Gruen was going to have my undivided attention for as long as he wanted it.

I leaned back and looked up at him. Even in five-inch heels I had to look up at him. He was perfect. "Tell me you live near here."

It took a few seconds for Gruen to crack even the tiniest smile at that. "Closer than you do."

"I'll follow you."

"Why?"

"Because I'm going to take my own car. Wherever you are in L.A., you should have your car nearby."

He grinned. "Good point." He leaned down and tilted his mouth over mine.

In the middle of our second, really fantastic kiss, my phone rang. While I wouldn't have been surprised at all at Stevie having the amazing timing to block things finally progressing with Detective Gruen, the ringtone wasn't for my sister. It was for Anne.

Two hours ago, Anne had been screaming bloody murder at

me. I didn't need more of her rage at why I might be keeping secrets that had nothing to do with her. I ignored it and the phone stopped ringing.

"What's your address in case we get separated?" I asked.

He told me. And my phone started ringing again. Once again it was Anne.

"Let me get this and tell her to go take a flying leap off a short pier," I said.

"Something happen?" he asked, his voice deep. That was a good register for his voice. I could get used to him talking to me like that.

"She's upset I'm a material witness to just about everything on the planet. And I didn't share that information."

"You didn't tell her?"

I shrugged as I answered. "You made yourself clear—"

"Hey, so, we're supposed to meet up for frozen daiquiris?" Her words were rushed and she sounded excessively festive. Desperately festive, even.

"Only if they have *real* whipped cream," I said.

Gruen narrowed his eyebrows.

"Of course with *real* whipped cream!" she said.

I held up an index finger at him, and mouthed, *Wait*.

Anne didn't stop to take a breath. "Listen, can you come here and pick me up? My car is making this funky noise and I need to take it in."

She must have thought I was still in the Palisades. But I was in Hollywood, less than three miles from her house. "It'll take me an hour to get there, depending on traffic."

"Always takes an hour to get anywhere!" Anne said. "Hurry!"

I hung up.

Anne was well aware that my definition of frozen daiquiri is "the alcoholic drink for people afraid of alcoholic drinks." The only way I'd drink one is if someone were holding a gun to my head.

The only reason Anne would ask me to go drink a frozen daiquiri was if someone were holding a gun to hers.

And the only likely candidate for that position was Roger Sabo.

What had I told her when she came by to scream at me? That Sabo had a much bigger meth business than we'd suspected...and he was an undercover cop. She'd probably decided to spring her sudden knowledge on Sabo. And he'd decided to return the favor.

My date with Gruen had just ended. I wondered what the odds were on getting a raincheck from him was. Probably not good.

Did I tell him? I should, I supposed. Except what was the response time going to be? And the second the cops showed up, everything was going to go to hell fast.

I shouldn't have told Anne those things when she was so angry, because angry people do stupid things. I had to see if I could help her.

"I have to go," I said.

Gruen turned my face up to look at him. "Tell me what's going on."

I was going to give him some crap excuse about having forgotten about plans with Anne, but not only was he not stupid, he knew I wasn't. "I have to go." I kissed him again. Hard. I had a distinct feeling this was going to be my last opportunity.

"Tell me now," he said. "You know. Before I happen to run into you again."

If he got too suspicious, he was going to send someone to check Anne's house out. Or he would do it himself. I had to get moving.

"You probably won't believe me," I said, "but I am really sorry."

What was the best way to buy her time and ensure that she would be alive when I got there?

When I got into my car, alone, I pulled out my cell phone. She answered with a timid, "Hello?"

"Should I bring those files I have? You know, the ones on our meth-dealing friend?"

There was a moment of silence before she said, "Yeah, do that."

"I'll call you when I'm almost there," I said.

I changed my shoes before setting off. I was also going to need to change my clothes into something less constricting.

I picked up the clothes I was planning on wearing tomorrow and put them on the passenger seat.

CHAPTER TWENTY-TWO

I DROVE BY ANNE'S HOUSE and didn't even slow down as I passed by.

Her white VW convertible was in the driveway. On the left-hand side, where it normally was. So, if she had run into a problem in her house, it was after she walked in the front door.

The house was dark. She hadn't turned on the outdoor lighting or the porch light. The drapes on her living-room window were drawn and no light spilled around the edges. No lights seemed to be on upstairs, either.

Perhaps she'd come home and fallen asleep while it was still light out, before she'd turned on any lights.

I rather doubted it, however.

Anne's street started as a left turn off of North Beachwood Drive, twisted and turned through the hill, gave birth to a couple of offshoots, and then some ways up the hill rejoined with North

Beachwood. I didn't drive all the way to the join at the top. I turned onto one of the side streets that wound up a rise in the hill. The backs of the houses on that street overlooked the houses on Anne's street. More importantly, their properties adjoined.

A charming—meaning "tiny"—light blue French Normandy-style house stood up the hill from Anne's house. It was a small house, right up against the side of the road, as all the houses up here were. The builders had probably looked at the setback requirements for the area and designed the footprint of the house to exactly fit within those lines.

There would be ten feet of land from the back of the house to the edge of the property line.

No one appeared to be home in the cute little cottage—if whistling dwarves returning from the mine had suddenly appeared, I wouldn't have been at all surprised—so I walked around the side and came to the chain-link gate that closed off the back garden from the front. I could have picked the lock, but I was in a hurry and some of those dwarves might come home from their jobs at the movie studios or financial products firms, and time was of the essence.

I climbed up and hurled myself over.

Since my landing was rather more noisy than planned, I waited for a moment to see if anyone was home and was going to come out. No one came. I continued to the back.

Where a large, bearded man wearing a t-shirt and jeans and holding a cell phone was waiting for me. He'd walked out the back of the cute little French Normandy house, probably having heard something and wanting to know what was going on.

"What the hell are you doing?" he asked.

I held up my hands to show they were empty. "Would you

believe I hit my softball into your yard?"

"No."

"Well, it was worth a try. Terribly sorry. Didn't think anyone was home, and I'm in a bit of a rush."

"Get off my property," he said.

"Will do." I headed toward the back fence.

At the edge of the bearded man's property was a waist-high wooden fence, with posts spaced widely apart and an attractive light brown stain on the boards. The fence wasn't there for protection. It served mostly as a visual cue for people not to go any further, because on the other side of the fence was a steep drop down the hill. One false move and you would be toast on the concrete patio off of Anne's kitchen.

Most of the side of the hill facing Anne's house had been replaced by a cement retaining wall, which served the dual purpose of shoring up the hillside, and cutting down on the amount of brush Anne was responsible for clearing every year, in order to keep down the fire hazard.

"I'm calling the police."

"That's a very good idea at this point."

"You'll kill yourself," the man said to me.

"Quite possibly," I told him. And then I ran. Toward the fence.

Toward the cliff, to be exact.

The distance from the edge, the very edge, of the property of the cute blue French Normandy house to the corner of Anne's house below would be the setback required ten feet. Generally, the setback from the edge of a property line to the building on that property was supposed to be fifteen feet—especially in the fire-prone Hollywood Hills—but much like the blue Normandy cottage, the builder of Anne's house had gotten away with the absolute minimum space, which was ten feet.

Actually, it turned out to be slightly more than ten feet, because the design of the house included a small balcony off Anne's bedroom. A tiny, useless, decorative balcony that no one except her neighbor up the hill would ever see. A balcony that jutted out toward the hillside exactly fifteen inches.

So the jump from the edge of the bearded man's property onto the roof over Anne's bedroom, right above the tiny, useless balcony was a horizontal jump of approximately one hundred and forty inches onto a sloped surface, followed by a drop of about ten feet onto a tiny fifteen-inch-deep balcony.

And I was going to get one shot at it.

I was about to tell myself I'd done worse, but as I vaulted over the fence and then bounded off the two feet of ground between the fence and the cliff, anything that might qualify as worse didn't come to mind. The graduated slate roof of Anne's house came up at me much faster than I imagined. Although I managed to land with my legs taking the brunt of the impact, I still scuffed up the skin on the palm of my left hand. The slope of the roof, however, was steep enough that I had to spread my arms and legs out fast to avoid rolling off and down two stories.

My left side, where Roger had sliced me, got pounded by my collision with the house. I vomited up a mouthful of saliva and stomach acid and watched the liquid roll down the roof.

Then I pushed myself up on my arms and started working backward, toward the drop onto Anne's balcony. I looked over my shoulder to see how close I was to the edge.

The bearded guy ran to the edge of his property and grabbed onto the fence. "Are you fucking insane?" he said.

I craned my neck to look up at him. "Am I over the balcony?"

"What?"

"The balcony. Is it below me?"

He looked down. "Yes."

I pushed myself backward off the edge and dropped. My feet hit the balcony and then I careened backward into the wrought-iron railing, which hurt, although the railing didn't make the top ten list of hurts I'd given myself in the past ten minutes.

Once on my feet, I pulled up my shirt to check for bleeding. The bandage had held, so if I was bleeding it was all internal. That thought seemed worth heaving up the sole contents of my stomach, which was about half of my whiskey sour. Then I looked back at the bearded neighbor and made the universal sign for "phone call," meaning "Call the damn police already, if you're going to."

If the balcony door turned out to be locked, I was going to kill Anne. If she wasn't dead already.

It was locked, but it wasn't a tough lock to crack. The door used the type of lock that assumed people weren't flying squirrels. I slid the door open and slipped into Anne's darkened bedroom.

It was easy enough to make out where Roger Sabo and Anne were in the house: his voice was clearly coming from downstairs, the living room. He was yelling, "What was that? What was that?" and she was crying, "I don't know!" Then she added, "Maybe it's a raccoon! Or a rat! I have a roof rat!"

"Let's see this rat."

Anne shrieked and something fell over. He'd obviously grabbed her roughly, and he was probably marching her in front of him as a shield.

I picked up the dark green ceramic lamp off of Anne's bedside table and ripped its lampshade off. Then I stood in the tight wedge behind the open door and the wall, watching through the crack in the door opening. The only thing visible was a tiny bit of the landing where the stairs ended, right outside Anne's bedroom. As soon as Sabo and Anne reached the top of the stairs, I was going to have somewhere between three and five seconds to separate them, turn his attention toward me, get the gun he undoubtedly had, and maybe strangle him with the cord of the lamp.

Anne would know to get the hell out of the way, right?

Anne's foot and the shadow of her body were visible through the crack in the doorway, and then the toe of one of Sabo's sneakers. He was right behind her. He pushed her forward through the door, which opened further, pressing into me.

Anne's shadow indicated she was on the other side of the doorknob. I could hear her panicked breathing.

Close enough.

I reached around the edge of the door and grabbed the hem of her t-shirt. She screamed and fell forward, giving me the perfect angle to rear back and kick her out of the way. She went flying toward her bureau.

Sabo started yelling and I slammed the door. The door definitely hit him, because it hit something solid and I had to push.

I risked a glance at Anne, who was staring at me like I was the one who'd been holding her hostage. She just lay there, like she was winded from the kick I'd given her. I jerked my head toward the closet and then hopped onto Anne's lowboy dresser.

After a certain point, people really need to learn to fight for themselves.

From the sounds behind me, Anne was crawling, probably into her closet. Which was her best option, under the circumstances.

The door flew open and I used the base of the lamp as a bludgeon to Sabo's face. He raised his arm to ward it off, but it was too late. I struck him right across the cheekbone and he flew backward into the balustrade at the top of the staircase, knocking his head against one of the balusters.

He had a gun in his right hand. A Kel-tec P-32. Small, black and silver, and a real impediment to us finding an amicable solution. It had to go.

I jumped off the bureau and kicked him hard, once, in the stomach. He tried to raise his right arm toward me. I reached out and slammed his hand up against the top of the handrail, bending his wrist backward against the wood.

He wouldn't let go.

So I dug into the exposed flesh of his wrist with my thumbnails, using as much force as I could. If slashing his wrist was the only way to do it, then in through the tendons it was. It's also a move that hurts like hell, the receiver slightly more than the giver.

Sabo let out a series of expletives as his fingers eventually loosened their grip on the gun's handle. I shoved the back of his hand against the handrail and used my fingers to tip the gun over the side of the railing.

Whereupon he managed to kick me and I knocked backward into the wall, the back of my head slamming against the sheetrock. While I tried to regain my balance, he scrambled off the floor and rammed into me, his forearm against my throat.

My head already hurt. So I slammed my forehead into his, shoving him back just enough that I got his arm off of me.

He rushed me again and I leaned back, letting most of his momentum rush past me. Then I planted my legs and shoved forward, pushing him backward, toward the top of the stairs.

He grabbed my arms and pulled me along with him.

I slammed onto him, my elbows hitting his torso, and we slid down the staircase, me riding him like a kid riding a flattened box down a snowy hill. At the bottom, his head hit the landing first, and he used the leverage to throw me off of him and into the wall. I managed to avoid having my ear pinned between my skull and the base floor trim.

He crawled off the bottom of the stairs and looked around the edge of the steps toward the kitchen.

The gun. He was looking for the gun.

Despite my deep need to take a breather or vomit again, I heaved myself up and launched myself over the side of the railing, landing on Sabo's back. He crashed to the ground, me once again on top of him. On the one hand, this stopped his progress.

On the other hand, I was certain the stitches in my side had opened up.

And his hand was about three inches from the gun. His entire body stretched toward it, taking me along for the ride.

I slammed my fist on the back of his wrist and then dug one of my thumbnails into his eye and pushed.

"Just stop, okay? Stop. Moving. I will fucking kill you, here and now. Stop."

His body stopped moving, but it was a feint. Every quiver told me he was waiting for an opening.

"Stand down." I pushed my fingernail into his eye socket a tiny bit further. Blood from where I'd scraped my hand after my jump smeared across his cheek. "Bend your right arm back here. Come on, do it."

He couldn't. His arm was shaking with adrenaline, which was only right and normal.

I took my hand off his eye and pounded the back of his shoulder blade as hard as I could. Which shook him up enough that his arm dropped against the floor. Which gave me enough time to dive for the gun.

I grabbed it, and somersaulted forward, and then I twisted around and onto my stomach. He was preparing to lunge at me.

Aiming from my prone position, resting on my elbows, wasn't ideal. But we were close enough that I'd take out a nice chunk of some part of him without much effort.

"I know how to use this. Also, I have no philosophical objection either to you dying or me being the one to kill you. So sit yourself against that wall and stop moving."

It took eons for him to finally choose the side of the wise and decide I was serious. His body moved like it was made of sludge and he set himself up against the wall, staring at me. Waiting for me to throw down the gun and maybe burst into tears about how horrible all this violence was.

Instead, I jackknifed my body, hips rising, legs drawing underneath, until I could get myself into a sitting position. The gun stayed trained on him the whole time. In case he thought I wasn't serious.

"We have somewhere between five and twenty minutes before Los Angeles's finest get here."

A smirk ghosted across his lips.

"You're not going to get out of this one this time. I recently had a conversation with Detective Samuel Gruen. You know him, I believe. Anyhow. He's kind of tired of your bullshit. You're dragging down the name of the rest of the force, and given the problems the LAPD's had recently, you get an A for effort."

Sabo stared at me, panting.

I knew what he was going to do, a second before he did it. He gave off some involuntary signal, whatever it was. Did he flex his fingers? Did his eyes flash to the side for a second? Lick his lips? He did something, and my brain translated that into: *he's going to go for it.*

He lurched his body forward, and I aimed at the stained-glass lamp that stood by the coat closet, maybe six inches in front of where his left hand would land. Maybe five inches. Anne's uncle had given her the lamp as a housewarming gift. I pulled the trigger. The stained-glass lamp exploded. So did the drywall behind it. Sabo cowered, protecting himself from the spray of glass and plaster.

The Kel-tec had nice handling. Good choice on his part. Loud, though.

I swung the gun back to his face.

He scrambled back to the wall opposite.

"I know how to use these things." My feet pushed me backward until my back hit the doorframe of the entrance into the kitchen. "Your death is not a moral issue for me, you moron. In fact, the smart money says I would be helping humanity in my own tiny way. So we're going to sit here, and, while we sit here, you're going to explain a few things. Like what the hell you're doing here at Anne's house."

"Fuck off."

"I have the gun," I said slowly.

The sound of his jaw grinding shut was audible in the foyer.

"You held a gun at my friend Anne. That makes me want to hurt you in delicate places. Talk and keep going until I tell you that you can stop."

He laughed and shook his head.

I aimed the gun at his foot. "I not only can cripple you for life,

I will. So talk."

"About what?"

"Why did you kill Courtney?"

"I didn't kill her! I loved her!" His voice was hoarse with desperation. "She was everything to me."

"Funny way of showing it."

His whole body shook like he was a rag doll in the grip of an invisible giant. "Sometimes she made me crazy. But I loved her. And she came back. She came back to me and now she's dead."

"So why did you kill her?"

"I didn't, you stupid bitch!" he yelled again, his eyes wide as he stared at me. "She came back to me and we were going to be a family together. She was going to be on TV again and we would have our family."

"So who did kill her?" I asked.

"I don't know!" Sabo yelled. "I'll kill whoever did it, I swear to God."

"Maybe Hitchcock did it."

Sabo muttered under his breath. "That stupid prick."

"Can't be that stupid. You do business with him."

"He knows his shit about money. He didn't know anything about Courtney."

I wondered what Sabo truly knew about Courtney. "He drove her to the motel that afternoon."

The look on his face was tragic and amusing all at once. "No," he said. "No, he didn't. She wouldn't have—"

I nodded. "She left her purse and keys in my car and didn't even notice until I called her about it. He took her to her motel room. What do you think happened?"

"She loves me!" he screamed.

"Did you know Hitchcock was paying her off, Roger?"

"Yeah," he said, nodding. "She lied to him, said it was his. I didn't care. Easy money. More for both of us."

"Said what was his?"

"The baby," Sabo said. "It wasn't. It was mine. My family. And she was back."

Was that the reason Courtney had left Los Angeles after the show ended? She'd had a baby and told a couple of men the baby was theirs and collected money from all of them.

And with my attention elsewhere for a fraction of a second, Sabo moved.

He jumped up and flung himself at me, knocking me back against the wall. His knee pinned the gun and my hand to the floor. Then he pulled his fist back and hit me hard.

In the side.

Where he'd stabbed me a few days ago.

Oh, Ares the magnificent, I thought, *please* let the endorphins kick in before I pass out from the pain.

I managed to bring my other hand up and sock him in the side, which moved him just enough for me to get my knee up underneath and kick him back. He launched himself toward me again. I brought the gun up and held it with both hands. As he landed, I jammed the gun up under his jaw, hard, into the esophagus. It dug into the soft tissue and he started choking. Right over me. He had bad breath.

"We can make this look like self-defense," I said. "I'll be the 'self' in that arrangement. You, on the other hand, will be dead."

I had to tell myself to wait for him to make the choice. I was mildly worried at how badly I wanted him to choose wrongly.

When I was sixteen, I killed someone. Since then, I had let

another person die—to be fair, he'd been trying to kill me, so it had been him or me and I'd chosen me. And on other occasions—too many other occasions—I'd watched people die. Not once did I fling myself forward to try to save them.

Life and death. There are no takebacks if something goes wrong.

I raised my eyebrows at him. "Nod if you'd like to proceed with dying. Oh, you can't nod. Move any muscle at all and that's how we'll do it."

He stayed absolutely still. The feeling of disappointment worried me briefly.

"Okay, good. Get off of me, and sit in that corner."

He crawled backward, still trying to cough away the bruise I'd left on his throat. The gun had left a red, angry imprint on his skin.

As I slowly rose to my feet in front of him, I whispered, "Don't even breathe hard."

The front door shook with violent banging.

The cavalry was here.

I wondered if Gruen was with them.

"Please don't shoot!" I yelled, with as much waver in my voice as I could manage. "Oh God, please don't shoot!"

Sabo was staring at me, his mouth open.

"Was that good?" I whispered. "Was I believable? Don't fucking move."

I threw the gun into Anne's living room and then opened the door to two uniformed police officers who had their guns drawn. I put up my hands, bloody palms out, showing they were empty. I ducked, submissive, and crouched away from the one coming through first.

"Oh, thank God you're here!" I yelled. "He's there, he's there!"

"This bitch is crazy!" Sabo yelled.

I looked at him and raised one eyebrow. Then I painted on a look of terror when I turned back to the cop. "He tried to kill us! His gun's in there!" I waggled my arm at the living room—and suddenly it was everything I had to keep my arm in the air. Every muscle hurt. At the moment I wasn't quite sure how I was standing, let alone pointing things out. "I threw it in there! He was going to kill us."

"Who else is here?" one of the cops asked.

"Anne. Her name's Anne. This is her house. She's upstairs. Check on her! Check on her, please!"

The cop put his hand on the stair railing and then looked up. "Is that her?"

Anne was leaning over the railing by her bedroom and looking down at us.

No.

She was staring at me.

Like she'd never seen me before.

"Yes, that's her," I said.

⁂

Nathaniel Ross didn't talk to me. He didn't even look at me. And I knew the drill: don't talk to anyone.

From the moment he showed up and assured the officer in charge that any questions would have to be directed toward his office and not toward his client, any time he appeared to be looking at me, he was in fact focused on a spot over my shoulder. I put my hand out toward him and he shook me off. Even the lieutenant in charge of the operation seemed to notice Nathaniel's hostility.

But he kept me out of police custody anyhow, despite what he clearly wanted to do. He seemed to be calculating how hard it was to kill someone and dump their body in the desert.

While Nathaniel did legal-fu on various officers, I tried to talk to Anne, who was holed up in the master bedroom upstairs. Every time I asked to visit her, the police came between us. To be more exact, they didn't intervene so much as provide a convenient excuse for Anne not to talk to me. While Nathaniel shot me glares, Anne refused to meet my gaze at all. Every time I approached her she turned her back and huddled away from me.

I stayed downstairs, in the living room.

Nathaniel talked to the lieutenant in charge. He had to do that an awful lot whenever I was involved in things, it seemed. When the lieutenant left to take a call, I sidled up to Nathaniel.

"Where's Anne going?" I asked.

"Her parents' house," he told me.

Anne's parents were rich. She wasn't very close to them, despite letting them help her buy this house. This lovely house that I'd put a bullet into. No wonder she wasn't meeting my eyes.

"I thought maybe she'd come with me."

"Yeah. That's not in the plans."

I nodded. Anne was avoiding me as hard as she could. "Let's go."

"Where's your car?" Nathaniel asked.

I began to lift my arm to point to the general vicinity of the blue French Normandy house that loomed over Anne's backyard, but my arm seemed strangely loath to cooperate. I shook my head. "A couple of streets away."

The most unfortunate thing about Anne's property was that there was only one way out of it: from the front and onto the street.

Nathaniel peered out through the living-room curtains to the cameras that had been set up on the street outside. "Let's see if we can get out of here without getting on TV."

"Isn't your raison d'être to be on TV?" I joked.

"Jesus," he muttered. Then he yanked me by the arm—which hurt—and pushed me into the tiny powder room, which was characterized by floral everything: sunflowers on the wallpaper, flowers in the vase on the toilet tank cover, a series of flowers lacquered on wooden plaques that lined the wall by the light switch. The mirror on the medicine cabinet revealed what everyone else had been looking at: I looked like shit. The cut at my hairline had opened. I had a scrape on my temple. I probably had a few bruises working their way to the surface on my throat and shoulders.

He wadded up a handful of tissue and ran it under the faucet. He lightly dabbed my forehead. I winced. He opened the medicine cabinet. It was empty. "Okay, let's see if you're bleeding anywhere else."

"I always knew you wanted to get my clothes off." I gripped the hem of my shirt and tried to pull up, but my back muscles spasmed. I couldn't lift my hands more than an inch.

"Relax," he said, and he pushed my hands down to my sides. Then he slowly pulled my shirt up to my breasts before turning me around. Checking me on all sides. An awkward activity made worse because of how small the powder room was. Every time I brushed up against him I winced.

He gently lowered the hem of my shirt. "You have to go to a doctor," he said.

"All they're going to do is give me Vicodin," I said. "And while I appreciate that sentiment mightily, I already have some at home."

"You could have internal—"

"I probably would have lost consciousness already. I'm also certain I didn't break or fracture anything."

"You can barely move right now."

I shrugged. "Because the adrenaline's worn off."

He turned my head from side to side, checking me over again. "What the hell were you thinking?"

"Anne was in danger."

"And your first move is to break into her house and confront the guy? A guy with a gun?"

"I didn't know for certain there was a problem."

His grin didn't indicate much amusement. "This is me, Drusilla. Come on. You knew better than to use the front door."

"I'm very observant."

He stared at me. He gave me that vibe I sometimes get from Stevie, where she's computing the 4096 possible responses and needs to pick from amongst the two or three best ones. "Next time, call the police and walk away."

"She would have been dead by the time they got here."

"You could have got yourself killed. You could have got her killed. Or you could have killed him. Are you fucking stupid or something?" He slammed his hand against the wall and the entire series of lacquered flowers lifted and dropped in unison. "You have a death wish."

I thought about that.

"No, I don't," I said. "I'll save you the sob story about my poor unhappy childhood and point out that not only did I save Anne's life, I kicked that son of a bitch's ass. He gets no more Get Out of Jail Free cards."

Nathaniel leaned toward me. "Courtney's still dead, and nothing you can do will change that."

"This wasn't about her! It was about Anne!"

"Everyone's best guess is Sabo killed Courtney. And no matter what you do or you don't do, she's still dead."

I suddenly realized I was crying. When had that started? "He didn't. He didn't kill her. I don't know who did, but he didn't."

"Okay, he didn't do it. Who cares? It's none of your concern. Do you get that? None of your business. Sabo isn't suing you for assault anymore. You don't need to worry about him or Courtney or any of these people, not now, not tomorrow, not ever."

We finally left the powder room and Nathaniel took me into the living room. Through the windows we could see a couple of cameramen. Usually that sight has Angelenos come running.

"We'll wait," he said.

I shrugged.

The police handcuffed Sabo and took him out. When he left, some of the TV cameras did.

Then a couple of police officers walked Anne down the stairs and out the front of her house. She seemed very small and frail as she walked by, her eyes locked on a point straight ahead of her. She didn't look into the living room. Most of the rest of the cameras followed her as well.

Nathaniel dropped the curtain. "Come on."

We walked out of Anne's house and no one paid any attention to us. I followed his lead and looked as professional as someone in a t-shirt, jeans, and rubber-soled shoes could next to a man in a five-thousand-dollar suit.

Chapter Twenty-Three

AFTER NATHANIEL DROPPED ME OFF at my car and I managed to get away from the police cars clogging up Anne's neighborhood, I took city streets instead of the freeway and I drove over the hill to Studio City.

When I drove by Micah Schlegel's production office, I saw the lights were on and the door was propped open with a giant fan. Micah was hard at work on a Saturday. No time to sleep in this town. If you took a day off, someone else might get ahead of you.

Schlegel was alone in the office. He sat at his desk, back to the doorway. His t-shirt was wrinkled. Also sweat-stained, but given the heat in the room, that wasn't surprising. The wrinkles, though, that was an interesting twist. How on Earth could a person wrinkle a t-shirt?

He was probably putting in some marathon hours hustling his producing projects. Because that's what he did. He hustled.

Was Courtney's death a hindrance or a door opener for him? Like that was even a debate. If he could capitalize on her death for anything involving his projects, like the *Girls Becoming Stars* reunion, he'd do it.

I knocked on the open door. "Hey, Micah." I leaned across the entrance because my legs were having a hell of a time keeping me upright.

He looked up and his startled reaction was so over the top I wondered how deep in concentration he'd been. Then I realized what his visitor must look like to him, with my clothes messed up and my hair in a tangled, messy ponytail and bruises and scrapes I hadn't had last time and probably bruises that hadn't bloomed until I'd left Anne's house. I'd just been in a fight, and now I was looming in his doorway. He probably thought I was there to mug him.

"What do you want?" he said. Nervous. One hand reached for his cell phone.

"Need to ask you something else about Courtney." I took a step over the giant fan.

"Sorry about the AC. The whole building's out. Goddamn landlord." He grabbed the phone, his hand shaking.

I reached over and took it out of his hand. "Micah, let's not do this."

"You don't look so good. I can call somebody."

"I feel fairly awful to boot, thanks. I need some answers and then I'm going to leave and you can sit here doing whatever it is you're doing until the cowboys come back to Studio City. Whatever." I pulled a chair from one of the other desks across the room over to Micah's desk. "Neither of us wants to be here right now. You want to go home and shower or maybe you don't, and I just got into yet another fight with Roger Sabo."

"Yeah?"

"Yeah. We got into an even bigger fight this time. His name isn't really Roger Sabo, by the way. It's Broderick Tennyson. He's an undercover cop. Or he was. Did you know that?"

His eyes widened. "Oh, God. He is?"

I held up my hand. "We're not going to talk about Roger. Just thought you might want to know, that's all. No, I need to know about the reunion show. Is that still happening?"

"Yeah." He bowed his head instead of looking excited, the way I would have guessed. "Yeah, we got the order. They want it bad. They want it fast."

"Because of Courtney's death."

He nodded.

"Are you going to be at the memorial service tomorrow?"

He licked his lips and nodded again. "Yeah, that's going to be a big part of the show. That's really powerful visuals."

"Are all the girls going to be there?"

"As many as can be in Los Angeles in time, you know?"

Anyone who could get their ass to that memorial service had guaranteed air time. "When you were originally putting the reunion show together, you didn't have enough space to feature every girl, right?"

"Yeah. Only got eighty-four minutes, you know."

Out of one hundred and twenty. Ah, the joys of commercials. "Was Courtney going to be one of the girls in the show?"

"Yeah, absolutely."

"*Originally*, Micah. When you originally put this idea together, was Courtney going to be one of them?"

"Oh. No. We were going to go with Randi. You know, she's

not the greatest or anything."

"But she's done some work in movies. And she and Courtney were both the nice girls with accents, so..."

"We didn't need two." Micah shrugged, as though he were talking about chess pieces, not actual women.

"What changed your mind?" I said.

"Well, Courtney called me this week. Maybe it was last week. Anyhow, right after she came back to L.A."

"And she had a new story."

"Yeah. It was something she hadn't wanted to tell anyone about before, but—"

"But if it would get her on the show, she'd talk about it. She'd let you in on it in great detail."

Micah nodded. "Surprised the hell out of me, let me tell you."

I had no doubt about that. "Courtney called to tell you the reason she went home to Oklahoma two years ago was she'd had a baby."

"Yeah. Can't imagine her with a baby, you know." He got a sour look on his face and he started to fidget, cleaning under his fingernails with such a vengeance I was afraid he'd draw blood.

"Did she tell you that you were the father?" I asked.

He shook his head of curly brown hair and looked almost sheepish. "No. I mean...you know."

"No, Micah, I don't know. Did she tell you that you were? Did you wish you were?"

He looked wistful for a moment, like he might say something, but then he smiled to cover it up and moved some papers around on his desk. "I kind of thought for half a second she was going to say I was. But she said Greg Hitchcock was."

"Just like that."

"Yeah, she said his name."

"Was she going to say that on the show?" I asked.

"My thing was, she needed to not do that. I mean..." He dropped his hands. He'd given himself a magnificent hangnail on his thumb. "Can you imagine the lawsuits? And when it was just us talking she said it was Roger Sabo. That's not even what's on the certificate. So, no, no mention of anybody. Just going to have her and the baby."

"Did she tell you where the baby is right now?" I demanded.

"Her mom is raising it. You know, she took the kid so Courtney could come back to Los Angeles and get back to TV." It finally dawned on Micah that maybe, just maybe, wily little Courtney had sold him a bill of goods. "Oh my God, there was no baby, was there?"

"Where were you going to film her and the baby?" I asked.

Micah shrugged. "I don't know. We hadn't worked it out. But she said we needed to do it soon, because her and Sabo, they were going to leave soon, them and their kid."

And as soon as Courtney could get Hailey back, she was going to use her for TV.

"Give me a copy of the birth certificate," I said.

"I don't—"

"I have fired a gun today, Micah. Would you like to smell the powder on my fingers? I am not in the mood."

After a couple of seconds he said, "Whatever," and rolled his chair over to one of the freestanding file cabinets. He used his huge keyring to unlock it and then dig through the middle drawer. He pulled a couple of papers out and stuck one on the glass of a small printer-fax-scanner combination machine. Stevie always told me those things were poorly made, which didn't stop her from asking for one periodically.

The copy he made came out of the side of the machine. He whipped it toward me like he was fly-fishing. "Here. Go away."

CHAPTER TWENTY-FOUR

SATURDAY MORNING STEVIE LOOKED AT the birth certificate.

"The father's listed as Jonathan Ricciardi."

Which was what I thought the words had spelled out. I thought about Jonathan and Alison, and little baby Hailey. Jonathan and Courtney both had Scandinavian blue eyes. I was fairly certain neither of them wore contacts.

"Is it possible for two blue-eyed parents to make a brown-eyed baby?" I asked Stevie.

"Genetic traits aren't passed on quite as cleanly as it's presented in biology class. Yes, it's possible."

I described Jonathan's and Courtney's bright, light-colored eyes, and Hailey's dark brown ones.

"Then that's not as likely, no."

"Why would he put his name on the birth certificate if he

wasn't the father?"

Stevie shrugged. "Because it's easier than adoption?"

Couples traveled far and wide to adopt. Everyone in Poland had stories about Western couples looking for babies "who looked like them." Courtney and her baby were much closer to home. And what an opportunity for Greg Hitchcock: he managed to cover up his little transgression with Courtney (if he was, in fact, the baby's father) and to bind Jonathan to him ever more tightly.

No wonder Jonathan was afraid of losing Hailey once all his fiscal sleight-of-hand was revealed.

How worried had he been about what Courtney might do? For that matter, what about his wife, Alison?

Stevie asked, "Can we go shopping for clothes?"

I looked up. "Who are you and what have you done with my sister?"

"I'll need a dress for church tomorrow. Also, the weather's warming a bit. My clothes are quite stifling out of doors."

"Your clothes were fine for you in Las Vegas."

"Yes. Because I was indoors with the air conditioning running."

For six months straight she had stayed in that apartment, never once leaving until the day we split.

She wasn't staying indoors all the time anymore. And if we had to move again, we might not find a place she'd want to hide in this time.

Stevie and I went to the Out of the Closet thrift store on Santa Monica. Everyone said they had the nicest vintage clothing, right down to calling it "vintage" instead of "used discards."

I'm a fabulous older sister: nothing but the finest previously owned clothing for my girl.

We scooped up slacks and jeans and long skirts, along with several short-sleeved and long-sleeved blouses made of a lighter-weight fabric than most of the things she currently wore had. Of course, we'd had those since Montreal. We didn't buy new clothes for either of us very often, and we got them for Stevie much less frequently than for me. But everything was, as usual, floppy and oversized. Easy to wear, easy to clean, easy to get lost in. Just the way Stevie always wore her clothes.

One of the employees, a middle-aged woman named Carla, checked Stevie into one of the changing rooms. "Does she need some new bras?" Carla asked.

"Previously worn bras? No, thank you." I shook my head.

"Those we have new," she said.

Stevie hadn't had new undergarments in a while. "Oh. Brilliant. My sister wears a 32B."

Carla blinked at me. "Your sister's a 30D, honey." I must have looked stunned, because she nodded. "Trust me, I've been doing this a while. 30D. I'll get her some."

Carla's assessment of my sister's figure wasn't even the biggest surprise of the afternoon.

No, that award went to the piece of clothing I hadn't even seen Stevie bring into the dressing room. The sweet ivory-colored dress with a princess neckline and large flower prints on the fabric was so unlike anything I'd seen her in for years that when Stevie came out of the changing area with it on, I honestly didn't recognize her for a moment. It took me several breaths and what seemed like several years to figure out why.

Because despite having three-quarter sleeves and a hemline two inches below her knees, this dress wasn't as shapeless as most of the clothing Stevie generally wore. And it was suddenly very obvious to everyone, even me, that my little sister was now in her early twenties and not a little girl anymore.

Her smile was so bright as she turned around in front of the mirror. She didn't twirl or giggle or do any of the things most girls might do when modeling a beautiful dress, she just looked at herself and smiled.

My sister's quite pretty when she smiles.

Beautiful, even.

She didn't smile nearly often enough.

"What do you think?" she said.

Probably I should have told her what I'd just seen: how pretty she looked. Possibly I should have pointed out that the dress was even a little too old for her, something more fitting for a woman working on the twenty-seventh floor in an air-conditioned office building, paired with sensible shoes, than a twenty-two-year-old who ought to be out having fun.

Anne hated me. Gary might be talked into getting rid of me. I seemed to cause mayhem wherever I went. And now my little sister, the person I had been taking care of for eleven years, wasn't a little girl anymore. She might not need me, either.

Instead, I shrugged and said, "Where are you ever going to wear that?"

Her smile wavered. "It's not expensive."

"Stevie, we need clothes we're never going to use like a hole in the head. Put it back and find something else."

"Okay," Stevie said. She touched the seam of the skirt gently.

My phone rang. Nathaniel. "Come here immediately," he said, and he hung up.

"Stevie, we have to go. Let's get this rung up."

I was so bothered by Nathaniel's abrupt phone call I didn't

even pay attention to what Stevie put on the counter. She kept our money, she paid for the clothes.

Only after we were in the car did I see, folded at the top of one of the bags, the ivory dress with the large flower prints.

I let it go. After Courtney's memorial service, she didn't have anywhere to wear it, so there was no harm in it.

Century City was deserted on Saturdays. The streets by Nathaniel's office building that were one large logjam during the week had moving traffic on them. The garage under the building was almost completely empty but I still had to stop at the lone valet, sitting at the desk near the elevators. He handed me a ticket, as though it was going to be hard to remember which car was mine. The only car visible was Nathaniel's Mercedes, parked next to the valet's desk. Mine he drove around the corner, so it wasn't visible right away.

The doors on Nathaniel's floor opened to silence. No receptionist at the oval-shaped desk with the high-tech headset. No one waiting in the lobby. I called Nathaniel's number: he didn't answer.

I didn't know whether to sit down or not while I waited. Maybe I wasn't supposed to come here? I'd always thought the reception area of the law office was quiet during the week, but in contrast to this silence, the regular day was a symphony of phones, low voices, and footfalls on the carpeting.

I compromised between standing and sitting by perching on the armrest of one of the chairs. The pain through my tailbone immediately let me know that maneuver was not appreciated, so I settled for leaning against the wall near the giant letters of the law office's name.

After a few minutes the door into the inner sanctum opened and there was my lawyer, in a suit and tie. No Carmela with her clipboards or efficiency. Just Nathaniel.

"Come on," he said.

The office was empty. I would have guessed that people would be there, finishing up paperwork, making phone calls, whatever, but every cubicle and glass-walled office we passed was dark. Even the computers were off.

He didn't say a word as we walked, his shiny shoes slapping in regular rhythm down the hallway to his office. I got the feeling I had better not try to lighten the mood. Or talk to him. Maybe ever again.

The meeting room nearest Nathaniel's office was the first light on in the place. Several notebooks and legal pads were strewn around the tabletop. There was a Starbucks cup, lid still on. I thought we were headed in there, but then Nathaniel opened the door to his office. Where the overhead lights were off. The giant windows looking out at Santa Monica Boulevard below provided plenty of indirect sunlight. I sat in my usual visitor's chair as Nathaniel turned the computer monitor around toward me. He hit the spacebar key and then walked out.

The picture on the monitor showed me a blank wall.

"Hello?" I said.

The image on the screen whirled around, making me feel sick to my stomach. When the picture stopped moving, the computer's camera finally focused on its subject, Roberto.

His face looked completely calm and placid, which told me I was in very big trouble indeed. Anger and rage I can deal with. Lack of emotion is terrifying.

"Are you all right?" he asked.

No need to ask what he was talking about. We were past that now.

"Yes," I said.

"Is your friend all right?"

I nodded, not very enthusiastically. "I think so. Not sure."

"And why aren't you sure, *Drusilla?*"

Oh, good. Sarcastic Roberto. My favorite kind. "Because she wouldn't talk to me afterward. After it was all over."

"Can you blame her? What you did was both terrifying and very stupid."

I opened my mouth to reply.

He snapped his fingers in front of the camera. "No. Not interested. Whatever rationale you have this time, save it. He could have killed you or your friend or both of you. You could have killed him. You could have fallen off that goddamned roof. And why? Because it seemed like a good idea at the time? Exceptionally stupid. You are going to get yourself killed."

And then I felt a calmness spread through me. Not my usual desire to snark, or to push back, or to start an argument. The best word for how I felt was "settled."

"It wasn't stupid. At all. I knew what I was doing. There are plenty of things I am terrible at. We can all name those. But the ones I do well? I do them very well. And when I'm good at something, I know exactly how good I am. So don't sit there and lecture me like I'm some naughty schoolboy who nicked a Crunchie down at the shops. Talk to me like I'm an adult, Roberto. A very capable adult. If I were more like Chance, everyone's life would be easier. My brother has always been fantastic at school and learning algorithms and getting degrees and probably negotiating over boardroom tables. My abilities lie elsewhere. You want to talk about how my skill set is a problem? Let's do that. But don't talk to me like I got lucky yesterday. Because we both know that isn't what happened."

"Would you have killed that man yesterday?"

Easy. "Yes."

"Why?"

"Because I make decisions and I don't spend a lot of time thinking about them after I've made them. Didn't you always say that was one of the most important traits in a leader? Decisiveness? Well, there you go. You want to get angry at someone about how I've turned out? Get angry at the bodyguard who was highly overqualified and bored shitless guarding a fifteen-year-old. Get angry at your wife, for not dealing with my issues when I was little because she was too busy getting married to assholes. Getting angry at me is like getting mad at the ocean: too little, too late."

Roberto stared at me for a few seconds, his mouth set in a severe line. So many possible responses he could give to my impassioned speech—at the very least, I'd just slagged off the love of his life, who also happened to be my mother.

And then he smiled.

Well, okay, maybe it was more of a grin, but that response hadn't been on the list of possibilities.

"I'm not angry at you," he said, and I felt an icy grip around my solar plexus.

Roberto angry at me I could handle. Roberto being proud of some of my more extreme behavior was scary.

The better part of valor yelled at me to shut up until he was done talking.

"Actually, that's not entirely true. Making what happened

yesterday go away is expensive and time-consuming and a waste of Nathaniel Ross's talents. But he can do it and I can afford it. The LAPD gets the credit for rooting out one of its own and your friend gets publicity and a really great story. She's been told not to include you, by the way."

Roberto stopped talking and I started counting the seconds. The highest I've ever gotten before someone else speaks first is eighty-two.

I reached forty-five before I blurted out, "And?"

"And now I know how far you will go to protect a friend, or to find an answer that's bothering you, or just to get what you want."

"You set Roger Sabo up to do that?" I yelled.

His wince was immediate. "No, good Lord, no. I had no idea. But nudging you in the direction of the answer you needed was more than enough to bring all of these things out into the light. To bring out your best. Or your worst. You not only figured out who Roger Sabo was, you took care of him. Brilliant. By the way, Chris McClanahan called Anson Villiers yesterday to complain about your negotiating technique. And to reconfirm that Erica Rose will be at the party tonight."

"The party hasn't happened yet."

He shook his head. "I'm not worried. Speaking of Villiers, you will start visiting him. Once a week, every week, starting this week. Call him for the appointment time—"

"Roberto, I can't—"

"Not ten minutes ago you assured me you're nothing but *can*. So you can, and you will. You will begin training for your future responsibilities. There are things you need to learn to expand your skill set."

Roberto wanted to teach me the business. All of the business.

And he wanted me to learn as fast as possible.

Either he really cared about me as a person, or Roberto needed me.

"What's going on in New York, Roberto?"

"Simply being fantastic at negotiating over boardroom tables is not going to be enough to succeed in the future. The family's companies are getting bigger and more attractive to outsiders every day. Your brother is very good at picking out the snakes in the office down the hall."

"And my job will be to take care of the other ones."

"If the two of you can keep from killing one another after you return, yes."

"I bet Chance doesn't have as much experience at actually killing people as I do."

"No, but he has more experience with money and power."

Roberto was worried about my brother. Not for my brother.

My stepfather had to set up the pieces on the chessboard before the whole chess set got taken away from him. He needed me on his side and he needed me in New York, as soon as possible.

Dammit. Not only did I have to go back to New York, now I really wanted to. For no other reason than to find out what the hell was going on.

"So where do we start?"

Roberto swallowed, which meant he was relieved. He hadn't known for certain how I was going to take his admission that lines were being drawn. Awesome. "You work with Villiers. Periodically I will give you things to learn. To study."

"Or to do for you."

He nodded. "Think of it as doing them for yourself. Learn a few things you need to know. And get very good at them. See you on Monday."

The screen went black. I had been dismissed.

Roberto had better enjoy the power differential between us now, because when I returned to New York, things were going to be different.

I left Nathaniel's office and waved to him outside the meeting room. He capped his pen and got up.

We might both be Roberto Montesinos's lackeys, but I ranked higher than he did, and I didn't need to listen to his lecture. "All done. You can go back to what you were doing. I know the way out." And I smiled.

Because he might hate what he had to do for me...but he had to do it for me.

CHAPTER TWENTY-FIVE

THE MEMORIAL SERVICE FOR COURTNEY Cherise Cleary was scheduled for 2:00 p.m. at the Tarzana First Christian Church. Stevie and I decided we would arrive early and wait inside, see who was attending. If the police were there, then Sabo hadn't confessed and they were still looking for the murderer. I wanted to find out who it was. The likeliest suspect would undoubtedly be attending the service.

Micah had given Greg Hitchcock a hell of a motive for killing Courtney. Expose him for being a hypocrite and having a baby out of wedlock, and who knew what secrets might come tumbling out afterward.

My only problem with that was that Hitchcock had clearly not been the man on the motorcycle. So had he gotten one of his workers to do it for him? What would be worth doing that?

The parking lot was still full, so we parked a few blocks down

Tampa Avenue and walked. Stevie was in her new dress with the large flowers on it. The hem was nearer her knees than it had been in the store, which meant Stevie had broken out her sewing machine sometime last night. It was now one of the shortest skirts she'd ever worn. She looked quite nice. I wondered why this bothered me so much. The only thing I owned that qualified as proper church attire was my lightweight dark blue wool dress. It was too hot, but the heat would still have been unbearable if I'd been in a bikini. Welcome to the San Fernando Valley, where the sun was shining full force with no clouds for miles and no wind blowing through to lessen the discomfort.

Quite a few people in their Sunday best were walking toward us, away from the morning church services, and they were very friendly to everyone they walked past. Lots of smiles, lots of parents holding hands with their children, all of whom seemed to be in much better spirits than I ever had been after suffering through Sunday services.

Parents holding their children.

"Everyone's leaving," Stevie said. "Will anyone come to the service?"

"If there are television cameras there, they will."

Coming down the street toward the church was a white van with a satellite dish on top.

"Courtney would be so furious to miss this," I said.

"Let's get into the church," Stevie said.

Micah stood near the van, which was parked near the door to the church. Two cameramen and two sound guys stood in a semicircle around him, while he explained the game plan, using expressive gestures. Micah wore a lightweight, relatively wrinkle-free black blazer and a nice shirt, which made me think he was attending the service as well. He wore the young, hip Hollywood version of dressing up. He did a double-take at me and his hand began to move up, as though he were going to wave. Then he shook his head and went back to what he was doing.

Immediately inside the church was the foyer, a plain square box. A large picture of Courtney with a black wreath around it stood on an easel. On the wall was a picture of the pastor, a nice-looking chap in his thirties with curly hair and a round face. Stevie whispered his name to me: Bernard Janek. A table had a guest book on it with a pen ready. Next to the guest book was a stack of release forms, authorizing Micah's production company to use the signer's likeness in a broadcast show.

I didn't sign either one.

The doors into the reception room were open, and Jonathan and Alison were in there, setting up the refreshments table. Hailey was in a bouncy saucer, hopping up and down. Jonathan looked up and saw us.

"Anything we can do to help?" I asked.

Jonathan looked at his wife, who shrugged. "Well, okay, then," he said. He grabbed a box of booklets from the corner. "If you could pass out the flyers in the pews, that'd be great."

Stevie didn't make a move to take the box, of course. I'm the pack horse in our relationship.

I took the box. It was heavier than I expected. My muscles told me exactly how much they did not appreciate my carrying anything right now. "How many people are you expecting?"

"Maybe a hundred," he said. "There should be a hundred and thirty in there."

I took a moment to wonder how many people would show up at my funeral and blanked out after counting to one. Possibly two, but Roberto would just be making sure I was really dead.

"Did Courtney have a lot of friends?" I asked.

"When she lived in L.A., she was active in the church," he said.

Stevie and I walked toward the assembly room. "Active in the church?" I said. "Doesn't seem like her at all." I dumped the box by the door.

"People are complex, Dru. They're never just one thing." My sister picked up a handful of the booklets. "Everyone has many facets."

That was my sister, always looking on the better side of things and using big words to do it. But then I've given the advice not to mistake people's religious beliefs for their behaviors, and perhaps the opposite was true as well.

The main area of the church was behind two large plain doors with square handles. The pews were set up with an aisle down the center. I put the box down on one of the front pews and Stevie picked up one of the pamphlets.

Courtney's picture was on the cover. Stevie quickly summarized what was written inside: a little bit about Courtney's life, who would be speaking at the service, where donations could be made to a charity that meant a lot to her.

I took the left hand pews and Stevie the right, and we distributed the pamphlets fairly easily among the first twelve rows. I put a pile of the remaining booklets on the pew at the back.

The door opened and Pastor Janek walked in. The noise of a variety of conversations followed him in, leading me to suspect attendees had started to arrive. He introduced himself and we shook hands. He told us they were going to open the doors soon, and was there anything else we needed to finish up with? I said no, we were almost done here, and he smiled as he escorted us back out to the foyer.

Which was filling up with guests, as the noise had indicated. Greg Hitchcock was there. The woman next to him was about his age, shorter, plumper, with her short black hair in waves around her face. Probably she was Mrs. Hitchcock. Every time she looked at him she seemed annoyed, and I wanted to assure her she didn't know the half of it.

Micah Schlegel was chatting away with a beautiful girl—undoubtedly one of the *Girls*—and when he saw me, he nodded. I didn't go any nearer.

Alison walked over to her husband, Hailey in her arms. The little girl reached for Jonathan, who gleefully took his white-blonde daughter from Alison's arms. He rubbed noses with her and she laughed.

The person in the foyer who surprised me both the most and the least was Randi Narvaez.

Stevie saw her well before I did. My sister stared at the crowd of people milling in the lobby of the church, her lips pressed together. It took me a few moments to recognize Randi in a relatively conservative black dress, with her long black hair swept up in a French knot. She greeted Pastor Janek with a handshake and she gave a slight smile when he offered her sympathy.

"She came back," I said. "She came back early from her little holiday for this."

Stevie scrunched up her forehead and the lips got pressed even harder.

Randi had left the weekend away she'd pressed so hard to go on. There was the lure of the TV show reunion, of course; Courtney's funeral was going to make a fabulous framing story. But she'd been so eager to go away.

I put my hand on my sister's shoulder. "Stay here."

Randi joined a trio of other young women, all of whom I guessed were other girls from the show. They all had the same physical type—young, with toned bodies, and too much makeup given how pretty each of them was — differing only in the details. One was shorter than the others, with straight blonde hair, one had long, wavy red hair, the third had purple streaks in her chin-length black hair. The short blonde stepped into the middle of their circle, widened her eyes, and started telling them what I could only hope was interesting gossip. She stopped talking when she saw me approaching.

Randi smirked at me, turning her head to talk to me, rather than her whole body. "Surprised to see you here."

"Why's that?"

She shrugged. "Oh, you know."

The other girls, after a few seconds of their conversation having been interrupted, each took out her phone and stared at it.

"I'm likewise surprised to see you."

"My boyfriend understands how much Courtney meant to me." She looked around the circle. "Did I tell you guys I'm dating Sir Gareth Macfadyen?"

The way the woman with the purple streaks in her hair rolled her eyes told me that Randi was making sure to drop that tidbit early and often.

"You hated Courtney," I said.

"Courtney meant a lot to me." Randi took out her phone, the modern way of indicating a conversation was over. "I wish Sir Gareth had gotten a chance to meet her. Oh, by the way. After the service Sir Gareth wants to talk to you. So be sure to stop by the house."

Of course I would stop by the house. I lived there. But Randi was so certain I was going to be out of the picture.

"Hera, you're an idiot," I muttered to myself. I grabbed her phone and held it away.

"Hey!" she said.

"What are you doing?" asked the redhead.

"I'm willing to wager actual folding money that the call history will show you rang Roger Sabo... Must be right after you'd talked Gary into going away for the weekend. You told Roger I'd be there alone on Friday night. Only he showed up early, on Thursday, before the two of you had left and you had to let him onto Gary's property."

"Give me my goddamn phone!" she said, her voice rising in pitch. Bingo.

"I only met you Wednesday," I said. "Thursday you'd already figured out how to get rid of me. That is fast work. What did Sabo promise you, Randi? Because he's in police custody now."

She grabbed the phone out of my hand and immediately entered her passcode—easy to memorize, stupid to show me—and started hitting buttons.

"You know that call records are logged by the mobile companies?" I asked mildly. "You can't erase them. Aiding and abetting is not going to be good for your career."

I pulled out my own phone and called Gary. "Turns out your new girlfriend is the one who let the psycho onto your property. I don't feel particularly safe with her around. Perhaps it's best if Stevie and I moved on."

"Good God," he said.

Randi's phone rang a few seconds later. She glanced at it and answered it quickly. She wandered away from the other girls, and within seconds she was messing up her carefully coiffed hair and reacting very badly to whatever her caller was saying. Seconds later she was glaring at me as she put the phone away.

I nodded at her and smiled. As I walked back to Stevie, I told myself that if she'd had anything to do with Courtney's murder, I was doing Gary a favor anyhow.

Stevie poked me in the side. I followed her gaze to the front door.

Detectives Samuel Gruen and John Vilar had entered and were standing along the back wall, taking their time to focus on each person who was there. Gruen noticed me immediately, of course. He didn't return my smile. I probably wasn't his favorite person at the moment. Or maybe ever.

I lifted my hand to wave at him. He turned his back on me to talk to Vilar. I'd tell Vilar about Randi's call to Sabo.

Stevie tugged on the sleeve of my dress. "It's time to take our seats," she said, and we headed in.

※

The first two-thirds of the service was quite beautiful.

Stevie and I sat about seven rows back from the front. Gruen and Vilar, I noticed, stayed at the back.

Pastor Janek spoke for a while about Courtney's life: she went to high school, she had big dreams, she came to Hollywood and had a tough time of it, she returned to her family, and then she decided to return to Los Angeles, a little older and wiser and surer of why she was here. She had some problems, but she was already returning to the community. She had attended church the previous Sunday and had signed up to volunteer at the preschool two days a week.

Greg Hitchcock went up and said a few words about how wonderful it had been to know Courtney, what a great help she'd been at the Financial Counseling Center. I could tell he meant to talk about her as though she were the cute high schooler who'd come in to tidy up the office once in a while, but some of the words he used—darling, sweet, loving, attentive—combined to give an overall impression that he liked her in a whole different kind of way.

People always give away their secrets in what they say.

Micah went up to the podium and spoke. He droned on at some length about what Courtney had been like while they were making *Girls Becoming Stars*. He told an embarrassing anecdote about how she'd fawned over some guy thinking he was a movie producer. Then he exhorted us all to watch the reunion show "for Courtney."

It's never too early to work the promotion for your TV show, I guess.

In a surprise twist, Randi went up to speak. She talked about how close she and Courtney had been, how they'd both been nice church-going girls blah blah blah. It was all completely sincere and yet totally Hollywood fake at the same time. Randi was a survivor, with Sir Gareth Macfadyen at her side or not. She had a long and storied career ahead of her in Hollywood.

Then she looked at me. "Drusilla, you were close to Courtney. Would you like to say a few words?"

I made a note to avoid getting someone who didn't like me dumped right before a funeral service. Payback's a bitch.

Lots of the people present turned around to look at me.

I looked at Stevie. "What do I do?"

She gave me a tiny smile. "Do you know anything about Courtney other people don't?"

Thanks for the lack of help on that, sweetie, I thought. I patted her hand and then walked to the front of the room.

As I walked the thirty feet to the podium, I wondered if I should try to be funny. Or sentimental. If there's one time you have free reign to be sentimental or even outright maudlin, a funeral service is it. Or I could try to go against the grain and talk about what a pain in the ass she'd been in the short time I'd known her.

Something other people don't know about Courtney.

Normally I'm good at making stuff up on the fly, but I was out of words. My fingertips slid along the oak base of the podium. The papers there were probably what Pastor Janek had read from during his statement. I tapped them for a bit and wondered what my sister had meant by what she said.

The hundred or so people present were all staring at me, wondering who I was. Greg Hitchcock had his arms crossed and he was glaring at me. Like I was going to say anything about his proclivities here and now—despite the vast majority of the behavior my parents taught me, they did teach me better than that.

Randi's mouth was screwed up in a wry smirk, like she was waiting for me to make a terrible mistake

She wasn't at all worried about what I might say. Interesting.

Micah also had his arms folded, his hands practically at his shoulders, giving himself a tight embrace. Maybe he was worried I was going to have another chat with him.

Detective Gruen's gaze was directly on me, arms folded across his chest. Detective Vilar, next to him, had his hands in his pockets, watching the parishioners.

"I didn't know Courtney very well." That wasn't a great start.

The second sentence didn't simply flow out from the first one. "I only met her during the last week of her life. My biggest connection with her is quite strange, actually. I was with her when she was murdered—"

And that was all I needed to say. Stevie had been absolutely right. I did know something other people didn't.

The shooter had seen me, clearly lighted inside the motel room. I had had trouble seeing the shooter. I couldn't tell for certain whether it was a man or a woman. Men tend to have bigger upper bodies that narrow to the hips. Women tend to be fuller below the waist or curvier all over. But there are always the ones, both male and female, who have slighter bodies, with less variation between the upper and lower bodies.

The shooter had a slender body, straight up and down.

Everything that had happened in Courtney's motel room had happened so fast. It was serendipity I had noticed anyone outside the window at all.

The shooter had most definitely noticed me. There was no way he couldn't have.

He must have assumed I could see him as well. And then every time we talked after Courtney's murder I hadn't said anything.

Had Stevie figured that out? Or was this what she'd call divine intervention? I wondered.

Because the revelation that I was the only witness to Courtney's murder was a huge surprise to everyone in the church. Except, of course, the only person in the church who knew I'd been there. Because I'd been clearly visible through the window.

Greg Hitchcock lurched forward.

Randi's smirk faded away.

Micah's eyes widened.

Alison put her hand over her mouth and hugged her daughter just a little tighter.

Even the detectives at the back of the room moved, startled that I would reveal that in public.

Jonathan Ricciardi, though, barely reacted.

⁂

I finished with some kind of summary -- I probably babbled incoherently, although a childhood spent giving impromptu displays of precocious cheek at your parents' cocktail parties does provide some training—and immediately returned to Stevie, who put her hand over mine. My sister leaned in. "What did you see?" Stevie asked.

"Something I didn't want to," I told her. "People have facets. You were right. How did you know?"

She shook her head. "I didn't. But I thought maybe you might."

Pastor Janek hurriedly finished up and asked us all to join him for refreshments in the parlor. Everyone left the assembly room politely, although with heads together and a rising murmur. Stevie and I tucked our ankles beneath our seats and let others in the pew pass by us. A couple of people stopped to console me—or ask for gossip, same thing—but I shook my head and refused to speak with them.

When it seemed as though everyone else had left, I finally exited the pew, Stevie behind me.

Detective Gruen blocked my path. "Tell me what you remembered from that night."

"Don't you have a job to do, Detective?"

He stalked past me, not giving me a second thought. We were

never going to meet up for that second drink. *Tant pis.* Just as well, really. It wasn't like I needed a boyfriend at this point in my life anyhow. I was having a hard enough time holding on to my fake boyfriend.

Was there alcohol at the reception? I wondered.

Stevie and I walked out into the foyer, which was now opened onto the side room, forming the reception area. Everyone noticed when we joined the party, either by staring at us and whispering or by pointedly not looking in our direction.

Jonathan and Alison were standing by the table with the platter of freshly cut fruit. Alison carried Hailey and the little girl had her arm slung around her mother's shoulders. Jonathan kept glancing over at me, perhaps wondering what I was going to do. Or say. Alison definitely knew he'd done it. I wondered if they'd talked about it openly, or if it was one of those things married couples accept as given.

Greg Hitchcock walked over to Jonathan, who was getting more upset every step I took toward them. Hitchcock reached out to touch Hailey on the back of her head, even as Alison hugged the baby to her tighter.

Courtney told Micah she wanted to change her story: the young mother in Oklahoma. She was going to need to produce the baby to prove it, of course. And then Sabo expected they were going to leave and go play happy families somewhere.

The afternoon that I met Hitchcock, Courtney had stopped by the preschool, which she'd done all that week. She'd mentioned Hailey directly to Jonathan. Then Hitchcock left with Courtney to drive her back to her motel. Did Jonathan worry that Hitchcock was going to try to help Courtney take Hailey back? After all, Hitchcock had a fairly large club to wield over Jonathan—the financial house of cards Jonathan had signed off on. Plus, Hitchcock thought he was the baby's father. While he clearly didn't want to acknowledge paternity, some men just get a kick out of thinking that the kid is theirs to do with as they please.

Was Jonathan hoping to find both of them in that motel room? Take both of them out, end all of his problems at once?

"What are you going to do?" Stevie said. "What will you say?"

I shook my head. "What is there to say? Where is the proof? I'm exactly as certain of who did it as I was ten minutes ago."

A woman standing next to me said, "You know who killed Courtney?"

The conversation near us cut off abruptly. Jonathan and Hitchcock, standing as far away as they were, simply stopped talking and looked at us. This was, after all, exactly what everyone expected from me after my little performance in the church.

I shook my head. "No, absolutely not. I don't know who killed her."

Probably no one else heard Gruen's snort of disagreement over the murmuring of the crowd.

I looked at Jonathan. He waited for me to say something. He'd been waiting for it since the day I showed up at his doorstep, thinking I was going to point the finger at him.

Instead, I pointed at the meeting room we'd all just left. "You need help cleaning up in there?"

After a second's hesitation, he nodded. We walked together, quietly, back in.

Gruen was going to know what to do with that, even if he didn't know how to prove it.

We started picking up the leaflets, which most people had left there. A couple of tissues.

"You want to talk about it?" I said.

"What Greg was doing...I knew where it was going to lead. I was trying to leave."

"Where what was going to lead? The women at the financial center?"

Jonathan straightened a few of the chairs at the side of the room. "With the women. With the meth business. He got involved with the drugs to get the money to pay the women. I didn't even realize what was going on at first." He tried to laugh, but it didn't work. "I thought we were doing really well in the middle of a recession. Took me a while to figure it out."

"You're the accountant. It's your job to figure it out."

"A lot of people kept working good jobs in the middle of a recession. We kept working. And we helped people at the counseling office, we did."

"Except for the ones Hitchcock asked to be nice to him."

"I didn't know he was doing it. I knew he saw other women. But...not like that. And the center was my idea."

"You went and got the documents when I told you about it, didn't you? That's the kind of thing he'd keep track of."

He nodded.

"How many women are there?"

"Hundreds," he whispered.

The thought of being part of a setup that took advantage of that many women...he was crumbling in front of my eyes. His shoulders were folding inward and he kept shuffling the programs he'd picked up like he was picking a card in a magic trick.

"Why'd you do it, Jonathan? Why did you kill her?"

It was like watching a carefully constructed stone facade turn out to be crêpe paper and burn up from a stray spark. Jonathan slid onto the nearest pew, dropping the pamphlets he'd picked up. The only thing holding him up was his hand, gripping on to the back of the pew in front of him. And everything he'd been holding inside came out.

"She was going to change the birth certificate. The birth certificate I signed for her. Two years ago the only thing she wanted was to destroy her baby. She was going to. She didn't, because I said I wanted the baby and Greg was happy to pay her to go away. And then she came back and all she wanted was to destroy my family. She was going to take away the most wonderful thing Alison and I have together."

If all Jonathan had had to deal with was Hitchcock's predilection for sex with lots of young women, he could have handled it. If the only thing Jonathan had had to face was the connection with Sabo and the meth trade, he could have bargained a way out of it. If all he'd had to deal with was Courtney's insane demand to take Hailey back with sole custody, he could have figured out some way of dissuading her. But the money and the drugs and Sabo and Courtney happened at once and he lost his mind.

"How did you find her?" I said.

Jonathan shook his head. "The kids at the construction site were out drinking after work, and I took one of the bikes that had been left. Easy to get the gun out of the trailer. Then I just followed Greg's location on his phone. You must have just missed him." He shook his head. "You weren't supposed to be there."

Lucky me.

Had he been hoping to find Courtney and Hitchcock there together? Two birds, a couple of bullets.

"You did the wrong thing, Jonathan."

"Don't you think I know that?" he yelled. I wondered if they could hear us outside. He wiped the tears that had rolled down his cheek. "I know that," he said quietly.

"I understand why you did it. People do crazy things for people they love. And I can tell this is eating you up inside, Jonathan. You want to talk to someone and confess what you've done. You can't."

"You have no idea how this feels inside, knowing you've done something like that," he said.

This wasn't the time to explain that yes, yes I did. "Do you want Alison to keep Hailey?" I said.

"Yes."

"Then you will shut your mouth until you get yourself a lawyer. A good one. Because how this plays out might be the difference between your wife keeping Hailey and not."

No matter what happened to Jonathan now, he was going away for a very long time.

"I don't hang around with lawyers," he said.

"I do." I took out my phone. I hit the button for one of my top three most dialed numbers.

"Please tell me this is just to wish me a happy Sunday," Nathaniel said.

"Do you know any publicity-hungry defense lawyers who'll work pro bono?" I said.

"Specifically?"

"Christians, sex for money, drug deals, accounting fraud, undercover cops selling meth, beautiful young women, and a baby theft."

"So this lawyer isn't for *you*, then."

"You're off the hook this go-round. You can marry me with a

clear conscience."

He ignored me, as usual. "I'll call you in ten. Tell the accused not to say a word."

I put the phone away. "He'll call me in a few minutes. Those detectives out there are going to tell you they're your friends. They're not. They're doing their jobs. So I'm going to give you a friendly piece of advice. Don't volunteer information. Ever. I know you want to. I know you need to. You can't."

Finally, Jonathan nodded. I wondered if he would follow through. He was desperate to talk to someone.

A few minutes later, my phone rang. Nathaniel gave me a name and number, which I passed on to Jonathan. When Jonathan was in the midst of dialing the number, I headed back out to the foyer, where the remaining guests were standing around gossiping like their salaries depended on it. Alison stood in the center, jostling a fussy toddler and ignoring Greg Hitchcock, who kept trying to talk to her. I walked straight to her.

"You should probably go wait with your husband," I told her. "Tell him to follow my advice, no matter what the gorgeous detective says to either of you. No matter *what*. No matter what you think or believe is the right thing to do, tell him to do the smart thing. Especially if you want to keep this one."

Alison looked at me, and only then did I realize her eyes were brown, like Hailey's. No one was ever going to doubt that girl was theirs, except for Courtney. Yes, Hailey wasn't biologically theirs, but biology isn't the most important thing in a family. And a mother who was right there was better than an unknown arrangement with people she'd never met.

Alison hurried to join her husband in the church. Hailey, looking over her shoulder, waved at me.

Someone's hand landed on my upper arm. I turned, expecting to find Gruen. Or even Greg Hitchcock. It was Micah Schlegel.

"Hey," he said. He waved a form in the air. "You didn't sign this." It was the broadcast and likeness release form.

"And I'm not going to," I said.

"The production company only pays a small fee for promotional—" he said.

"You don't have my permission. You don't have my sister's permission. Sorry. This memorial service is not going to be part of your tacky little reality TV spectacular."

He stepped in front of me. Micah was territorial when it came to protecting his little show. "You can't do this."

I smiled. "Watch me. I have better lawyers than you do, Micah, so don't even think about leaking this video footage anywhere."

The look of shock on the producer's face at my refusal to parlay the discovery of Courtney's killer into a newsworthy event was hilarious and sad, all at the same time.

I clapped him on the shoulder. "Think of it this way, Micah. You can interview yourself for the show. Turn yourself into a TV star."

CHAPTER TWENTY-SIX

JONATHAN RICCIARDI WAS ARRESTED FOR murder and accounting fraud. The charges were somewhat mitigated by the fact that he'd been trying to blow the whistle on what Greg Hitchcock was up to. He had a really good lawyer, albeit one who wanted to be on the evening news every night. The murder charges were reduced, provided he testified against everyone, which he did.

Greg Hitchcock was arrested and charged with accounting fraud, embezzlement, solicitation, possession of narcotics with intent to distribute, actual distribution of narcotics, and several counts of inciting other people to break the law. The name of his lawyer meant nothing to me. Nathaniel rolled his eyes when I asked, but he refused to say his opinion of his colleague out loud.

Broderick Tennyson was a police officer who got sent to jail. I didn't ask what happened to him.

Samuel Gruen never did call me back.

Anne opened the door to her new apartment, a sublet in Santa Monica. Over her shoulder I could see most of the apartment: tiny living room, tiny kitchen and dining area, tiny hallway leading back to what was probably a tiny bedroom. She didn't even greet me. She just stared at me for fifteen seconds. "How did you —"

Ah. It was going to be that kind of conversation. Where, if one thing seems weird, everything seems suspect.

"You told me the apartment number. Someone had propped open the front door. Happy housewarming." I handed her the bottle of Shiraz Stevie had picked out for her.

It slowly seemed to dawn on Anne she should let me in, since she'd asked me to come here. "Come on in. Belongs to my friend Don. He's headed to Europe for a long contract and needed to sublet this place for at least six months. Lucky timing for me."

Lucky wasn't the word I'd use. After my interaction with Sabo, Anne needed to get some work done on the house and had decided to remodel while she was at it. She wouldn't live there for a while. If ever again.

"It's a totally illegal sublet, so don't tell the landlord."

The living room was no more than three meters by two meters, and the main wall of the living room was taken up by a three-cushion sofa. There were a few framed prints by Ansel Adams on the facing wall. None of the decorations or furniture were Anne's type of thing. The place must have come furnished. I took a seat on the far end of the sofa. "Anne, are you okay?"

Anne didn't sit. She stood somewhat awkwardly by the wall decoration that marked the division between the living room and dining room. She pushed her glasses up on her nose. "With all the excitement recently—"

Oh, to hell with this. "Come on. Cut to the car chase."

"Now I know the worst thing you've done for money," she said.

I shook my head. "I wouldn't do something like that for all the money in the world."

"There's so much information about people out there."

Two sentences in and I already did not like where this was going.

"Then you...at my house. You know. With Sabo. You said it didn't bother you whether he lived or died."

"I remember."

"You were telling the truth."

"Anne, listen, I was—"

"You were telling the truth," she said, loudly, right over me. "You didn't care one way or the other. And I thought, where did she learn to be like that?"

Oh, fabulous. Psychoanalysis 101. Although in my case, most of my problems can in fact be traced back to my parents. "And what did your Google search tell you about that?"

She shook her head. "People can hide stuff from Google if they know how. Someone who can do the things you can do can probably hide stuff on the Internet. Or your sister could. She's good with computers. I asked a guy to see if he could find anything. About you, I mean."

"A guy," I prompted.

"That private investigator. From the magazine. He never did help me with Sabo."

She must have used her own funds and hired him on her own. She'd wanted some answers. "And?"

"So Drusilla Thorne isn't your real name."

"I would have told you that if you'd asked. Doesn't even sound like a real name, does it?"

She took another drink. "You've never filed taxes. The only job you've ever had was in Vegas with Colin. You've never—"

"Is this going somewhere?"

"Your social security number is real and it was issued over a decade ago, but it was never used until last year."

Until shortly before Stevie and I arrived in Las Vegas and I met Colin Abbott. True, all true.

"Who are you?" Anne said.

"My own sister calls me Drusilla. Don't sweat the name."

She smiled nervously and gave a short, repetitive, hysterical chuckle. "He couldn't find anything about Stevie. There's no one named Stevie Thorne. It's like she's never existed. She told me once that she's British, but he couldn't find any record that she's ever entered this country."

What kind of search had this man done? I wondered. "You checked our fingerprints." The idea that she had come into my house—Gary's guest house, whatever, the place where I was showing her hospitality—and taken things with Stevie's fingerprints on them made me very angry. I could take care of myself. But she had brought my sister into this. "You did, didn't you? You checked our fingerprints." I allowed myself a few seconds to worry about the implications of our fingerprints showing up somewhere, and then I pushed it away. This wasn't the time.

She didn't answer.

"Oh, sorry, let me be more exact. What did he find when he checked our fingerprints?"

"Are you in witness protection?"

Would it make my life easier or harder to say "Yes"?

"No, Anne, I'm not with the Mafia. I have met some people in the Russian *Mafiya*, but they probably just want to kill me, so I avoid the Hollywood Farmer's Market for a reason."

"What?"

"Haven't you noticed how many Russians live around Hollywood? Look, you can either trust me when I say who I am doesn't matter and accept that you'll never know, or we can be done being friends and you can accept that you'll never know." I shrugged. "I'm good with either decision."

She stared at me through her cat's-eye glasses and her jaw started to tremble. Anne was about to lose it.

I don't let myself get too caught up in friendships for a reason. Generally the reason is I need to move to a new country and get a new name, but there are others as well. Know thyself.

"Why did you go with me?"

"To interview Courtney?" I asked.

"All of those things we've done recently. Like…Baldwin Park."

"They were fun. Outside the norm of my everyday life. Spending time with my mate, Anne. And of course, you were paying me. That's always a nice add-on."

"Friday. At my house. I was so scared. Were you?"

There was absolutely no way I could answer that truthfully and make her understand that what scares me is pretty basic stuff, like losing someone I care about. "Yes," I said. "That wasn't reason enough to stop."

"Would you do it for other people?"

Was this an interview? Was she working on a story? I stood up. "Anne, you asked me to come by and talk. I hope you're recovering from what happened with Sabo. Tennyson. Whoever. But I'm not doing this."

"Would you be willing to help a friend of mine with a problem she's having?"

I opened the front door. "The answer is you're not recovered, because you've clearly gone insane."

Anne ran to me and grabbed my hand. "Have I ever mentioned my friend Maisie to you?"

I shook my head. "No and I don't care."

She clutched my hand. If she thought that was enough force to keep me from walking, she was sorely mistaken. "She needs help. Just one day of help, nothing big or illegal, and she's willing to pay you. A lot."

I removed my hand from her grip and took her by the shoulders. "Much as I appreciate your trying to help me financially —"

Anne blurted out a number. A rather large number. In dollars. How much Maisie was willing to pay me to help her. For one day.

"Come again?" I said.

She looked sheepish. "I may have exaggerated how much I was paying you."

"Does 'nothing big' include murdering someone?" I asked. "Because she can hire some professionals for less than that."

"Her ex-boyfriend has some of her stuff. He's a total dick and she's scared of him. She needs someone to go with her to get it. When he's out of the house. I didn't even mention half the things you can do and she's like, Oh my God, can I talk to her?" Anne began to giggle. "You come with a great personal recommendation."

Holy Zeus. That amount of money would pay for a lot of therapy. That would pay for a few months of an apartment for

Stevie and me. That would make me less needy in my dealings with Roberto.

On the other hand, there wasn't a chance there wasn't something very, very dodgy about this setup. Few things are worth that much money.

Six of one, half a dozen of another. Keeps life interesting.

"Half up front," I said. "Cash."

About The Author

Diane Patterson has an MFA in Film from the University of Southern California and a BA in Linguistics from Stanford University. She's been a shill in a magic act, a production assistant on a science-fiction TV show, and a tech writer at Apple. She lives with her family in the San Francisco Bay Area.

Want to get an email when my next book is released? Sign up here: http://eepurl.com/uP4yD

Books By Diane Patterson

The Sound Of Footsteps

You Know Who I Am

Everybody Takes The Money

Visit DianePatterson.com for up-to-date information.
For news about new releases, join the mailing list: http://eepurl.com/uP4yD
Follow Diane on Twitter: https://twitter.com/dianepatterson
Diane's Author page on Facebook: http://www.facebook.com/pages/Diane-Patterson/331432836956998

www.ingramcontent.com/pod-product-compliance
Lightning Source LLC
Chambersburg PA
CBHW070653180626
46817CB00006B/2350